MW01125294

# NO ROOM FOR REGRET

CULLEN/BARTLETT DYNASTY BOOK 1

JANEEN ANN O'CONNELL

*CHILL WITH A BOOK Readers' Award – May 2018*

*This book is dedicated to the memory of my maternal grandfather,*
*Hector Ralph Werrett*
*1905-1986*

.

# AUTHOR'S NOTE.

This is a work of fiction; however, the main characters are real, they existed: their births, marriages, criminal convictions, travels, and deaths, are real.

Thanks to subjects in the Diploma of Family History run by the University of Tasmania, I was able to locate the convict ancestors who had long ago been buried, literally and figuratively, by my grandfather's family. Years of genealogical research fell into place when the brick wall surrounding Elizabeth Blay, was broken down.

**Records were sourced from:**

- Tasmanian Archives and Heritage Office (Libraries Tasmania)
- New South Wales State Archives (Colonial Secretary's Papers)
- University of Tasmania Library
- Trove – National Library of Australia
- Public Record Office of Victoria
- Old Bailey online

- UK Convict Hulk Registers and Letter books 1802-1849
- British Newspaper Archives
- And many hours on Ancestry.com.au

Please visit my website at
https://janeenannoconnell.com/
Like my Facebook Page:
https://business.facebook.com/JaneenAnnOConnell/_

This novel would not have been completed and published without the help of my alpha readers: Ashleigh Hutton and Denise Wood. And my beta readers: Heather Hubber, Luc Mackey and Julie-Anne Jordan.

Amazing encouragement and support was received from: Wordsmiths of Melton, author Isobel Blackthorn, and Liz Virtue, owner of Glen Derwent, Hamilton Road, New Norfolk, Tasmania, setting of the book launch on 28th April 2018.

# EXILED: TO NOWHERE, WITH NO-ONE, WITH NOTHING

# Descendant Chart – James Bryan Cullen – First Fleet – *Scarborough*, 1788 and Elizabeth Bartlett – *Marquis Cornwallis*, 1796

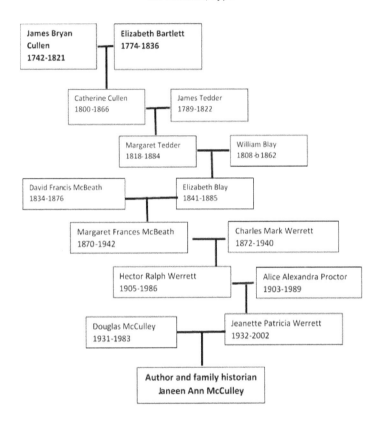

# 1

*"There were confined in this floating dungeon nearly 600 men, most of them double ironed; and the reader may conceive the horrible effects arising from the continual rattling of chains, the filth and vermin naturally produced by such a crowd of miserable inhabitants, the oaths and execrations constantly heard amongst them..."*

*[The Memoirs of James Hardy Vaux.] James Hardy Vaux described the conditions on the hulk Retribution Written by himself in 1819 re his time on the hulk <u>Retribution</u> in 1810. Conditions on board the floating gaols were appalling. The standards of hygiene were so poor that disease spread quickly. The sick were given little medical attention and were not separated from the healthy.*

*The living quarters were very bad. The hulks were cramped and the prisoners slept in fetters.*

*The prisoners had to live on one deck that was barely high enough to let a man stand up. The officers lived in cabins in the stern.*

*[www.portcities.org.uk]*

## February 1811

He wanted two things: the fetters on his ankles and wrists gone, and to kill the cheating, lying, evil old man who put him here. James Tedder trembled; the chains around his wrists rattled.

It was perishingly cold - the norm for winter in London – but even the cold damp air couldn't dilute the stench. It made his eyes water; he could taste it. Was it the prison hulk itself, the water it floated on, the men crowded into every available space, or a combination? He vomited on his breeches and shoes.

'Don't matter 'bout ye breeches, convict,' sniggered a guard. 'Ye'll be losing them soon anyways.'

James Tedder hobbled along the deck of the prison hulk *Retribution* with the 50 or so other men he had travelled with from Newgate Gaol. The weight of the shackles made his arms ache and his legs longed for the ability to take powerful strides, instead of degrading powerless shuffles.

The guards manhandled and pushed and shoved until satisfied that the line of bedraggled souls met requirements. One by one their chains were unlocked. Tedder rubbed each wrist, taking it in turn to massage and soothe.

'Strip!' Bellowed a guard.

Confused, the convicts looked at each other for clarification. It was freezing on the deck of this old ship; the wind mocked as it lashed at them.

The guard cracked a whip as he again bellowed the command.

'I said strip!'

Tedder removed his once handsome jacket, the once clean shirt and his vomit covered breeches and shoes. He stood with the other convicts, shivering, naked, waiting for his flesh to be scrubbed with a hard-bristled brush and his hair to be cut back almost to the scalp. Looking longingly towards the river bank of the Thames, and Woolwich, Tedder felt the bile again rise from his stomach; this time it carried with it the realisation of what was to become of him. He'd one more year of his apprenticeship to go, with plans to be a master tinsmith himself, but "justice" intervened. That life belongs to another, he thought.

A boot on his bare backside and raucous laughter from the guards brought Tedder back to reality. A bald, toothless guard shoved him towards the barrel of water. He stumbled on the slippery, cold deck, finding it difficult to get his frozen feet to obey his brain's instructions; lumbering over to the water barrel, he managed to climb in. A convict took the caustic soap and brush, then scrubbed Tedder until he thought he must look like a boiled lobster, whilst another took to his once beautifully groomed hair with shears. The mocking wind again played with him, biting exposed ears and neck so that without the need of a mirror, Tedder knew his hair was cut as close to the scalp as the shears allowed.

'Get out, convict,' bellowed the guard as he threw some coarse, grey clothing at Tedder. 'Ye got 10 seconds to put 'em on or they be mine.'

Dressed in breeches and a shirt that scratched and rubbed against their skin, the convicted men huddled together, teeth chattering, arms squeezing their torsos trying to find warmth. Stick wielding guards again pushed and shoved the hapless group into a line. Tedder watched them coming, the bile crept from his gut to his gullet and his ankles ached in anticipation; the chains were being reattached, but this time his wrists were spared.

Standing quietly looking down at the worn boards on the deck underfoot, pondering the loss of identity and dignity, Tedder felt the savage strike of a cudgel across his back. It took the air from his lungs and his legs crumbled beneath him. The convicts either side picked him up and put him back in line. Struggling to stand up straight and breathe he shuffled with the other men toward a gaping black hole in the middle of the old ship.

'Please God, be that not where we are going.' On this occasion, like so many others recently, God didn't appear to hear him.

Making their way down the ladder the prisoners tried to avoid the arbitrary strikes of the guards. Reaching the hold below, most cowered, none with the strength required for defiance.

It took time for James Tedder's eyes to adjust to the gloom; he didn't think he would ever become accustomed to the stench. It required every ounce of strength to hold the tears to a trickle, but the tears stopped, and he spun when James Blay slapped him on the shoulder.

'How are you holding up, Tedder, my lad?' probed Blay – a cellmate from Newgate Gaol. 'Dark and stinky down here. Suppose we'll get used to it. It's got to be better than hanging at the end of a rope.'

'Are you sure about that?' Tedder asked. 'The way I see it now, hanging at the end of a rope might be a better end.'

'Easy to see you don't have a wife and boys to think about, Tedder. See how you feel about being strung up by your neck when you got a family counting on you.'

Tedder understood Blay's relief at not facing the hangman and being transported instead, but he didn't share his optimism.

'We'll stick together Tedder. Try to get in the same work gang and sleep near each other. We've got to protect one another from the guards and the other convicts. They'll steal anything you've got. If one of us gets sick, we help the other.'

It seemed to Tedder that Blay had it all worked out. He was twenty years older and ready to take charge to protect them both. Tedder wasn't sure he needed a protector; however, he needed a friend, and it was a friendship on offer.

Four guards lurched through the prison deck waving cudgels, hitting men indiscriminately. 'Line up agin the sides, convicts. Make it snappy,' bellowed the guard with the least number of teeth. Rotting teeth, Tedder knew, was a sign of too much rum. He also knew to do what they told him, and to keep his head down if he didn't want a beating or worse, a flogging with the cat-o'-nine-tails.

'Get yaselves inta them cells. 'Hurry up 'bout it.'

Tedder dubbed this one *Toothless*.

Twenty at a time, the men were herded into cells big enough to house eight to ten. Two men shared a sleeping space, with a threadbare blanket between them. The one Tedder shared with Blay held the rank smell of stale vomit. The guards locked the doors, the hatches closed, and desperate darkness enveloped the men. The only visible light peeped at them through the tiny cracks in the ship's old hull. With nothing to eat, a thin blanket to share with Blay, and a constant battle to keep the rats from crawling on his face; James Tedder didn't sleep.

The first full day on the prison hulk *Retribution* began with a breakfast of the coarsest boiled barley Tedder had ever seen.

Again, the bile crept into his throat as he tried to force himself to eat. He couldn't.

After breakfast, at seven am, with chains rattling around their ankles every able-bodied convict struggled up the ladder to the deck and clambered into tenders, to go ashore to work at the Royal Arsenal on the south side of the River Thames. Attached to each group of twenty convicts was a guard wielding a weapon.

The prisoners hobbled one behind the other into the work shed which stank almost as much as the hulk. Tedder could identify perspiration, urine, dirt, dust and the over-powering tang of rusting metal. He'd hoped working would ease the terror and give him something else to think about, but the overseer wrapping the whip around his back put a renewed focus on his misery. He doubled over as the pain reverberated from his back to his chest, and down his arms. Stumbling into the man in front saved him from falling face down into the piles of metal on the floor.

Struggling to breathe, with the pain in his back pulsing and increasing with every step, Tedder eventually took his place at the bench, ready to chip rust off old cannon balls.

At the midday call to return to the *Retribution* for dinner, Tedder took a moment to examine his hands. The split skin had trickles of blood mixed with black / red rust to make a colour not unlike the floor of the shed they worked in: it was the colour of Hell.

Under the ever-watchful eyes of the brutal guards, the wretched convicts lumbered to the tenders for return to the hulk. The midday meal was a broth Tedder didn't recognise, a small piece of tough, overcooked beef, a mouldy hard biscuit, and a half pint of ale. Ravenous hunger overtook his taste buds, regardless of the quality of the food, his stomach ached to have something in it. Tedder gagged on the first mouthful, he coughed and spluttered on the second, but managed to swallow the rest; his grumbling stomach settled a little. Within a minute or two of the convicts forcing themselves to eat the muck disguised as a meal, the bell sounded for return to the tenders, and the Arsenal.

By the finish of the first day at labour, Tedder had established a steady rhythm for cleaning the cannon balls, but his hands suffered: they burnt, cramped, and had tiny pieces of rust and metal ingrained into the scratches the cannon balls left on his skin. His feet, already uncomfortable in the ill-fitting shoes assigned to him, ached and throbbed; he wasn't used to standing all day with fetters on his ankles. At the sound of the bell to end the day the convicts were manhandled, hit, and shoved into line. Chains rattling, they trundled along the pier, heads bowed in defeat. Tedder could feel the air of desperation and hopelessness as they crawled, one by one into the tenders to return to the hulk.

'That was hard work, Tedder. I don't use my hands to work with metal. Leather is softer on the skin,' Blay complained in Tedder's ear.

Tedder grunted, he was too tired to speak.

Supper on the *Retribution* was broth made from boiling the left-over beef they had for dinner, a small piece of cheese, a piece of bread so hard Tedder thought a nail wouldn't penetrate it when banged with a hammer, and another half pint of ale. He and Blay ate greedily, neither tasting the muck that made its way into their still empty stomachs.

Longing for the loaf of fresh bread, cheese, potatoes and salted pork the master tinsmith's wife used to bring him for dinner in the middle of the day, Tedder looked at the plate in front of him, trying to imagine the good food he once ate. Staring, he could see himself in the tinsmith's foundry. Making plates and mugs like these. Hands trembling, he turned over the plate to find the maker's mark underneath. Through tears welling in strained, red eyes, Tedder saw the mark of his master tinsmith. Near the edge of the plate, where you had to look hard to see it, his own mark as the maker of the plate. The irony was mind-numbing. He remembered making about fifty of these plates over two or three days without giving the ultimate users a first, let alone a second, thought.

Supper ended, and the hatches closed on the men crowded below deck. The day was over. Darkness descended on Tedder as he wondered how long he would be on this floating hell before being transported to the other side of the world. He lay in the cot next to Blay, burning with such hatred for Bagram Simeon, the old man who had ruined his life, that he could hear his heart pounding in his ears and see the pulses of rage inside his eyelids.

This nightmare began the day Tedder told his older brother Henry, what the Jewish diamond merchant, Bagram Simeon, had done to him.

'No! James!' Henry had wailed. 'It's a sin. You must get the money and tell him no more. Why would you even go along with him?'

The 70-year-old well-respected diamond merchant had come to Islington to conduct business with Tedder's employer. When introduced to the apprentice, Simeon smiled and patted his hand. At day's end, the old man sat outside the tinsmith foundry in his carriage, waiting.

He beckoned. 'Come on, young James, come along and I'll give you a ride home.'

At 17, the attention flattered Tedder, and he accepted the businessman's offer. But Simeon didn't take him home, he took him to a quiet place by the Thames and instructed the carriage driver to go for a walk. Sliding onto the seat next to Tedder, Simeon picked up his hand and squeezed it. Tedder pulled away. 'What are you doing?' was the obvious question, but he was too stunned to speak. He sat, open-mouthed, staring at Simeon. The old man grinned. Conflicted, Tedder instinctively felt uncomfortable, but social norms indicated he should show the older man respect.

'How long have you worked for the tinsmith, James?' Simeon queried.

'Why do you ask, sir?'

'I am trying to make conversation, James so we can be friends,' Simeon smiled at him.

Tedder squirmed on the seat.

'I might help you once you finish your apprenticeship, James. Help you set up your own business. Would you like to have your own business?' Simeon continued.

Confusion swirled in Tedder's mind, the chaos of thoughts like leaves being thrown around in the wind. He didn't know how to respond to this stranger, the old man trying to befriend him.

Simeon pressed on. 'How long did you say until you finish your apprenticeship, James?' he asked again.

'I have one year to finish, then I will be a craftsman, a tinsmith.'

'I'm sure you are an amazing craftsman already, James. But how long will it take you, do you think, to make enough money to set up your own business?'

'I haven't thought about it, but many years, I'd say.'

Simeon lent back in his seat, looked fondly at Tedder, and asked 'Do you have a lady friend in your life, James?'

'No, not yet, I've been too busy working. Maybe someday soon I'll meet someone.'

Tedder often thought of meeting a girl he could love and marry. He wanted to build a life; a life such as his parents had built for him and his siblings.

'The problem with girls, James, is that a young man like yourself has desires that need to be met but meeting them with a girl results in her becoming with child. I can satisfy your desires, James, with never any worry about an unwanted infant. I will pay you 500 pounds for your time. I will look after you.' Simeon sat back on the seat studying Tedder for a reaction.

Tedder didn't like what the old man was doing to him, but it was easy to talk himself into cooperating; 500 pounds was a lot of money. After several rides in the carriage, he asked when he would receive the promised payment.

'Soon, James,' murmured the 70-year-old. 'Just a few more trips and I'll get the money for you.'

Frustrated by Simeon's stalling tactics, Tedder told his brother, Henry, about his arrangement with the diamond merchant. With Henry's encouragement, Tedder wrote to Bagram Simeon:

> *"Sir – Having innocently informed my brother of what a friend you had promised to be to me, if I would let you do something to me, which you have done with me several times, I not knowing what a horrible crime it was; but having discovered its wickedness, and refused to suffer you to repeat it any more, you*

*seem angry, and want to get off your promises to me. My brother is determined to see me righted.*"[1]

Tedder's younger brother William delivered the letter to Simeon on 22nd August 1810.

The devious businessman took the letter to the constable [2] and they planned a trap. Simeon wrote to Tedder asking him to his home to discuss the matter.

In the early morning of Monday 27th August feeling buoyed by the old man's encouraging reply, Tedder dressed in his finest clothes. He put on a clean white shirt, breeches his mother had tailored for him and his best jacket. He polished his leather shoes until the beautiful summer sun reflected from the surface. His heart light, head spinning, a huge grin on his face thinking about his 500 pounds, Tedder walked the short distance to Simeon's home and place of business in Sydney Street. He tapped on Bagram Simeon's door, and the old man invited him in.

'Good day to you, James,' Simeon began. 'I beg you to explain the meaning of the letter you had delivered to my hand this last week.'

Tedder, unaware that the constable hid in an adjacent room listening to their conversation, spoke candidly.

'You promised me 500 pounds if I let you do those things to me, that you did on many occasions. Each time I brought up the subject you told me you would give me the money soon. If you do not give me the promised money, you leave me no choice but to go to the constable and have you prosecuted for the abominable acts you performed on me.' He took a deep breath.

Tedder was still breathing deeply, waiting for a response from the old man, when the constable, having all the evidence he needed to prosecute for extortion, stepped out from the adjacent room and arrested him. His efforts to get the 500 pounds and have the old man leave him alone, resulted in a trial in October 1810.

'James Tedder, the jury has found you guilty of the extortion of Mr Bagram Simeon in the amount of 500 pounds,' announced the judge. 'You are ordered to be transported beyond the seas, for the term of seven years.'[3]

The truth didn't matter, Simeon had a position of influence and power; he won.

Tedder pulled his knees up into his body, folded his arms around them, and turned away so his friend, James Blay, would be less likely to hear his sobs.

# HAMPSHIRE CHRONICLE (ENGLAND) 5 NOVEMBER 1810

(BRITISH NEWSPAPER ARCHIVES)

*Middlesex Sessions – James Tedder, a young man about eighteen years old, was indicted for writing letters to a Mr Simmons, a diamond merchant, on the 22nd of August last, threatening to prosecute him upon a charge of an abominable offence, for the purpose of extorting from him the sum of £500.*

*Mr Simmons is an Armenian of the Jewish persuasion and a diamond merchant, living in Sydney Street, Goswell Street; the prisoner is an apprentice to a tinman at Islington with whom the Prosecutor had dealt for some small articles in his line of business. On the day above stated, the Prosecutor received a letter signed in the Prisoner's name, demanding the 500L, which it alleged he had promised him; and threatening, in failure, of performance of the pretended promise, to prosecute him for the alleged crime. The Prosecutor, astonished at such a letter, went immediately to the Public office, at Hatton-garden, stated the circumstance, and asked advice how he should proceed. It was advised that he should answer the Prisoner's letter, and appoint an interview; which he accordingly did, and the Prisoner in consequence promised by another note to come to his house on the morning of* the 27$^{th}$, at which time Hancock, the police officer, attended, and was within hearing in an adjacent room, while the Prosecutor entered into conversation with the Prisoner, and elicited from him a distinct explanation of his object and intention. Immediately after which the Prisoner was taken into custody, and the letter of Mr Simmons was found in his possession. His own two letters to Mr Simmons were also produced in evidence, and proved by a little boy, his fellow apprentice, to be his hand writing, and that this witness left them at Mr Simmons's house by his desire.

A number of witnesses attended on behalf of the prisoner and gave him a most excellent character; but the jury found him guilty, and he was sentenced by the Court to seven years transportation.

# 2

## THE SHOEMAKER

*The Bloody Code had a major effect on the American Colonies and later Australia. Judges frequently offered transportation, i.e. being sent to one of the overseas colonies and indentured as a servant for a term of years, as an alternative to execution, by some accounts at a rate of 10:1.*

From: http://theglitteringeye.com/the-bloody-code

James Blay could hear Tedder's sobs. He could feel the young man's body shaking with grief and rage. The sobs didn't quieten or lessen. Lying in the cot next to Tedder, listening to his heartbreak, made Blay brood over his own situation. He ached for his boys and wife, Sarah. Once we leave England, I'll never see them again, he thought. His mind wandered to the chain of events that brought him to be lying in squalor, on a prison hulk, on the River Thames.

## January 1811

'What's happened to the maker's mark on the boots?' Alexander Wilson, a footwear trader, asked Blay. 'It's been inked over and can't be read. Where did you get them?'

'I don't know the man I got them from, or how he came to have them. They could be cabbaged,' Blay declared in defence.

In the blink of an eye, Wilson grabbed Blay around the neck and dragged the shocked shoemaker into the store-room, locking him in. Wilson then sent for the constable who arrested Blay, and charged him with :

"*burglariously breaking and entering the dwelling house of George Hobey, about the hour of twelve in the night of 3d January, and burglariously stealing therein, a pair of boots, value two pounds, his property.*" [1]

Head reeling from the speed at which he'd lost his liberty, Blay found a clear space on the floor in the cell at Newgate Gaol between two pitiful looking prisoners. Going over and over the events in his mind, he became convinced the jury would see his innocence; he'd soon be home with his wife and three boys. One of the pitiful souls sitting on the floor next to him was staring.

'What are you looking at, you snivelling shit?' Blay demanded.

The boy shifted position but didn't answer.

The slowness to respond infuriated Blay; he shoved the boy who then fell onto the prisoner next to him. Blay noticed there was no indignant reaction from any of the prisoners who were knocked about by the effect of one falling on another. His palms became clammy, beads of sweat appeared on his brow, he recognised, in the eyes of every man and woman in the cell, the mark of hopelessness. It smouldered like the dregs of a fire.

The young fair-haired boy he'd shoved into the others came back to his position. Defiance emanating from his being, he sat on the floor as close to Blay as he could, without touching him.

Curiosity piqued, Blay began a conversation. 'Why you here, boy? And what's your name?'


'It's a long story.'

'I have nothing else to do.' quipped Blay.

Tedder told his dismal story and James Blay listened without interruption.

'Doesn't matter if it isn't fair, does it?' Blay commented when Tedder finished speaking. 'The rich and powerful always win.'

'Why are you in Newgate?' Tedder asked.

'I did something very foolish. I took a risk. I had a good business, I'm a respected craftsman, belong to the Cord-wainer's Guild,[2] have an apprentice and feed and house my family and pay for my boys' schooling. But I thought I could make quick, easy money. Not unlike you when you accepted the diamond merchant's offer. Now I face court, and like what happened to you, I don't like my chances of anyone believing me.'

Blay wrung his hands so hard, the knuckles were bone white and the flesh fire poker red. Tedder didn't press for more information, and Blay offered none.

**10th January 1811.**

Dawn crept through the grates that masqueraded as windows in the cell. The watery steaks of sunlight promised warmth but delivered the cold hard light of day. A day that Blay knew would see him in court.

Standing in the dock with the other accused on the day's list, terror crept into Blay's soul as the three prisoners before him were found guilty and sentenced to various terms of transportation.

If it wasn't his life in the balance, Blay would have been impressed with the way the prosecutor, Mr Ally, elicited information from the various witnesses called for the Crown. Alexander Wilson described the scene where Blay had offered to sell him the boots; even remembering the alias Blay gave, along with the false address.

When the witnesses for the defence took the stand Blay hoped justice would prevail and they would reduce the charge to receiving the stolen boots. He thought he had a strong case. He lived an hour and a half's walk from George Hobey's shop in Piccadilly, where the boots were stolen from. Being accused of walking this distance, on a bitterly cold London winter night, breaking a window, stealing three pairs of boots and walking home again carrying the boots, made little sense. His lodger, Mary Wood testified that he had to pass her to leave the house and she did not see him leave. A customer of Blay's, Thomas Fuller, testified that he took a pair of shoes to Blay for repair and as he waited saw another man, unknown to him, sell the boots to Blay. He saw Blay pay twenty shillings for the boots. [3]

James Blay concentrated as the defence and prosecution badgered the witnesses. As he listened, he became more confident of being charged with the lesser crime. He even managed a small smile in his wife's direction as she sat in court waiting, like him, to find out his fate.

He didn't remember the closing remarks of the defence or the prosecution. He remembered the judge's gavel thundering on the bench and declaring him guilty, with a sentence of death. His wife put her hands to her face and sobbed. Blay's knees went from under him and he collapsed onto the chains attached to his ankles. Striking Blay with his cudgel, a guard ordered him to get up. He dragged himself to an upright position while trying to hold down the terrible scream that wanted to launch from his throat. The judge was talking again and Blay cleared his head enough to make out what was being said.

'James Blay the jury has found you guilty, you are hereby sentenced to death. The sentence can be commuted to transportation for life if you so agree. A decision is required immediately.'

Blay blurted out that he would be transported. Sarah's anguished cries penetrated his soul.

# 3

# THE SHOEMAKER'S WIFE

*"By the eighteenth century, most guilds did not include women, though sometimes widows who took over their husband's businesses became members by default and took over the training of their husbands' apprentices".*

*[https://www.londonlives.org/static/Guilds.jsp]*

## 8 Crispin Street, Spitalfields, London.

### January 1811

'I couldn't look at him; he was wretched and I'm furious. We were getting along fine. There wasn't heaps of money left at the end of the day, but there was enough to feed and educate the boys and pay the rent. Now he's being sent to New South Wales and I've got to bring them up on my own.'

Sarah Blay sat in the tiny kitchen of her Spitalfields home with her mother and youngest son. Using her hands, she wiped her reddened, sore eyes. Eyes that had been dispensing tears since her husband's sentence that morning.

Her mother picked up three-year-old John who was pulling Sarah's hands away from her face, trying in vain for her attention. John was the youngest; Sarah wasn't worried about the effect her husband's transportation would have on him, but the older two, James Jr, eight, and William, six, would know their father's predicament.

'Ye'll have to find a way to keep the apprentice on,' Sarah's mother reasoned. 'He can keep workin' for ye till ye can sell the business. Then at least ye'll have money comin' in. The lodger will stay too. She's nowhere else to go.'

Sarah knew her mother was right; an immediate solution could be found. The long-term worried her.

'He'll be moved to one of those prison hulks in the Thames before he's transported. It'll be harder than Newgate to see him, to bring him food and clothes.' Sarah said.

Her mother thundered 'I don't know why ye worried about him going to them hulks. Ye'll never see him again after he's sent to New South Wales. How many of them has ever come back? Do ye know? None, that's how many.'

The tears again welled, they ran down Sarah's already sorrow stained cheeks. John, whimpering at his mother's distress, climbed up onto her knee, and flung his arms around her neck. Sarah hugged her youngest child and wept into his little shoulder; overwhelmed with anger and fear.

Ignoring her daughter's distress, Sarah's mother continued: 'The lodger, what's 'er name?'

'Mary Wood.'

'Well, Mary Wood's goin' to have to help with the boys so ye can see to the business. Ye'll 'ave to concentrate on the here and now to keep the boys fed and a roof over ye heads.'

Her mother's pragmatism forced Sarah to focus on what

had to be done. Planning the survival of herself and the boys, her mind turned to the necessary steps. The apprentice had one year on his indenture to serve, and the Cordwainer's Guild sometimes allowed widows to take over the training of apprentices. She would have to convince the master of the Guild that James being transported for life made her as good as a widow.

---

In the hat and dress, she wore to her husband's trial and wearing a smart pair of boots he'd made for her two years earlier, Sarah walked the mile from her home in Spitalfields to the Guildhall in Gresham Street London, where she was to meet the Master Cordwainer. She waited in the great hall, fidgeting with the buttons on her bodice and straightening her hat. The much-rehearsed speech went around and around in her head. She knew it would take an effort to hold back the tears when she reinforced that James wasn't coming back.

Her mother demanded to know the outcome before Sarah had time to take off her hat and close the door.

'Yes, mother. The master cordwainer agreed that because James was sentenced to death, and is now being transported for life, that makes me as good as a widow. I'll supervise the apprentice and keep the business running.'

Sinking into James' chair by the fire Sarah's mother let out a huge sigh 'It will not be easy, mind.'

'I know, but as you say, the lodger will help with the boys while I supervise the apprentice and the shop.'

In bed that night, holding John close, Sarah prayed her thanks.

## May 1811

'I can't bring the boys to see you anymore, James.' Sarah struggled to keep the steady voice she had been practising. 'They'll see you one last time before you get sent away for good, but not here, not anymore, not on this rotten hulk.'

Before he could rein it in, James Blay's voice bellowed disappointment and anger. 'What do you mean, you can't bring them anymore? They're my boys, I'm entitled.'

The emotions Sarah had kept subdued like a simmering volcano for months, erupted into her husband's face. 'You are not entitled. You are a convict on a filthy, floating prison. You are leaving us for good. So, they are my boys, and I will do what I see fit.'

Stepping back from his wife's fury, Blay took a deep breath, stared at her expression, let out the breath and swallowed. 'Your words stab at my heart Sarah, but I must consider them,' he told her. 'I've been on this hulk for three months. Rats crawl over me while I sleep, many fellow prisoners have the bloody flux. [1] Gaol fever spreads, then goes away, and then spreads again. I'm wearing the same clothes I got that first day on this stinking hell hole. You are right, Sarah, this isn't a place the boys should endure. But I fear the sadness of not seeing them will swallow me whole.'

Sarah considered the brown eyes of the man she had married eleven years earlier - the spark had gone - replaced with misery and fear. She cupped her hands around his face, noticing the sallowness of his complexion and the wretchedness of his expression. She wanted to hug him like one of her boys and tell him everything would be all right, but that would be futile. Instead, she kissed his lips and told him she would see him next Sunday.

Along with other visitors, Sarah climbed down the ladder to the small tender and headed back to shore, away from the bleakness of the prison hulk and the desperation of her husband.

# 4

# FAREWELL

*Indefatigable*

*"Before embarking on the vessel <u>Indefatigable</u>, many prisoners had been held on the hulks moored at Woolwich and were transferred to the <u>Indefatigable</u> between 21<sup>st</sup> - 25<sup>th</sup> April 1812.*
*The Guard consisted of Lieutenants Pook and Lascelles of the 73rd Regiment with a Detachment for Hobart.*
*The <u>Indefatigable</u> sailed from England on 4<sup>th</sup> June 1812 in company with the Minstrel.*
*They arrived at Rio de Janeiro on 29<sup>th</sup>. The <u>Minstrel</u> and the <u>Indefatigable</u> kept company until the 17<sup>th</sup> August and then separated in a gale of wind.*
*The <u>Indefatigable</u> sailed direct to Hobart arriving there on 19<sup>th</sup> October 1812. <u>Indefatigable</u> was the first convict ship to be sent directly to Hobart. One prisoner died on the voyage out, from the accidental explosion of a musket."*

*From https://en.wikipedia.org/wiki/Indefatigable_(1799)*

## 2nd June 1812

Fettered at the ankles, the prisoners had twenty minutes to say goodbye to family gathered on the Woolwich dock.

James Tedder wept, gasping for breath, as his mother hugged him and caressed his now re-grown, but filthy, hair. His younger brother William stood aside trying to be strong, but the red, swollen eyes and the clear tears trickling down his snow-white face exposed the masquerade.

Older brother Henry appeared solemn and composed, but eyes brimming with tears highlighted the attempt to conceal his distress.

Henry Tedder Sr stood to one side behind his wife. His heart ached, and his head throbbed. He didn't try to hide the tears; they ran down his face like rain dripping down the window. He stepped forward, and for the first time since Tedder's imprisonment, Henry touched his middle son. He put his hand on his face and the boy collapsed into his father's arms. Tedder's distraught cries and sobs drew the guard Toothless, who waddled over to the little group.

'Stop ya whinin' so loud ya baby,' he yelled at Tedder.

Henry Sr stepped between his son and the guard. He didn't speak but stood his ground with the air of one who held a higher station in life. The guard backed away, mumbling about making life difficult for the snivellin' baby and the uppity shoemaker in Van Diemen's Land.

Esther Tedder the youngest of the siblings, had been standing with Henry Jr and could no longer contain her heartbreak. She threw her arms around Tedder's neck and sobbed into his shoulder. They held each other for a few minutes before Tedder stepped back to see her face.

'You never know, Esther,' he said. 'It might be all right in

Van Diemen's Land. I might find my way back when my time is served.'

At the end of the quickest twenty minutes of his life, they ordered James Tedder onto a tender and sent him back to the *Indefatigable,* where he had been confined for the last five weeks, waiting to sail. He didn't look back at his family on the dock. He hunched over and folded himself into an almost foetal position, crying, knowing he would never see his parents or siblings again.

James Blay's emotions played havoc with his mind. As much as he was eager to see his wife and boys, he knew the parting would be more painful than any event of the last year. Keeping his composure for his children, he hugged his wife, taking in the rose smell of her hair, and feeling her breasts against his chest.

She hugged him back, but didn't cry, or bend to the emotional tidal wave that emanated from her husband.

Moving the chains around his ankles so they were behind him, he knelt to speak to the boys calmly and comfortingly. 'We'll be together again soon, boys. Don't you worry, this isn't forever,' he reassured them. 'We'll all be together again before you know it. You James, you're the eldest; you've got to be a man and look after your Mama, and William and John.'

James Jr scowled, folded his arms in front of his chest in defiance, and refused to look at his father.

Blay left him and hugged the other two twice as hard. He knew Sarah to be a strong woman, and that she would look after the children. As he kissed his wife for the last time, he pushed the random thought of her remarrying out of his chaotic mind and prayed that his promise of reunion would happen.

Shoved onto the tender for the return to the *Indefatigable,* Blay could no longer hide his anguish. He let the tears run down his cheeks unchecked. Mouthing 'I'm sorry,' he waved a final goodbye to Sarah, James Jr, John, and William. Overcome with despair, he sunk down into the small boat, so the children wouldn't see his body racking with sobs.

# 5

# THE OTHER SIDE OF THE WORLD

"*Major-General Lachlan Macquarie: 31 January 1762 – 1 July 1824) was a British Army officer and colonial administrator from Scotland. Macquarie served as the fifth and last autocratic Governor of New South Wales from 1810 to 1821, and had a leading role in the social, economic and architectural development of the colony. He is considered by historians to have had a crucial influence on the transition of New South Wales from a penal colony to a free settlement and therefore to have played a major role in the shaping of Australian society in the early nineteenth century. An inscription on his tomb in Scotland describes him as 'The Father of Australia'.*
*On a visit of inspection to the settlement of Hobart Town on the Derwent River in Van Diemen's Land (now Tasmania) in November 1811, Macquarie was appalled at the ramshackle arrangement of the town and ordered the government surveyor James Meehan to survey a regular street layout. This survey determined the form of the current centre of the city of Hobart.*"

From: https://en.wikipedia.org/wiki/Lachlan_Macquarie

**19 October 1812**

The birds were the first signal that land was close. After four and a half months at sea, James Tedder and James Blay jostled other convicts for a position on the rail of the ship's deck, scanning the horizon for their first look at Van Diemen's Land.

'Land ho,' roared the sailor in the crow's nest.

A brief glimpse of mountains covered in green was all the human cargo got to see.

'Get below convicts,' thundered the marine in charge. 'The chains be goin' back on before we land, so get to ye bunks and don't leave. If ye get up from the bunk, ye'll be flogged.'

Crowded below deck on their cots, the convicts heard the marines' wives and children leaving the ship, while they were cramped below, waiting. Excited voices marvelled at the blue sky, comments on the bright sunshine and clear blue water of the estuary, and exclamations about how warm the breeze was for October, filtered through the boards of the deck to the prisoners below. They waited again while someone guided the livestock off the ship. They waited while the marines collected their belongings and left the ship to catch up with their families. They listened while the sailors readied *Indefatigable* for a stay at anchor.

'Stand lively,' came the order from a guard. 'The fetters are goin' on, and ye'll all be chained together. Can't be watchin' every one of ye single like, easier to watch ye all in one nice long line. Don't want to lose any of ye to the natives, now do we?'

Tedder didn't know what to expect. He didn't know what Hobart Town would look like. His imagination showed him a city like London, even though he knew it wouldn't be as big and he hoped, not as dirty. It showed him paved streets, buildings of different heights, shops and people meandering along talking, shopping, and going about their different business.

With no time to establish their 'land legs', the convicts struggled to walk in the fetters. The guards marched them up dirt tracks, between tents and timber and stone buildings under various forms of construction. The reality of Hobart Town stunned Tedder, the ramshackle, ad hoc arrangement of dwellings and business premises and the tracks masquerading as roads, took his attention away from finding his land legs. His heart ached with despair at the sight of convicts from earlier voyages working, fettered, digging up rocks to make the untameable landscape yield tameable roads.

Four and a half months on *Indefatigable* and before that the prison hulk, *Retribution*, had left Tedder, Blay and their fellow convicts, covered in lice, and scabs and sores from picking at bites. They were thin, dirty, and exhausted.

Apart from his fatigue and a general feeling of wretchedness, once he could walk, albeit still in chains, on a surface that didn't move, Tedder noticed the air: it had a smell that included the sea, trees, dirt, and sunshine. He knew it was spring on this side of the world – marines and sailors who had been here on previous voyages told of how the seasons were upside down – so Tedder allowed himself to breathe deeply, to breathe in the crisp, clean air that felt like clouds going into his lungs. He didn't understand the bushes and was mulling over why, in spring, they didn't sprout flowers, when someone shoved him in the back with the end of a musket. Falling on his face in the dirt, he brought the convicts either side of him down too.

'Get up ye maggots,' roared the marine who had inflicted the musket damage.

Tedder and the two men either side of him were struggling to get to their feet, with Tedder being kicked and punched during the attempt. His tired legs finally found the strength required to stand with the others. He didn't speak, didn't move. Until now, he had been almost as invisible as he had planned. Blay caught the attention of the marines on *Indefatigable*. They beat him for insolence, for talking when the hatches were closed, and for complaining about the chains rubbing into his flesh. For the last complaint, they fit new, tighter chains. Blay stopped complaining, but Tedder knew his spirit hadn't broken.


The convicts shuffled their way to a makeshift dormitory at the foot of a small rise, overlooking the bay where the *Indefatigable* rocked gently on the swell. They were the first convicts sent directly to Hobart Town and were to be housed in tents that offered no protection from strong winds or heavy rain. Tedder looked to the sky, praying he wouldn't see dark clouds forming. He knew this time God heard him because the sky was the azure colour they saw over the skies in Rio de Janeiro, with a few fluffy, white clouds scampering along in the breeze. The strike of a cudgel across the back of his legs took Tedder by surprise, but this time the convicts either side were ready and braced themselves against his inevitable fall.

'Gonna have to see if we can't find out what's in ye head,

convict. Seem to spend all ye time lookin' around ye. If ye canna use ye ears to listen, ye might lose 'em,' sneered the guard through rotten teeth and corpse smelling breath.

Tedder knew the expected response 'Yessir.'

'Yer better not go off on yer dreamin' here, convict. Ye'll be hanged for bein' lazy. I be watchin' ye close like,' the guard snarled. 'Won't stand for any snivelln' like you did in Woolwich, either.'

There were two chain gangs of about thirty men in each, dumped into the large tent. They were left alone in the silence. For the first time since stepping off the ship just before the supplies were unloaded, Tedder wondered about Blay.

A roaring voice from the other end of the other chain gang had all heads looking in one direction.

'I imagine they'll be feeding us at some point. I imagine we'll be sleeping here on the dirt at least for tonight. We all have to sit down as one and piss in our pants cos we can't get up without dragging the fellas either side of us up part way too.'

Tedder was happy to hear Blay's voice.

'When I say three, we all sit down,' Blay ordered. 'And hope we get some food and water before much longer.'

The convicts slumped to the dirt floor as one. Exhausted, hungry, thirsty, and some like Tedder, in pain. No food found its way into the tent. Tedder reckoned it had been about thirty-six hours since they'd eaten, but they were grateful to see a convict bringing around a ladle which he filled from a bucket of water. Each, in turn, drank thirstily. Tedder thought the water tasted like fresh snow; it was crisp and clean, but one ladle wasn't enough. He wanted to down the whole bucket.

# 6

# THE TINSMITH IN VAN DIEMEN'S LAND

It was strange sleeping on a surface that didn't move with the rise and fall of the sea. Tedder had been on water for two years and often let the ship's roll ease him to sleep. Odd as the stationary feeling was, he went to sleep as soon as it was dark, astonished to wake to bright sunshine and the marine sergeant yelling at them to get up.

'Line up ye wretches,' bawled a cudgel waiving guard from the ship.

The convicts shuffled into a line of sorts and as seemed fitting to their station and situation, stood with heads bowed and hands clasped in front. Like the other prisoners, Tedder was hungry and exhausted. He did not have the energy to be whipped or kicked or shoved; he was too miserable. So, he stood still and listened to instructions.

'Get outside and turn ye worthless selves to the sun and start walkin',' came the order from Toothless.

A marine corporal in a crisp, clean uniform took up the lead and the thirty souls who formed the convict line Tedder was part of, shambled along behind, still with heads bowed. Tedder couldn't have known how far they trudged, but he knew his ankles were raw, bleeding, and bruised from the relentless weight of the metal cuffs. Without food and with no more water, and with the heat from the sun intensifying, men collapsed and pulled others down with them until most were on the ground, too exhausted to continue. The marine leading the way strode toward Toothless just as he was about to sink the boot into Tedder who had collapsed with everyone else.

'Keep your feet to yourself guard,' roared the corporal. 'Have these convicts had any food and water since disembarking *Indefatigable*?.

'Don't know that sir,' responded Toothless. 'We's just collected 'em from the tent and got 'em lined up.'

Tedder wanted to let the outwardly more amenable corporal know that this same guard had taken them to the tent the night before, he knew they'd had one cup of water and no food. He decided against speaking out.

The corporal marched halfway down the line, stood up straight, and addressed the prisoners. 'You'll have to find the strength to get up and walk to the Government buildings. It's about another fifteen minutes. You'll be given something to eat and drink, an opportunity for a wash and clean slops. If you think you can't make it, let me know now, I'll unchain you from the others and you can stay here, in the sun, on the dirt. The ants won't take long to get into your ears, eyes, and nose, but it'll still take a long time to die.'

Toothless grinned. His few remaining rotten teeth bared in jubilation.

Tedder forced the bile back down his throat.

After a few minutes, all thirty convicts were again on their feet, facing the same way, and shuffling towards the said rewards.

The buildings the corporal called 'Government' were

made of some type of wood and looked primitive compared with the buildings in Islington and Newgate.

Led into a barn-like building with a stone paved floor, timber walls, spaces where window glass should be, a timber roof and a long, wooden table down one end, the convicts stood, awaiting their fate. The corporal had a black-smith remove the fetters and chains from their ankles and they were at last able to sit down individually. It was a relief to have their legs freed from the weight and constraint of the shackles. Some convicts sat on the stone floor cross-legged, some sat with their legs in front, others tucked them under for reassurance. Tedder sat cross-legged on the floor, rubbing each ankle to try and relieve the soreness the fetters left behind.

'This is the last time you'll be given food that isn't rationed,' lectured the corporal to the grimy, fatigued men sitting on the floor. 'When it comes in, eat slowly. Don't scoff it down in one go, because you'll be sick, and you won't be getting any more until supper.'

Unshackled men appeared with water barrels and tin mugs. Tedder assumed they were convicts as they were all dressed the same, in calico trousers and striped cotton shirts. The convicts on the line gratefully accepted the clear, fresh water. Tedder remembered with a shudder the four and a half months on the *Indefatigable* where water was often scarce and the more than twelve months on the *Retribution* where water was brown and made men sick.

Leaving the water barrels, the attendants returned with loaves of bread, cheese, and dried pork. It became clear that most of the prisoners hadn't heard the corporal's advice about eating slowly, or had decided through the pangs of hunger, to disregard it. Tedder hadn't yet received his allot-ment when the vomiting from the start of the line began. It was difficult to eat slowly, he hadn't realised how hungry he was. But eat slowly, he did. He didn't look as the man on the line next to him brought his food up almost as soon as he had scoffed it down. Tedder moved away from the vomiting men, shut out the smell and sound, closed his eyes and relished every slow mouthful.

'The corporal told ye'all to eat slow like. Now ye have ta wait five hours for anymore,' sneered Toothless.

Tedder knew this man enjoyed the deprivation of others. There were men like this in the world, his father had warned him when he was going off to be apprenticed to the tinman in Islington.

'There be some who will enjoy the lowliness of others,' his father, Henry had lamented. 'Be not one of them my boy. Be kind to people, do as your master orders, take pride in your work and you will be a fine man someday.'

Tedder sniffed and swallowed hard; he knew his father was heartbroken.

'Oh, look the little one o'er 'ere is cryin' like a baby again,' Toothless had caught Tedder daydreaming. 'Don't ye worry yeself about tings little baby,' Toothless whispered into Tedder's ear. 'I'll make sure ye'll be awright. I'll keep me eye out fer ye.'

Dread crept up Tedder's back.


On his return, the corporal ordered the thirty men to stand. Those who had scoffed down their food struggled.

'There is much administration to be done,' the corporal bellowed 'you will wait here until someone calls you. If you do not keep your position, you will be flogged. When you hear your name, come up to the desk and answer all questions with honesty and truthfulness.'

Their names were called alphabetically by surname. Some were reluctant to step forward. Some were reluctant to step forward, worried about their fate at the end of the interview. Hesitation was met with a ram to the back, from the butt of a musket. William Barrett was first, followed by Clements, the one next to Tedder who had vomited up his lunch. There was a long gap between names, and to keep himself focussed and upright, Tedder counted the minutes in between. When his name came up he didn't hear it, he was still counting after they had summoned William Smith. It amazed him how many in this group were called William.

Toothless didn't speak. He crept up behind Tedder and slammed the cudgel across his back with as much force as he could generate. Tedder landed face first on the stone floor, instantly tasting blood. Too dazed to stand, he lay there, blood pouring from either his nose or his mouth, he didn't know which.

Toothless was about to sink in the boot when the corporal's voice rolled over the stone floor and rattled around in Tedder's head. Two marines shoved and dragged him to the corporal's desk. With his eyes full of water, Tedder couldn't see the corporal or the desk. Random thoughts rattled in his brain while he tried to focus and stand on his own. Was that chair for him? He hadn't sat on a chair since he left *Indefatigable*, and then it was one that moved with the swell of the sea. He hadn't sat on a stationary chair for two years. Two other men he assumed were convicts, helped Tedder to the chair. They cleaned up his face – it was his nose that was bleeding – broken according to one man. His right eye swelled, and his lips bled, but he didn't appear to have lost any teeth. That was a relief, he didn't want to be toothless, too. He chuckled.

'I'm going to ignore your stupid cackling, Tedder,' the

corporal admonished, 'the crack on the head might affect you for a few days. Right, my name is Corporal John Black-bow, you will call me sir. Clear?'

'Yes, sir,' mumbled Tedder.

'We need to get done some paperwork. Then you'll be assigned to either a work gang or a settler or the Government, depending on your skills and character. Says here your sentence is seven years so I know you didn't kill anyone. Also says your crime was a felony – so you're no angel either.'

Tedder was about to explain the circumstances of his being charged and transported but Corporal Blackbow's raised hand in his face silenced him.

'I did not give you permission to speak. I don't give a shit what your crime was. You are here, in Van Diemen's Land and you will serve your time.'

Tedder stood still as his height was taken, 5ft 3 inches, average. He was examined for tattoos and other markings. The colour of his hair, his eye colour, and skin appearance were noted. He knew the record would show no tattoos or markings, light brown hair, and grey eyes. His mother had loved his grey eyes. The tears rolled down Tedder's cheeks as the image of his mother holding him and looking into his grey eyes when he said goodbye to her on Woolwich dock, swamped his mind. He noticed the corporal wrote 'sallow' under the complexion heading. He wanted to scream and spit in the corporal's face that since October 1810 he had been in prisons, not eating properly, not having access to clean water and not enough sunshine. Yes, his complexion was fucking sallow. The tears continued from his eyes and meandered down the dirt on his face, forming tracks as they rolled.

'Christ, Tedder. Stop your cryin'. Do as you're told, keep

out of trouble and the time will go quickly enough. You might even like it here – at least the weather is better.'

Tedder didn't attempt to explain his tears, and he wasn't asked. He was grateful it was the corporal and not Toothless witnessing his distress.

Ordered to return to the chair, the corporal asked questions about his education, his upbringing, what his father did for a living, where he lived, what sort of dwelling he had lived in, how many siblings he had, and his trade. He answered the questions truthfully without elaborating. The corporal just wanted the facts. He showed interest in Tedder's profession, even though he had one year left on his apprenticeship when the tragedy struck.

'You'll know enough surely, Tedder?' the corporal queried. 'After six years an apprentice you must have learned something.'

Tedder was staring at the door on the north side of where he sat, wondering if England was that way.

'Jesus, Tedder, snap out of it, man. I'm asking you a question.'

Embarrassed, Tedder faced the corporal. 'Sorry, sir. Yes, I learned much when apprenticed in Islington. I can fashion fine objects for stately homes and items for everyday use.'

'I don't care what you made for stately homes. We don't have stately homes in Hobart Town. I am more interested in your being able to read and write.'

'Yes, sir. I went to school.'

'You'll be assigned to the Commissariat Provision – our Issuing Store - God knows Williamson can do with the help.' The corporal dipped his pen into the ink and scribbled a comment next to Tedder's name on the paper. 'Mind you, if you don't pull your weight or get it in your head you're too good for the Stores, you'll be assigned to the chain gang digging roads or lugging stone for buildings. Clear?'

'Yes, sir.'

'Follow the guard out the door over there,' said the corporal pointing to the door on the north side. You'll have a wash in the estuary and get clean slops. Take care of the slops, don't know when we'll have any more to distribute.'

Joining the assembly of processed convicts outside the corporal's office, Tedder smelled the despair clinging to their threadbare clothes. Glimmers of hope faded with each step toward the water's edge.

'Take off them *Indefatigable* slops, wash in the estuary water, and put the clean slops on when you're dry. Yes, the water will be cold, just get in there and get it over with. It's seawater, mind.'

It was one of Toothless' band who issued the orders and warning, Tedder noticed he had more teeth and more hair.


With the washing, drying, and dressing completed, the line of thirty prisoners followed the lead guard - heads bowed, arms by their side. Tedder wondered at the difference between what he and the others were experiencing to the treatment of slaves.

# 7

# THE SHOEMAKER IN VAN DIEMEN'S LAND

*Those transported in the first few decades had a greater chance of long-term economic success than those transported later when labour markets were glutted and access to land was more difficult.*

From http://www.utas.edu.au/library/
companion_to_tasmanian_history/C/Convicts.htm

Relieved his name started with 'B', Blay took a glance back at the line of prisoners as he made his way to see the corporal; they were all struggling to stand, especially those who'd vomited up their dinner. He'd lost sight of James Tedder.

'Stand up straight,' bellowed the corporal as Blay took a position in front of his desk. 'So, you've got life, eh? Burglary of boots, even though you can make your own. Are your boot making skills no good, Blay?'

James Blay didn't know whether he was expected to respond or remain silent while the questioning continued.

'I asked you a question, convict,' roared the corporal.

'I'm sorry, sir. I am a good shoemaker, sir. I have my own shop in Spitalfields.'

'No, you don't convict. You are in Van Diemen's Land, with nothing.'

Blay felt crushed. 'You are right, sir. My wife is running the business with the apprentice, to keep herself and the three boys fed.' Blay caught what he thought was a slight change in the corporal's attitude.

'Well, then, let's get on with the processing and get you assigned to work.'

Blay's complexion, like Tedder's, was listed as sallow. His eyes listed as brown and he had no tattoos or other marks. He was 5ft 6 inches tall – above average, but underweight.

Blay received instructions about his new slops, the rationing of food, equipment, including tools, and clothing.

'We have enough shoemakers in Hobart Town, Blay. There's not enough leather to keep you all busy. You'll be assigned to a settler, James Bryan Cullen. He'll collect you in the morning.'

# 8

# THE SHOEMAKER'S BOOTS

*Convicts found in breach of the rules and regulations of the
convict department could be brought before a magistrates' bench.
Punishments awarded varied from fines, cautions, floggings (of
from 12 to 100 lashes) and sentences to the cells, treadwheel and
the public stocks. Sentences to road and chain gangs could also be
awarded...*

*From: http://www.utas.edu.au/library/
companion_to_tasmanian_history/C/Convicts.htm*

They slept on bunks in a large wooden dormitory the
second night in Van Diemen's Land. With no shackles it was
easier to find a comfortable position. Guards were around
the perimeter rotating during the night. James Blay could
not care less about the guards; he was sleeping in a bed that
didn't move, that was reasonably clean, and he was unfet-
tered. He took a deep, satisfying breath.

Dawn broke through the cracks in the walls of the

building at the same time as guards stormed in bellowing for the prisoners to get up. Blay fumbled around for the boots they gave him yesterday; he couldn't find them. Panicked, he threw up the mattress, threw his blanket off the cot, got down on the dirt floor to look under the bunk, and turned the blanket over and over.

'What's yer problem convict?'

Blay couldn't mistake the slurring speech of Toothless. Heart racing, colour gone from his face, he turned to look at the guard.

'My boots are missing, sir,' stammered Blay.

Toothless laughed. Cudgel raised ready to strike, he was stopped by the growl of the corporal.

'What's going on guard?'

'Blay here has lost his boots, sir, and don't know where to find 'em.' There were four guards in the dormitory; they doubled over laughing.

'Well then, guard, I imagine someone in here has taken them unless you and your men were not watching the quarters all night and Blay slipped out and sold his boots.'

'No sir, he did not slip out. We guarded all night long.'

'Then search the quarters, find the boots and the thief, and we'll have ourselves a trial and an execution. Or, we can go outside for a bit of fresh air and see if the boots turn up.'

Blay was relieved to no longer wear shackles, the chains would have rattled in synchronisation with the shaking of his body. He wanted no one executed on his account, but his boots were missing. The men in the quarters milled around, talking, and pointing in different directions at imagined suspects. Blay could not have been more miserable. He got down on all fours and looked under the bunk again, the boots were there.

The corporal and guards returned to the quarters as Blay was slipping his feet into the boots.

'Find them, did ye?' sniggered Toothless.

'They appeared under the bunk when you were outside,' testified Blay.

'Take him out and give him 25 lashes with the "cat" for wasting our time,' ordered the corporal.

Toothless grinned. 'Told ye when ye and Tedder were snivellin' at Woolwich that I'd make ye suffer, convict. Now tis the time.'

Grabbing Blay by the collar, Toothless threw him outside. It was raining a little. For some reason this brought comfort to Blay. The rain seemed appropriate.

'Don't rip his clothes,' warned the corporal, 'we are in short supply.'

'Well then, Blay, best you take off your shirt real nice like, and be careful not to get it dirty or to rip it.' Toothless was up against Blay's face spitting his instructions.

Determined not to let Toothless, the other prisoners, or the corporal see weakness or fear, Blay removed his shirt, folded it, and placed it on a small bush on the edge of the clearing; he stood, doggedly. Looking into Toothless' menacing and hate-filled eyes, seeing the cat o' nine tales swishing around at his whim, waiting impatiently to make contact with its victim, Blay held the vision of his wife and sons in his mind.

With his back to the aggressor, they tied Blay's wrists to a frame set up in the middle of the yard. He shook in anticipation of the coming agony. He had seen men – both convict and crew - whipped on the *Indefatigable* en route to this God-forsaken place. He'd been whipped too, but not with the "cat". Picturing the blood, the tearing of the flesh, he heard the screams of agony. His screams. After the third or fourth strike the noise stopped. Toothless cackled with satisfaction.

Blay made no sound as the rest of the cuts penetrated the fair English skin on his back. He didn't feel them; his brain took over the terror and he lost consciousness after counting twelve.

James Tedder's heart pounded in his ears like soldiers' feet marching to the beat of a drum. He'd been away from Blay for one night and the obstinate fool was tied to a frame waiting to be flogged with the cat o' nine tails. By Toothless, no less.

'What's he done?' Tedder asked the convict next to him.

'Lost his boots for muster and found 'em agin' volunteered the man.

'Why are they flogging him if he found them?'

'Cos, he wasted the corporal's and the guard's time when he could na find 'em.'

Jumping when the first strike hit James Blay's exposed flesh, Tedder felt sick as Blay let out a blood-curdling scream.

Toothless leered at the assembled group of convicts forced to watch the punishment. He swung his arm back as far as he could and struck Blay an almighty blow. The scream Tedder heard after the first strike was a muffled groan compared with the second and subsequent screams. As Toothless got to work, the blood spewed from Blay's back and the skin fell away in strips. Not one of the other 199 surviving convicts from the *Indefatigable* made a sound. Some had felt the wrath of the "cat" on the voyage from England. The marines and guards stood, quiet, motionless, cringing as the "cat" ravaged Blay's back. Toothless was the only man present who gained any satisfaction from the punishment. Tedder knew Blay had passed out; he thanked God for the mercy.

Scanning the group witnessing Blay's torment, Tedder noticed several men, who by their dress and stature were not convicts. As one, they frowned at the scene. With no obligation, they did not stay to watch Blay's misery, they moved into the superintendent's quarters, closing the door on the sorry scene behind them. All except one.

Tedder noticed him, older than his counterparts, wincing with each strike of the "cat" on Blay's back.

Watching one of the loathsome guards take pleasure in making this convict suffer, the skin on James Bryan Cullen's back prickled. He was about the same age in 1788 when Governor Phillip ordered his whipping. Shaking his head, he walked to the superintendent's office.

# 9

# THE SHOEMAKER'S ASSIGNMENT

*Upon arrival, a convict was usually assigned to a master, the Female Factory or to Public Works. To who and where a convict was assigned was recorded in an assignment register. Not all assignment registers have survived to present. Convicts were not assigned to a master in Western Australia.*

From: https://www.nla.gov.au/research-guides/convicts/convict-assignment

Lying face down on the cot in the hospital for three days, Blay dreamt of his home in Spitalfields, of his wife and his boys. Female convicts and the surgeon tended to him. Screaming in agony whenever they applied salt water was as fruitless an exercise as trying to convince the judge he didn't steal boots in Piccadilly. So he gritted his teeth, clenched his fists, buried his head in the mattress and waited each time for the agony to stop. By the third day, the expected agony had become a sting that was tolerable. He sat up on the fourth day, cringing as the skin on his back pulled and grabbed with each breath.

'Take your time, Blay,' the surgeon encouraged, 'it will be a while before the skin gets back flexibility. You won't have the time to heal in here, though. They'll come and get you before day's end.'

Even resting his head in his hands was torturous. The slight bending dragged the skin on his back, he felt sure the wounds were opening further with each movement.

'You must be careful, Blay,' continued the surgeon. 'Keep a shirt on all the time during the day; try to keep your shirts clean. Wash them regularly. This time of year you can sleep on your belly with your shirt off, there's no mosquitoes yet. But you must keep your shirt on during the day to keep the flies off your skin. Men recover from these floggings; it's the dirty clothes, fly strike and not keeping clean that kills them. If you can get fresh water on your back at the end of each day it will help. Sea water's even better.'

The surgeon moved away to his next patient, leaving Blay sitting on the edge of the cot, still with his head in his hands.

The first attempt to stand failed. Blay's knees went from under him. Putting his hands out to break his fall; the jarring reverberated up his arms and down his back. Breathless with the pain, he was on his hands and knees when Toothless strode in.

'Ah, look at ye Blay, already bowin' down to me and us aint even outta the 'ospital yet.'

The surgeon, looking up from another patient, glared at Toothless. 'Give him some time, guard. It'll be days before he is healed enough to work.'

Toothless ignored the surgeon and moved to stand over Blay. 'Get up Blay, put ye shirt on, and get outside. I'll be a waitin' for ye.'

Helping Blay with his shirt, the surgeon offered advice,

'There's no easy way to do this. Each day you get dressed it will be better. Remember to keep clean and you should be alright.' The doctor watched his patient shuffle to the door toward the brute of a guard waiting for him.

Squinting in the afternoon spring sun Blay found comfort in its warmth on his face. Toothless ordered him to the superintendent's quarters, shoving him in the middle of his back for good measure. Blay lost his breath and momentarily stopped. Toothless shoved him again. He could feel the blood trickling down his back.

'I told ye to walk, now walk.'

Blay could feel the pain induced tears running down his cheeks. They would have to run. If he wiped them away Toothless would see and hit him again. Toothless pushed him into the superintendent's quarters.

' 'ere's Blay, Sir.'

'Leave him and get out.'

Toothless gave one last menacing look at Blay and marched out into the spring sunshine.

'Find ya boots did ya Blay?' ridiculed the superintendent. Addressing another man in the room Blay hadn't noticed, the superintendent went on 'This is Blay he lost his new boots and has spent a few days remembering how important it is to look after them. Haven't you Blay?'

'Yes sir,' was the expected response, but Blay didn't reply. He was still catching his breath from the push in his back. The superintendent stood up, put his hands on his desk, leaned over and bellowed at Blay to respond.

'Yes sir,' he answered, 'I have learned to look after my boots.'

Finished with his intimidation, the superintendent sat back on his chair.

James Blay found it hard to come to terms with being

pushed around and ordered about by men, who if they were still in England, would be inferior to him on the social scale. He had been a member of the Cordwainer's Guild, he had been a respected craftsman, a respected merchant. He stared over the head of the superintendent, picturing the life he used to have.

'Well Blay,' the superintendent said, 'you should stay here in Hobart Town to dig roads, but the settlers need help.'

The superintendent addressed the man standing to the side. An older man with grey, thinning hair, with wrinkles on his face that danced when he changed his expression, and a colour on his skin that reminded Blay of the leather he'd shaped into shoes and slippers.

'He's all yours, Mr Cullen. But mind your boots now, he might just have a mind to steal them.'

Blay flushed as the Superintendent yelled 'Be gone with you, you're not my responsibility anymore.'

James Blay nodded at the superintendent and turned to look at Mr Cullen.

'Go get your things and meet me outside the Commissariat, Blay. Don't take too long, they have already held me up because of your flogging.' Cullen looked disapprovingly at the superintendent and left.

Blay trudged to the barracks to collect his spare breeches, shirt, and his jacket and cap. Half expecting his meagre belongings to be missing, he instead found Tedder waiting by his bunk, with his clothing bundled up ready for collection.

Putting his arms around Blay's shoulders Tedder gave him a gentle, comforting hug.

'I watched them whipping you Blay. We all did. We had to. Even the bastards who hid your boots on you were

56

feeling squeamish. Don't think they expected it to go that far. I've been looking after your stuff since.'

Tedder held Blay at arm's length and considered the face that seemed to have aged ten years. 'You're not looking your best, Blay. But I hear they have assigned you to a settler in New Norfolk. It's got to be better than a chain gang.'

'Blay,' came a call from outside. 'Get your stuff, we need to get sorted.'

Giving Tedder an awkward hug, Blay took his belongings and shuffled to the door of the barracks into the unknown. Again.

'Name's James Bryan Cullen, Blay. I'm going to keep callin' you Blay 'cos I'm a free man, and the name James belongs to me, on my property. Got that?'

'Yes, Mr Cullen,' answered Blay. Bewildered and confused, he followed along behind the older man. There were no physical chains attached to this relationship. No cudgels, no whips, no foul-smelling beings leering over him, but he was undoubtedly a convict. Clearing his throat to gain Mr Cullen's attention, Blay asked for permission to speak.

'What is it Blay? You got something to say, just say it. No need to tiptoe around me or mine.'

'I'm wondering,' blurted Blay 'Where we are going and what is to happen to me?'

Mr Cullen burst out laughing. 'Well Blay, you've been assigned to me to work on my farm. So, for the rest of your life, you'll work for me or if I die before you, another settler. Of course, if you behave, you might get a Ticket of Leave or a Conditional or Absolute Pardon. Then you'll be able to look after yourself.'

The incredulous look on Blay's face prompted Mr

Cullen to continue. 'Do you know what a Ticket of Leave is, son?'

Blay admitted he had no idea.

'If you do your time without any bother, if you don't break any of the laws here in Van Diemen's Land, you can apply to the Governor to have a Ticket of Leave. Means you can move about and work for someone else. You're free, but not quite - you can't leave Van Diemen's Land - and do one thing wrong, and your Ticket of Leave gets taken away.'

This is not what James Blay imagined his sentence to look like. He imagined the horrors of imprisonment being continued on dry land; of being shackled and worked almost to death.

'I'm wonderin' Mr Cullen if I could ask some more questions.'.

Cullen nodded.

'Will I be wearing shackles?'

'Not as long as you work hard and don't run off,' answered Cullen.

'What about clothes and food and medicine?'

'You're my responsibility, Blay. I'll look after your bodily needs.'

Blay was about to ask another question when Mr Cullen raised his hand to indicate silence. Obeying didn't stop his mind jumping from question to question.

'Keep up Blay,' Cullen ordered as they walked through the dirt streets of Hobart Town. 'We will stay in town tonight, at a friend of mine's, and make our way to New Norfolk early tomorrow.'

As the sun set, a chill crept into the air. Blay's body begged for rest and sustenance. He hadn't had a good night's sleep since the flogging, and he'd had nightmares about dying. Cullen knocked on the door of a small hut on the edge of the convict's and guard's barracks. Someone made the hut of a timber Blay couldn't identify, with a roof fashioned from tree bark. The door opened to a well-presented man with a beaming smile who welcomed Mr Cullen and him inside. The fire, placed in the middle of the eastern wall of the cosy room, was alight and welcoming.

'Good to see you James,' greeted the stranger. Blay, smiling at the welcome tone, looked toward the speaker, who he then realised, was addressing Mr Cullen.

'Might be some confusion in this convict's mind, Abraham. When you say James, he thinks you're talking to him. We're calling him Blay to save mix-up,' explained Mr Cullen to his friend.

'Blay, this is Mr Abraham Hands he is kind enough to let us stay at his Hobart Town home this night.'

Blay bowed slightly in acknowledgement of Mr Cullen's friend, then looked longingly toward the fire and the chair placed near it. He wanted to sit in a comfortable chair by the fire and have something to eat. He would close his eyes and remember his home and family in London.

As if reading his mind, Mr Cullen indicated that Blay should sit in the chair by the fire, while Mr Hands got some food together for the three of them. Exhausted, Blay found it difficult to stay awake, but his rumbling stomach ensured he did. Mr Hands and Mr Cullen ate at the small table to one side of the room and let Blay eat his supper in the chair by the fire. Ignoring the jarring pain in his back, he went to sleep in the chair.

Waking with a gasp of anguish, Blay remembered he was a convict in Van Diemen's Land. In a wisp of smoke, morning swept away the dream he had during the night of sitting by the fire in the kitchen of the home he shared with Sarah and the boys.

'You'd better get up, Blay, come outside and wash. Wash your dirty shirt and it will dry on the boat on the way home,' instructed Cullen.

Blay did as he was told, but Mr Cullen saying they were going 'home' brought a sadness that spread over him like a gust of wind in a snowstorm. He shivered.

'Have you ever been home to England, Mr Cullen?' Blay asked his new master. He thought of Cullen as a master because he was a servant until he earned his freedom, or until he died.

'No, I have not, and have no desire to. My life is here, although it was a better life on Norfolk Island, but we had to leave there.'

'Why was that, Mr Cullen?'

'That is a story for another time, Blay. Now go inside and help Mr Hands with breakfast. We need to be on our way as quick as possible.'

Abraham noticed Blay staring at the food in the bowls. 'What's the problem, Blay never seen oatmeal afore?'

'It's a very long, long time since I've seen oatmeal look so clean. I had it made with filthy water from the Thames for more than a year and mixed to a stodgy mess with hardly any water on the *Indefatigable*.' He caught his breath.

'Ah yes. I remember the muck we were fed on the *Alex*ander on our way to Sydney Cove in New South Wales. And the shit we tried to eat on the hulk in the Thames. Hard times those Blay. But life gets better when your time is up.'

'You were a convict?'

'Yes, I thought you knew that. But then again, if no one told you, why would you know? I came in what they call the First Fleet. Took us ten months at sea to get to Sydney Cove. But, you know what? Best thing that ever happened to me. I got seven years for highway robbery. In London, I would have had a shit life with no prospects. Here, I'm a landowner, I've got this little house in Hobart Town and my house in New Norfolk. I sell my goods to the Commissariat. I'm happy. Most importantly, I have no regrets.'

'What about Mr Cullen, was he a convict too?'

'Yes. Came on the *Scarborough* in the First Fleet. Lots of us in New Norfolk came in 1788. Many more came later. Been good for everyone who kept their head down and worked. Not so good for those who kept on breaking the rules.'

Cullen walked into the small house just as Abraham finished telling his convict story. 'Sit down and eat your oatmeal. We have to get started as quickly as possible after breakfast.'

'Blay here didn't know we were once convicts, James,' said Abraham Hands. 'Found it a bit hard to believe, I think. Didn't you Blay?'

James Bryan Cullen took a deep breath, swallowed hard and sat down to eat his oatmeal. 'Doesn't matter. Doesn't change anything. It was a long, long time ago. All turned out for us.'

Blay noticed Mr Cullen's colour change a little. 'Thank you for waiting for me, Mr Cullen. For waiting while I got a bit over the flogging.'

'Upsets me to see anyone flogged, Blay. I knew you wouldn't have done much to deserve it. The injustice is what shits me the most.' Cullen stood up from the table, washed his bowl in the bucket Abraham had provided for the purpose, shook his friend's hand and walked outside. 'I'll expect to see you outside with your things in two minutes, Blay.'

## 10

# THE TINSMITH'S JOB

'

'Mr Williamson, Tedder here is literate. Apparently, he wrote a very impressive letter to a well-respected London diamond merchant demanding 500 pounds. He said the gentleman had done illegal things to him and had promised him money. And yet, here he is, standing in front of us, in Van Diemen's Land, penniless and at our mercy.' The superintendent smirked at Tedder.

Tedder's face and neck turned fire poker red, his heart thumped hard enough to jump out of his chest. His breathing so rapid, he worried he would pass out. Clenching his fists by his side he tried taking deep breaths to calm down.

'But, Mr Williamson,' continued the superintendent 'I'm sure you'll be able to keep him so busy maintaining the records in the Commissariat, he won't have time to write mischievous letters. Mischievous letters here, Tedder, will see you working on a chain gang.'

The superintendent leaned back in his chair, arms folded across his ample middle, glaring. Although the superintendent's stare penetrated his thoughts, Tedder felt the heat of the poker red colour leave his face, his heart beat slowed, and his breathing returned to normal. Waiting like a rabbit in a trap, not knowing what was next, but certain it wouldn't be good, Tedder stared ahead.

The superintendent spoke to Mr Williamson, 'Get Tedder to his quarters and get him to work first thing in the morning. You'll start at seven in the forenoon Tedder, every day except Sunday when you'll go to church. You'll finish at five in the afternoon. Get out.'

The man the superintendent called Mr Williamson moved toward Tedder and indicated that he should be followed. Tedder walked just to the rear of Mr Williamson, outside into the sun and fresh air. Taking a deep breath he put his head back to make the most of the sun on his face. Mr Williamson kept up a brisk pace, and Tedder had to almost run to keep up.

'Go and get your shit from your barracks, Tedder,' ordered Mr Williamson. 'Hurry up.'

James Tedder, convict number 2028, had no idea what was going on. He trudged to the barracks to collect the rest of his convict slops.

While walking on the dirt tracks that pretended to be roads in Hobart Town, Tedder was shown the Commissariat building, then Mr Williamson took him to a little timber hut about one hundred yards from the water's edge. 'You'll be sleeping here, Tedder. These are your quarters while you do the record keeping for the Stores. You'll be looking after yourself. You'll get rations from the Stores like everyone else – make sure you record them proper like – and you'll cook, clean and manage yourself. Do that, and you'll get along fine. Break the rules, and you're on the chain gang.'

'There are two cots in here, Mr Williamson,' Tedder said.

'Oh, really? Gee, the superintendent was right, you are clever. You'll be sharing the space with another clerk eventually. You can see we don't have that many huts to go 'round. There's some food in there for tonight. Be in the Store at seven in the morning.' Mr Williamson left.

Tedder stood in the middle of the little space. It was quite comfortable. The windows had glass fitted, a stone fireplace on one wall had a fire going. The two cots on the other wall each had a pillow and blanket and a small timber table, and two chairs were in the middle of the room. The floor was timber. He would be able to sweep it and keep it clean. The table was set with tin plates and mugs and knives, forks and spoons. Tedder hadn't eaten with a knife and fork for two years. A small loaf of bread, salted beef, tea, and sugar were laid out in the middle of the table. A bucket in the corner had fresh water in it, and a kettle hanging over the fire was almost to the boil. A rail had been attached to the wall next to the fireplace where the heat would reach it; two towels hung over the rail. Tedder sat down on a chair, folded his arms on the table, rested his head on his arms, and cried. He hadn't had luxuries such as these, or privacy, for more than two years.

The fatigue that came with insecurity and fear nagged at Tedder to lay down on a cot and sleep, but hunger took over, and he felt obliged to take advantage of the provisions laid out for him. Tedder sat up straight in the chair, used the knife to slice some bread off the loaf, and some salted beef from the portion provided. He made a pot of tea, poured some into a mug and piled in three large spoons of sugar. Returning the kettle to its position, he stoked the fire, put on another piece of wood, moved a chair next to it, and enjoyed the first meal he had eaten alone, and in comfortable surrounds, since being arrested in October 1810. With no one around to care or see, he let the tears run down his cheeks.

Worrying about oversleeping and having Toothless sent to drag him to the Commissariat's Office kept Tedder awake.

Getting up at first light, not knowing the time, he put his head outside to see any signs of activity. Marines were moving around, and a few settlers were starting their day's activities. Walking to the water's edge to wash his face, he crossed paths with a settler leading a horse.

'What time is it please, sir?' Tedder enquired.

'I don't know. Don't have no watch.'

'I don't have one either. How do you know what time of the day it is then?'

'They ring the bell that's hangin' on the superintendent's door. First ring of the day is six. Then every hour til dark.'

Tedder panicked. 'Has it rung today yet? I'm afraid I might have slept through it.'

'No, not yet. Not proper daylight yet. You just get 'ere did ye?'

'A few days ago,' said Tedder. 'I start work in the Commissariat today and I have to be there by seven. Thank you for your help, sir.'

Nodding in appreciation to the stranger, Tedder moved to the water's edge, splashed cold clear water on his face, took a deep breath of the fresh, biting, morning air, and returned to his hut. The bell over the superintendent's door was rung. Tedder heard it. Managing to restore the fire to a flame high enough to boil the kettle, he smiled, daring to feel a little happy. He changed into his new convict uniform, made tea, ate some bread and beef, tidied up his little hut, closed the door and found his way to the Commissariat long before the bell was rung for the next hour.

The doors were locked. Tedder didn't know if someone was inside and he should knock or wait. He knocked twice.

Walking up behind TEdder, Mr Williamson said, 'No point in you knockin' Tedder. You're not in there, so no one can open it.' He laughed at his attempt to be funny.

Tedder smiled politely.

'First customers don't arrive till eight, Tedder. We need from now till then to get organised for the day. Everyone's on rations, settlers and convicts alike. That'd be includin' you. People buy their supplies, but they can only buy what's in their rations. Tis your job to keep track of what they buy and take it from the rations they got for the month. Clear?'

'Yes, Mr Williamson. How do convicts buy their rations?'

'With the money, they earn from workin'. Where did you think? From the faeries at the bottom o' the garden?'

'I get paid for working?'

'Yes, Tedder. Everyone gets paid. If you are bad enough to work on the chain gangs, you don't get much pay cos you can't go anywhere to buy anything. Governor Macquarie wants convicts to do their time and then help build up this colony when they are free. Money is needed to do that. Don't go smiling with that twinkle in your eye, Tedder. You must buy everything for yourself cos you're working for the Government. Government won't be feeding you. You'll get new uniform each year, and the hut you live in, nothing else.'

'What about the things that were in the hut when you let me in last night?'

'Something to get you started. The food comes out of your rations, the furniture, and other stuff is a loan; you'll have to buy your own when you get money saved.'

'How often do we get paid, Mr Williamson?'

'You don't actually get the money, Tedder. The Government puts it in a bank account and uses it to buy what you take from the Commissariat. You won't get actual money till you are a free man.'

Understanding how the system worked, Tedder didn't care that he wouldn't see any money. To be paid, as a convict, and to be partly responsible for his own affairs was liberating. He had hope in his heart for the first time in two years. He smiled, thinking that God was listening now.

The morning passed quickly, Tedder reminisced about his first day working in the Arsenal at Woolwich. How different this was. He wasn't free, he was a convict, but he felt free. No chains, clothes that he could wash, dry and keep clean. Responsibility for his own affairs.

Mr Williamson was a good teacher. He said he only wanted to say something once, so he said it clearly and made sure Tedder understood the processes before he moved on to something else.

Counting the bells during the morning, Tedder knew when it was time for dinner.

'You get one-half hour,' Mr Williamson informed him, 'when the bell sounds again, you better be here, waiting for me to open up.'

Walking to his hut with a new spring in his step, Tedder took his time to take in the different smells and sounds of the settlement. Boats travelled up and down the estuary, women collected water from the fresh water wells in buckets of different sizes, children played and splashed each other, the fish and eels could be seen just below the surface, the trees and the sky and clouds reflected in the water. The scents emanating from the trees cleared his head, the smell of burning wood from house fires gave the settlement a feeling of normality. He reminded himself to fill up the kettle before he returned to work.

'My first item to purchase is a lock and key,' he said aloud while checking to see that the food and towels and bedding were still in place. Knowing that the bread and beef would have to last until he was paid and could buy more, he ate sparingly. 'A list must be made of things that will make this little place comfortable. After food, I will need a chair to sit by the fire.' Tedder's mind wandered to a future where he was comfortably situated in Hobart Town.

He stoked the fire from the wood pile next to the fireplace, making a mental note to find out where the wood came from. He used a small piece of wood as a stopper for the top of the door, which would fall if someone broke in while he was at work.

Tedder learned quickly. Convicts and settlers came into the stores, identified themselves, he looked up their details, recorded purchases against the relevant name, and provided the goods. The ration sheet was always on hand, so he knew if customers were trying to buy more than their rations allowed. Each item of stock sold was itemised on the stock list. If a settler, approved to sell to the Commissariat Provence brought in supplies, they were recorded into stock and the settler was paid the agreed rate. Tedder had done a little bookkeeping when he was apprenticed to the tinsmith, which gave him the confidence to deal with cranky settlers and disagreeable convicts. Under his breath, he thanked God he was born to parents who sent him to school to read and write.

The bell over the superintendent's door rang six times. Tedder was surprised how quickly his first day had passed.

'Good work, Tedder,' complimented Mr Williamson. 'You learned quick. Keep it up and you'll be right as rain in no time.'

Tedder wasn't sure what Mr Williamson meant by right as rain, but it didn't seem important enough to worry about. 'Good evening, Mr Williamson. I'll see you in the morning.'

'Tomorrow is Sunday, Tedder. Best get your bearings so you know if you're comin' or goin'. I know we're at the bottom of the world, but the days of the week are the same, even if the seasons and the stars are upside down.'

'Thank you, Mr Williamson. What time does church begin Sunday?'

'You'd best be sitting in a pew when the superintendent's bell rings eight. We don't want an excuse for them to take you away from the Commissariat and put you to work on a chain gang.'

Grateful for Mr Williamson's help and advice, Tedder nodded and strolled toward his hut. He felt like skipping, like running, like jumping for joy, but his feet hurt, and he was tired. He did, however, allow himself to grin like a Cheshire cat.

A sigh of relief followed his grin when he found the door as he left it. He'd forgotten to ask about a lock and key. With his stomach grumbling at the sight of the beef and bread, Tedder realised he wouldn't have enough food for Sunday and Monday: a plan was needed, and part of that plan was restocking the wood pile and looking in the Derwent estuary to see if fishing was a feasible option.

He found a small stockpile of firewood behind the hut and stacked as much as he could carry in his arms. Walking around the edge of the hut back to the door, he tripped, dropped the wood, most of it falling on his worn-out feet.

'Oops, Tedder. Ye dropped somethin'.'

He knew the voice, he knew the sound of the spittle leaving the mouth between the rotting teeth. Toothless had tripped him. He struggled to his feet.

The guard was grinning widely, baring a few black, brown, and dark grey teeth. Tedder thought he looked like a freak from the carnivals that sometimes passed through London.

'Best pick up ye little supply of wood, there Tedder.'

He bent down to collect the wood.

'Oh geez, Tedder,' said Toothless as he kneed him on the nose. 'Did you get hurt at your precious, safe, cosy little job today, did ye?'

Tedder's nose erupted into agonising pain and the blood poured into his mouth.

'I asked ye a question, convict,' bellowed Toothless into Tedder's face.

'No, sir. I didn't get hurt at work today.'

'Ah, that's good, Tedder. I'm comin' in to see ya next week. I need supplies, and I need some extra little bits and pieces, Tedder. You'll be able to help me with that, won't ye?'

'Yes, sir.'

'Good, convict. I'll see ye next week.'

As a final gesture, Toothless slapped Tedder in the middle of the back before sauntering off.

. . .

Standing in the same place for a long time, he took quick, short breaths, waiting for the anxiety to subside. Several people walked past, watching as Tedder stood, breathing rapidly. No one offered to help. He bent to pick up a few pieces of wood, no longer focussing on the task. Managing to carry the pieces to the hut, he dropped them next to the fireplace. Three more trips were required before the wood-pile in the hut was replenished. Tedder sat at the table, resting his head in his hands. He marvelled at how things changed so quickly from a little happiness in the morning to physical agony and being in peril from Toothless in the evening.

Even though he cherished the privacy, Tedder was lonely. After two years living in very close proximity to so many other men: shitting, washing, eating, working, sleeping together, it was strange to be alone. He wondered what had happened to Blay, and if he was safe and in a good job.

He ate the last of the bread and had a weaker cup of tea with less sugar, for his supper. Looking at his limited supplies, he wondered how long they were supposed to last. He must find out how much he was to be paid, and how to buy his own supplies. He dragged his cot closer to the fire, using it as a makeshift fireside chair, making a mental note to put a proper chair on his shopping list. Intending to sit on the cot in front of the fire for a while before bed, the last thing he remembered was pondering how he could get some books to read.

Waking with a start at the sound of the bell ringing over the superintendent's door, Tedder hurried to his feet panicking that he'd missed church. He pulled on his boots, wiping blood away from his nostrils as his injured nose bled without warning. He splashed water from the bucket onto his hair and face, put on his jacket and stepped out into the clear Sunday morning.

He walked along behind a group of settlers, hoping they were heading to church. The little building with the cross over the door came into view. Tedder was surprised at how it had settled into its surroundings; looking as if it had been in the same location for years. Standing back, he let others enter ahead of him.

'Hurry up, then, convict,' a marine at the door was marking them off the list as they walked into St David's Church. 'What number are ye?' the marine asked Tedder.

'Twenty twenty-eight.'

'Right, here it is.'

Tedder watched the marine put a mark next to his name to prove he had come to church.

'Get over there, convicts sit on the left side.'

A church service was conducted every Sunday morning on the *Indefatigable*, but this felt good, sitting in a building fit for purpose even though its construction was basic. The Reverend Robert Knopwood urged them, convicts and settlers, marines, and guards, to be thankful for the things God had provided. Considering the journey he had been on since October 1810, Tedder was grateful to still be alive.

# 11

# THE DERWENT

## Convict administration - The Assignment Period: 1803-1839

*Convicts' food and clothing needs were transferred to private settlers during the Assignment Period. Landholders were required to take on at least one convict for every 100 acres. Recordkeeping practices were designed to record each convict's "career".*

https://www.linc.tas.gov.au/convict-portal/pages/convict-life.aspx

Blay recognised the type of boat. It was a wherry. They used them on the Thames to transport people and goods. 'Where are we goin' in that?' he demanded of Mr Cullen.

'You won't be speaking to me like that, Blay. You'd be advised to mind your tongue and your place. Don't you think my showing a bit of kindness means I'm weak. Don't you think that now you know I came here as a convict, changes things. I've been through a hell of a lot more in my years than you in yours, no matter what you think. Now get on board and pick up the oars.'

Doing as instructed, Blay climbed into the boat, nodding at another man who was already seated. Mr Cullen offered no introductions. He sat, with his back to Blay, in the middle of the boat, surrounded by what Blay could only imagine were supplies for the mysterious farm he assumed he was heading towards.

Blay and the man using the other pair of oars established a steady rhythm, guiding the little boat through the water. He felt at peace in the stillness and beauty and spellbound by the clarity of the water in the river and the trees and plants on the river's banks.

'What is the name of this river, please, Mr Cullen?' Blay ventured.

'It's the Derwent,' Cullen answered. 'Named after the Derwent in Cumbria in England. God only knows why. You won't find any of these trees and plants and animals in Cumbria.'

'It is very clean. Not at all like the Thames. And very wide. How far is it to your farm, Mr Cullen?'

'Twenty miles or thereabouts. The wind is starting to pick up, you can put the sail up, Robert.'

Blay realised Mr Cullen wasn't going to continue a conversation with him. 'It's going to be a long journey. I'll have to keep my head down and let him get over the shock of me knowing he was a convict. But I don't know what the problem with that is. I think it's amazing that he came here twenty-four years ago with nothing and seems to have built a good life for himself.' Blay kept himself entertained with his thoughts.

. . .

The sail swallowed the wind and gave Blay the opportunity to rest and take in the beauty that followed him along the river. Dancing on the water, the sun occasionally broke through the surface revealing an abundance of fish swimming carelessly around the boat. His breath left him in a gush as he noticed some amazing birds standing on the rocks. With practised technique they swooped into the water, coming to the surface with a fish struggling to escape the vice-like grip of their beaks.

'They are cormorants,' said Cullen 'They are good at fishing.'

Blay jumped when Mr Cullen spoke; he had been silent for a long time.

'We'll steer clear of the rocks they are resting on else we end up in the river with the fish they are hunting,' Cullen continued. 'The river widens out a bit around the bend. Keep your eye on the banks for the different creatures you'll see. There's nothing like it in England.'

Blay was mesmerised as Cullen named the birdlife, animal life and parts of this magnificent river.

'What's that? Looks like a rat,' exclaimed Blay.

'It's a bandicoot. Digs little holes in the ground. Eats worms, insects, and spiders. Good to have in the house garden at the farm. Lots of strange animals here, Blay.'

The solitude of the river was splintered by a crescendo of squawking white birds flying overhead. Blay looked up to see hundreds of birds with yellow crests on their heads, flying back towards Hobart Town.

'They are cockatoos. Live in those big flocks and make lots of noise when they are all together,' explained Cullen. 'Keep looking on the bank over there – there's some native hens scrounging around.'

'It's full of life,' Blay said. 'The river, the river banks, the sky. My boys would love it here,' he wiped his eyes before the tears had a chance to escape.

'Best tell me about your boys, Blay. It's another couple of hours before we reach New Norfolk. It'll pass the time,' invited Cullen. 'Robert will keep us sailing along nicely.'

He missed them every minute. These last few days in Van Diemen's Land he'd missed them more than ever. Seeing children running around Hobart Town, the children of marines and settlers, playing their games, being growled at by the adults, made the emptiness in his heart expand enough to almost swallow him whole. Again, he wiped his eyes before the tears escaped.

'It'll help to talk about them. Keeps them alive in your heart. You might even get to see them again one day.' Cullen encouraged.

'What do you mean see them again? I got life, remember,' this time the tears escaped and Blay didn't' try to stop them.

'Not very bright, are you Blay? Is that how you ended up getting knicked? I did tell you yesterday that if you work hard and don't break any rules, you can get a Ticket of Leave, or maybe even a pardon. You've got to have hope to keep going here.'

James Blay wiped his tears and stared at the older man's wrinkled, tanned face. 'Do you really mean that? I could see my boys again?'

'Hope is the only thing that is yours while you are a convict, Blay. Hope is the only thing they can't take away from you. You need hope to keep going every day. So, tell me about your boys.'

'The first is James Jr, he's nine years now I think. He's quiet but raises to anger real quick. I was going to start him off as an apprentice when he was the right age. Don't know what he'll do now.'

Cullen asked Blay how many boys he had. 'Three. Sarah was disappointed she didn't get a daughter. She wants a girl she can call Susanna after her mother,' he sniffed. 'The next one is William. He should be seven by now. He's quiet too, a good boy, loves his Mama more than anything in the world. He's good at the school work too. Likes numbers. John is the youngest. He'd be four, I guess. He wouldn't even remember me, still a baby really when I got thrown into Newgate. Noisy little bugger didn't stop talking. Followed his brothers around like he was their shadow.'

'What about your wife?' asked Cullen.

'She is a strong woman. A lot stronger than I ever gave her credit for. When I got sentenced, she went to the Guild to get permission to keep training my apprentice and keep the shop going. When they shipped us off on the *Indefatigable* she was running the shop and making sure there was enough money to feed the boys, pay the rent and send James and William to school. Made of tough stuff, that one.'

Blay had confidence in his wife. He knew she would take good care of the boys.

'You can tell me all about how you ended up in Van Diemen's Land another day, Blay. When the river widens out in a mile or so, we'll be in New Norfolk. It becomes fresh water then.'

It took his breath away. Blay had never seen anything more spectacular. The trees on the riverbank, the ones the cocka-toos loved so much nearer to Hobart Town, stood towering over their domain. Everything reflected in the water: the sky, the clouds, the sunshine, the trees, the plants.

As they rounded the bend, a little township came into view. It sat, nestled on the riverbank, overlooked by a towering rock formation that spread itself like arms, offering protection from the outside world.

Blay was mesmerised. 'I've never seen anything more beautiful,' he whispered.

'Did you ever leave London?' Cullen asked.

'No, born in Bethnal Green and lived half a mile away in Spitalfields.'

'There's much to get used to then, Blay. This is an unforgiving country and we have lots of land to clear and get under cultivation. We'll unpack the wherry and put the supplies on the cart to transport them up to the house. You will meet the family and get settled, and we'll start tomorrow at first light.'

Blay didn't know how he should be feeling. Excited? Happy? Wary? He did know he had an overwhelming sense of sadness lying in the pit of his stomach. The feeling was akin to the one he experienced when he said his final goodbyes to his wife and boys before the *Indefatigable* left England. He smiled at Mr Cullen. He wanted to indicate his appreciation of the change in the man's attitude toward him.

'What's the date, Mr Cullen?' he asked. He'd lost all track of time on the voyage to Van Diemen's Land and hadn't caught up on landing.

'October 22, 1812,' Cullen answered. 'Mark this day in your memory because it's the start of a new life. A life you can use to build and improve your lot, or one you can throw away. Up to you. But, don't have any regrets.'

Robert went up to the house and harnessed the horse to the cart for Cullen and helped him and Blay load the supplies. 'Thank you, Robert. Much appreciated,' Cullen said. Passing money into Robert's hand when he shook it.

'Up on the cart,' Cullen ordered.

Blay climbed up next to Cullen just as the reins were flicked onto the back of the horse. The cart lurched forward, and the horse took its first slow steps down the well-trodden track to the Cullen farm.

# 12

# NEW NORFOLK

*Prior to the arrival of Europeans the area around New Norfolk had been occupied by members of the Lairmairrener Aboriginal language group.*
*Between 27 November, 1807 and 2 October, 1808 some 500 people from Norfolk Island (23 were convicts) were settled at what is now New Norfolk. It was known as The Hills at the time.*
*On 30 April, 1808 the settlement became known as New Norfolk.*

**From :**
http://www.aussietowns.com.au/town/new-norfolk-tas

'Robert is not coming with us, Mr Cullen?' Blay asked.

'No. He's staying in town. He'll come out to the farm in a day or two.'

James Blay wanted to ask if Robert had also been a convict. He needed to feed his desire for hope. Reasoning that the more settlers he saw living on their own land and making a good living, the more chance there would be for him to improve his lot.

'I get the feeling you're busting to ask me something, Blay. Just ask, if I don't want to answer you, I won't.'

'I was wondering if Robert had been a convict, Mr Cullen.'

'Yes. He came on the Third Fleet, arrived in 1791. Got seven years. I didn't see him arrive, I was already on Norfolk Island by then. But, by God, I saw the Second Fleet arrive, and it's said that the Third was just as bad. Governor Phillip was so angry when the convicts started coming off the Second Fleet ships you could've cooked eggs on his hot, red face. Conditions on those old slave ships were so bad that nearly 250 men died on the voyage. There were only seventy-eight women on board the ships, and eleven of them died on the way out. When they got to Port Jackson, 500 of the convicts were sick or dying. We had to carry them off the ships; fleas were jumping off them onto us, they had dysentery, typhoid fever, the scurvy and God knows what else. They stunk, we had to throw ourselves in the sea after we put them down on the beach. That's one of the reasons Phillip sent some of us to Norfolk Island, there wasn't enough food, clothes or medicine at Port Jackson to do everyone.'

Blay's mouth fell open as he listened to Cullen's story. 'I had no idea, Mr Cullen, no one ever told us. Sounds like a rottener version of the hulks. At least on the hulks, we could see family and get supplies from them. *Indefatigable* wasn't so bad coming here, we usually had enough to eat but the quality wasn't good. We got to exercise, were allowed on the deck, had some education and some work each day.'

'Indeed, Blay. Our trip from England was long, but Phillip had prepared well, and we all arrived alive. But when we carried those poor souls off the ships and put them on the sand, Governor Phillip walked around with his red face pulsing fury, his fists were clenched, and he had tears running down his cheeks. None of us had ever seen that before. They said he wrote to Lord Grenville about the poor souls that came on those ships, but the next lot – Robert's - was sent out before Grenville got the letter. So, he wrote again. Things got better for convicts being transported after that.'

> *"Of the convicts mentioned by your Lordship to be sent out, 1,695 males and 168 females have been landed, with six free women and ten children. It appears by the returns from the Transports that 194 males, 4 females and 1 child died on the passage; and, although the convicts landed from these ships were not so sickly as those brought out last year, the greatest part of them are so emaciated, so worn away by long confinement, or want of food, or from both these causes, that it will be long before they recover their strength, and which many of them never will recover.*
>
> *Your Lordship will readily conceive that this addition to our numbers will for many months be a deadweight on the stores.*
>
> *The surgeon's returns of this day are: "Under medical treatment and incapable of labour, 626.... 576 of whom are those landed from the last ships."* [1]

'Anyways,' Cullen continued, 'Robert was in that lot that was starving and sick. Soon as he was well enough, he was sent to Norfolk Island with some others. The tropical air on that island, Blay, the sweetness of the trees, the beautiful clear skies, the nourishing rain, all helped Robert Bishop to heal and become whole again. He was assigned to me. We became good friends. Still works for me from time to time, but he's his own man now.'

The older man's stories had Blay in awe of him, and of what these old prisoners seemed to have achieved.

'You'll be surrounded by ex-convicts, Blay,' Cullen offered. 'Elizabeth, my wife, came on *Marquis Cornwallis* to Port Jackson and was then sent to Norfolk Island. She was assigned to me too. Poor little might was pregnant when she got to us. Never asked her how, or who the father was, and she never told me. Dear little boy – she called him William – died not long after he took his first breath.

'Surrounded by settlers who started their lives in this colony as convicts, you will be, Blay. All of us living here were moved from Norfolk Island where we'd all finished our time and made lives for us and our families. Governor Macquarie tried to call this place Elizabeth Town after his wife, but we kept calling it New Norfolk, and the name stuck.'

Just as James Bryan Cullen finished his sentence, a well presented, good sized, timber house, with good fencing, gardens, and animals grazing in the paddocks at the back, smacked Blay in the face.

Cullen pulled the horse to a stop. Blay couldn't take his eyes off the house and its surrounds.

'We'll get the horse sorted, then we'll go inside and get you sorted,' said Cullen. Blay followed Mr Cullen to the stable. He'd never tended to a horse before and hoped Mr Cullen didn't want him to do it now.

'You looked after horses, before, Blay?'

'No, sir. Didn't own a horse or carriage in London. Walked everywhere.'

'Well, today you can watch me, and then that will be put on the list of things you need to do to earn your keep.'

Finished with the horse, Blay helped Cullen remove the

supplies from the back of the cart and stack them in a shed next to the stable.

'Papa, Papa, Papa,' squealed a very excited little girl as she ran towards Cullen and threw her arms around him. 'Have you brought us a new helper, Papa?' she asked Cullen.

'Yes Betsy, this is Blay. He'll be staying and working with us for a time. That is if he is good. Do you think he will be good?'

'I don't know Papa, we'll see,' Betsy replied while looking Blay up and down as if he were a new pony.

'Betsy is our youngest, Blay, she is named after my wife, Elizabeth. We call her Betsy to save confusion. She is seven. Just four when we left Norfolk Island, so she doesn't remember much.'

Blay swallowed hard, keeping the heart-breaking realisation that Betsy was about the same age as his son, William, buried and silent.

'I'm pleased to meet you, Miss Elizabeth,' said Blay with a slight bow.

She smiled and skipped off towards the house. 'Mama has some food ready, Papa. And Blay, my name is Betsy,' she called over her shoulder.

'Let's go into the house, Blay. You can meet the rest and get organised.'

James Blay followed Cullen into the house, copying his movements so as not to get off on the wrong foot. Cullen took his boots off at the door, so did Blay. Cullen hung up his hat inside the door, and Blay put his convict cap next to it. The smell of a home hit all his senses at once. He could hear children squabbling, smelled the aromas of dinner simmering, saw the colours of a family, felt the warmth of the fire. He touched the back of a chair to make sure he wasn't on *Indefatigable* about to wake up.

Blay watched as Mr Cullen kissed each one of his girls on the forehead and did the same with his wife.

'Elizabeth,' said Cullen 'this is our new assignee – his name's James Blay – but we will call him Blay. I explained we can't have two men named James living here, and I'm the boss, so I make the rules.' He smiled at his wife.

Blay bowed towards Elizabeth Cullen 'Pleased to meet you, Mrs Cullen.'

'I hope I'm pleased to meet you, Mr Blay,' she responded. 'We don't want any breaking the rules while you're here. Plenty of our neighbours have sent convicts back to the barracks to work on the chain gang cos they can't follow the rules. Hope you're not goin' to be one of 'em, Mr Blay.'

'No Mrs Cullen. I want to see my wife and boys again, and Mr Cullen said if I follow the rules, do the work, keep my head down, I can earn a Ticket of Leave.'

Elizabeth Cullen looked quizzically at her husband. 'So, Mr Blay has a family, James?'

'Yes, he does and he's very keen to see them again.'

'Well, best wash up and sit down to dinner, Mr Blay so we can hear all about your family.'

For the first time in two years, James Blay felt human. 'I know I am a convict. I know I don't have my freedom. I know I'll have to work hard, but I also know I have some hope in my heart at last.' He sat on the seat Elizabeth Cullen indicated, and smiled at the girls. All three were staring at him.

'Best do some introductions, Elizabeth,' said Mr Cullen. 'Blay here is fascinated with our stories.'

'Well Mr Blay, you might be able to tell from my accent that I'm originally from Dublin. Arrived in Port Jackson on *Marquis Cornwallis*, and was pretty well straight away, sent to Norfolk Island. You know what they're reasonin' was? Fourteen of us girls were shipped off to Norfolk Island because they had a spinning wheel they were sending there, and they said, we bein' Irish, would be able to use it to spin the flax. I didn't even know what one looked like, let alone use it. But, as you know, you don't get to make your own decisions about where you go and what you do when you are transported to the other side of the world. Got seven years for stealing from my employer. I covered for another servant.. And you know what?'

Blay shook his head

'Best thing I ever did,' Elizabeth Cullen continued. 'No regrets at all about what I did. I would never have had the chances I got here, or the life I have if I stayed in Dublin. Woulda died in the poorhouse more than likely. Lucky for me, I got assigned to James here. Quite a lot older than me, aren't you, James? Still, I don't care, we done well for ourselves and our girls. Speakin' of girls – you already met our youngest, Betsy - the middle girl sittin on yer right is Catherine, and the eldest over here next to me, is Sophia. All born on Norfolk Island. James and me didn't get married till we were sent here to Van Diemen's Land, did we, James?'

'No, no need for a piece of paper. But Reverend Knopwood started nagging at all of us from the Island to get married. He said Governor Macquarie wanted us to be respectable. There were lots of weddings in a short time.'

'How old are your girls?' Blay asked Elizabeth Cullen.

'Betsy is seven, Catherine is twelve, and Sophia is thirteen. How old are your boys, Mr Blay?'

He felt the tears pooling in his eyes, he used his hand to wipe them away before they trickled down his face.

'He's crying', pointed out Betsy.

'No, he's not,' said Mr Cullen 'He's got something in his eye. Leave him be to answer the question.'

'I was a shoemaker in London,' Blay began. 'I bought

some boots off a fella. I knew they'd been cabbaged but thought I'd make a pound or two on them. Turns out the fella I tried to sell them to knew the bootmaker who'd made the boots. They charged me with stealing the boots – which I didn't do – made no difference. Because of the value of the boots, I got sentenced to death. But the judge said I could be transported for life, instead. Here I am. Missing my boys real bad, and Sarah, my wife.'

'Mama asked you how old they were,' Sophia reminded him.

Blay looked at the family sitting around the table and realised he had five bosses here in New Norfolk. 'Sorry, yes, Miss Sophia. James is the eldest, he'd be nine now, William is seven, like you Miss Betsy, and John is four.'

'How is your wife managing, Mr Blay?' asked Elizabeth Cullen.

'Surprised me how strong she is,' he said. 'She went to the Guild, got permission to keep on the apprentice and is keeping the shop running.'

'Sounds like the boys are goin' to be well taken care of, then,' said Elizabeth Cullen. 'Let's eat dinner. Then, Mr Blay, James will show you your quarters, and explain where you fit in here, and what you'll be expected to do.'

He could feel the saliva forming in his mouth as the Cullen's cook served dinner. It had been two years since he'd had a proper, cooked, meal.

# 13

# SURVIVAL

*Before 1840 the majority of prisoners were assigned to private individuals. Small numbers were retained to work at public sector tasks including working as clerks, flagellators, overseers, seamen, blacksmiths, masons, bricklayers and carpenters. Contrary to popular perception, convict Van Diemen's Land was anything but a vast gaol. Assigned convicts laboured under little or no restraint. Those who worked in the public sector were generally housed at night in secure accommodation, although as late as the mid-1820s it was not unusual for some skilled prisoners to rent rooms in town.*

From: www.link.tas.gov.au

Standing back, James Tedder waited until Toothless and his cohort left the Church. He then wondered if that was sensible, he worried that Toothless might wait for him. 'Surely with all these people around, he'll leave me alone today?'

Tedder took the chance and walked out of the little church making his way to the centre of a group of convicts dressed the same as him. Toothless was not visible. Tedder relaxed. He stayed with the group as much for the company as anonymity, glancing over his shoulder every few minutes to see if Toothless was around. Some of the convicts in the group were from *Indefatigable*, but Tedder didn't really want to strike up friendships with any of these men. He and Blay had avoided them on the voyage, and he was happy for things to stay that way. He did, however, need to know how to catch fish and eels from the river.

He spoke to the man next to him 'Morning. Wondering if you can tell me how to go about catching myself some fish for dinner and supper. I've got no rations.'

'I don't give a shit if ya got no rations, convict. Most of us in the same boat. Make yerself a spear and go for it. Happy huntin'.'

Tedder stood to one side as the group moved off towards the barracks. Instead of going straight back to his hut, he walked for a while through the tiny little town, wanting to get his bearings. He had seen little of it since he arrived a week ago. The roads were narrow and bumpy, it seemed to him as if they'd been constructed more from use than deliberate excavation. Dust swirled on the surface of the road, even though only a slight breeze from the river meandered through the trees. The buildings were simple: timber walls, timber rooves. But they did have glass where windows were fashioned. Lots of tents lined up in rows at the back of the government buildings, three buildings made up the Commissariat, Tedder realised. One for farming equipment, tools and farm supplies, one for clothing, and one for food. Tedder and Mr Williamson worked in the food stores.

Keeping his head down, looking for suitable pieces of wood to fashion into a spear, Tedder walked to the bank of the estuary. He smelled the sickly stench of rum before the owner of the stench spoke.

'Well, look ye here, it's Tedder again,' said a voice slurring from intoxication. 'What ye lookin' for convict?'

Tedder turned to face Toothless not responding to the question.

'I asked ye a question, convict,' roared Toothless. 'Don't you go thinkin' ya too good for me cos ye work in the stores, ye still a convict, and I'm in charge of ye.'

Thinking it best to keep the peace, Tedder answered the guard rather than have him riled up and unpredictable. 'I'm walking in the fresh air, Sir. Haven't walked on a surface that doesn't move, for a while.'

'Just so long as ye 'member ye place, Tedder.' Toothless spat as he walked with other guards back towards the centre of town.

'Where does he get the drink? Wouldn't mind a glass of rum myself.' Tedder asked no one in particular.

Relieved the confrontation didn't escalate, he continued his search, spending the best part of the morning walking along the banks of the estuary. He'd long stopped looking at the ground for wood, instead, he appreciated all this body of water had to offer. The water was dark, almost black, and yet crystal clear. He could see fish of all sizes frolicking just beneath the surface, tantalizingly close, yet out of reach. He had never seen birds like the ones squawking overhead or those singing in the trees. He remembered his first look at the trees when he arrived last week. Strange, covered in leaves but no flowers, all different heights, leaves of green but at least one hundred shades of green. Enormous trees you couldn't see the tops of, bushes covered in red berries. 'I wonder if you can eat those berries.' He almost stood on it. It looked like a rat, but much bigger and it had an infant looking out from a pouch on its belly. It looked at him as curiously as he looked at it, but only for a couple of seconds. Then it jumped, yes, jumped away, on its back legs. Tedder was dumbstruck; his little sister Esther would love to see this place. He wondered what games God had played on this side of the world to create such a menagerie.

Deciding he had walked far enough along the water's edge he turned to go back the way he'd come. He was hungry and still didn't have anything he could eat for dinner or supper. He found an appropriate piece of wood to use as a spear, just as he heard the bell over the superintendent's door ring twelve times. The morning had gone quickly.

As magical as this place was, it still needed to feed him. The stick he found was a good length and had a slightly pointy end, but not sharp enough for spearfishing. He didn't have a hook or line to use it as a fishing rod. Tedder considered the surface and could see the fish and the eels teasing him from the safety of their watery home. Taking off his shoes, he rolled up his breeches and gingerly put his foot into the water. The sand squished under his toes, he put in the other foot and reached back to the bank for his stick, losing his balance he fell into the water. Not being able to swim sent him into a state of panic. He thrashed and splashed trying to regain his footing, before realising his feet were on the sandy bottom. Regaining his balance, he saw and felt an eel swimming around his legs. Eyeing it for a few seconds, he thrust his hand into the water and grabbed it around the middle. It struggled for its freedom. He knew where the saying "slippery as an eel" came from. Determined not to let dinner and supper go, he held on and pulled the creature out of the water. Throwing it onto the bank he climbed out of the water after it, hitting the creature on the head with a rock he'd found. He wanted to kill it quickly. Wiping the sand from his feet, he put on his shoes, unrolled his breeches and put the eel around his shoulders.

Tedder was wet, cold and gritty with sand, but happy.

With the bushes and small trees as cover, Tedder scanned the roadway between the guards' barracks and his hut, and the water's edge. Running into Toothless would be the end of his meal. He kept to the very edge of the clearing where small huts like his stood as sentries leading the way to the centre of town, sneaking between huts and checking surroundings before moving to the next. 'This is the first time I have felt like a criminal, sneaking around trying to avoid detection,' he thought.

As his own hut came into view, Tedder's stomach jumped into his mouth. If he'd eaten today, he would have vomited. The door to his little hut was wide open. He swallowed hard and held his arms close to his side to stop his hands from shaking. He skulked around to the back of his hut to listen for any noises from inside. It was silent. Creeping to the front, he took the risk of looking in the window. The hut was empty. He forced the raging scream that was desperate to escape from his throat to hush. Standing up straight he stepped inside. All the small luxuries were gone: the table and chairs, kettle, bucket, cooking pot, his cutlery, pillows, and blankets. They'd left his convict clothes and the wood for the fire. They'd left the tea and sugar, but Tedder knew that was an oversight, he'd put the tea and sugar behind the woodpile with his mug and plate and flint. The desperation overpowered him. He sat on the hearth and rested his head in his hands. He didn't cry. What was the point? He was sure Toothless, and his cronies had helped themselves to his things, but then wondered if in fact, they were his things. 'They were here, but were they really mine? I am a convict, after all. Toothless is making sure I don't forget.'

Tedder rescued the plate, mug, tea, and sugar from behind the woodpile; he would hide things here until he had a lock for the door. He needed fresh water for his tea and to clean the eel, which was still around his neck. Water was stored in barrels near the Commissariat, he made his way without giving a thought to Toothless.

He filled up the cup with water, drank it, filled it up again, washed the eel with the water, filled it up again for his tea, and walked back to his hut with the wet eel hanging around his neck. As disappointed as he felt about all the stuff being taken, he still had the fire and something to eat. He got the fire going, balanced the mug of water so it wouldn't spill, lay the eel across the flames and pulled one of the cots over to wait for the water to boil for his tea, and the eel to cook. He put his boots, still wet from sliding his wet feet into them, and his wet shirt on the hearth to dry.

The hut filled with a smell not unlike the deck of the *Retribution*, he dry-retched. Using the stick he'd found at the water's edge, he lifted the eel off the fire, moved his boots and shirt and lay the eel on the hearth. Wondering if the flesh was the same orange colour as the skin, he broke a piece from the middle to see if it was cooked. Blowing it to cool, he peeled off the skin to reveal white flesh. It melted in his mouth. Despite the misery of the late morning, he was excited about the first meal he'd ever cooked himself. He thought about how proud his mother would be and determined to write to her.

His cup of tea wasn't as successful as making it in a pot, but it was drinkable and accompanied the orange coloured eel beautifully. Tedder saved half of the eel for supper. Waiting until it cooled down, he hid it behind the woodpile, with his cup, plate, sugar, and tea. Putting on his warm shirt and dry but still gritty boots, he went outside to collect some more wood.

Tedder loved the afternoons in Hobart Town, even though the sun was on the wrong side of the sky. He loved the crispness in the air as the day grew closer to the end, and the noises the birds made while they found their way to their favourite eating places. He looked up at the towering mountain that stood sentry over the town and the estuary. The skies were clear, the air was clear, the sun shone on his face, his nose was healing. He made his way to the water's edge, sat down on the sand and lifted his shirt so the sun could warm his back.

Voices came from behind. Slurred voices. Voices with that terrible cockney accent. Without waiting to see if it was Toothless and cohort, Tedder crawled into the undergrowth out of sight. Toothless and his mates walked to the water's edge and pissed into the beautiful clear water Tedder had just been admiring. Afraid to move, he waited to be sure they'd gone. When the clock on the superintendent's door rang four times, Tedder came out of his hiding place, stood straight, head high, and walked back towards town and his hut unnoticed by anyone.

For supper he repeated dinner's ritual, he made tea and ate the eel. This time he ate like a gentleman, savouring the smoky flavour, knowing there would be no breakfast except tea and sugar.

He stoked up the fire as darkness descended as quickly on the inside of the hut as it did outside. 'Candles will be on my list.' Moving the cot a little further away from the fire, he lay down with his back to the coals, curled up into a ball, and went straight to sleep.

· · ·

The cold woke James a couple of times during the night, restoking the fire each time, warmed him. Daylight crept through the little window, urging him to get organised for his second day on the job at the Commissariat. He dressed, put on his convict cap, and walked to the barrels to fill his cup with water. The first cup he splashed on his face; the second would be for breakfast – a cup of tea. Looking around to ensure Toothless was nowhere to be seen, he took his mug of water back to his hut, balanced it on the coals and sat on the cot, waiting for it to boil.

'Good morning, Mr Williamson.'

'Mornin' Tedder. Hope you had a good breakfast, it'll be a busy day today. Monday usually is.'

'I didn't have any breakfast, Mr Williamson,' Tedder offered. 'I ate some of the food left in the hut for me on Friday, and what was left got stolen after Church. I caught an eel in the estuary and had it for dinner and supper yesterday.' Tedder waited for a reaction from Mr Williamson.

'What do you mean it was stolen?'

'The food wasn't the only thing, Sir. The table, chairs, pillows, blankets, towel, kettle, pot and fire frame. All gone. There's no lock on the door,' said Tedder in his defence.

'Oh, for God's sake, Tedder. You got a tongue in your head, couldn't you have said you needed a lock for the door?'

'The day was finished, and I didn't know where to find you.' Tedder felt like a child that Mr Williamson was about to scold for his naughty behaviour.

'Don't have time for this now, Tedder. We've got to get ready. Day's end, we'll work out how much it'll cost to replace the stuff, and you'll get rations for the week. All the convicts get the same rations, the guards get the same as each other, the marines get the same, and the officers, well they get their share too.

'The furniture and stuff you've lost will come out of your pay each week until you've paid it back. I'll give you an advance cos, you need the basics,' Mr Williamson grunted. 'Now get on with ye work.'

Tedder decided against telling Mr Williamson about his problems with Toothless.

'Mr Williamson,' he said 'How long will the *Indefatigable* stay in port?'

'Why, you gonna catch her home again?'

'No Sir, I was wondering if I'd be able to write to my mother, and if *Indefatigable* was going back to England would she take mail.'

'You can write to your mother, Tedder. The paper and pen and ink and envelope will come out of your bank account. You won't be able to buy luxuries like that till you've got your first pay next Saturday. I'll give you an advance on the furniture.'

After his last comment, Mr Williamson had Tedder light the lamps in the Commissariat building, open the doors and windows, get the ledger books onto the counter top and fill the pens with ink. He felt like a man for the first time in a long while. He was hungry, but he had a real job, he would get paid, and he could support himself. He would write to tell his mother things weren't so bad after all.

## 14

# DEAR SARAH

*January 1813.*
*From: Cullen Farm, New Norfolk, Van Diemen's Land.*

*To: Sarah Blay, 8 Crispin Street, Spitalfields, London.*

*Dear Sarah,*
*I hope and pray this letter finds you and our sons well. My*
*heart aches every day for you all. I know you to be a strong*
*woman, Sarah, and I have belief in your ability to keep the shop*
*going and to feed and educate the boys. I know it's winter at home*
*in London, but here, in Van Diemen's Land, it's summer. Can you*
*believe that? Summer? The world is turned upside down.*
*It's been a surprise, Sarah. A nice surprise. I dreaded what life*
*would be like here, and you feared I would not survive. If convicts*
*behave and have skills, we get to live a useful life and even get*
*paid. There are convicts chained together working on digging*
*roads and chiselling out sandstone for buildings, but most of them*

*broke rules on the voyage here or broke the rules when they got here. I'm being careful to keep my nose clean.*

*I'm working on a farm. Can you imagine that? Me, on a farm? I'd never left London in all my life let alone rode a horse or rounded up sheep or goats or pigs or cattle. I'm in a place called New Norfolk, it's a day's ride or three hours' sailing up the Derwent estuary from Hobart Town. The estuary becomes a river at New Norfolk, it turns to fresh water. It's so different – the Thames has buildings and shacks all along its banks, the Derwent River and estuary have trees and animals and plants and the most amazing birds. I'm assigned to a fellow called James Bryan Cullen. Seems we're all called James. He calls me Blay, cos he says he's the one whose free and he'll use his name as he chooses. I live on his farm with his wife, Elizabeth and their three girls. I have my quarters in the stable, which suits me fine. It's a bit off to the side with a cot and wash basin. It's good. I'm enjoying my privacy; there wasn't much of that on the* Retribution *or* Indefatigable.

*I eat with Mr Cullen and his family. I don't wear chains, I work on the farm side by side with him. He has a friend, Robert Bishop who sometimes comes to help. Guess what, Sarah? Mr Cullen, Bishop, and Mrs Cullen were all convicts. Yes, convicts. Now they're called Settlers. I know Mrs Cullen's convict story, and Robert Bishop's, but not Mr Cullen's. He's been quiet on the matter. He will tell me in good time if he feels the need. Mr Cullen told me that if I keep my nose clean and work hard I can get a Ticket of Leave, that I won't have to do life. That means I can work for someone else, be my own man. Just means I can't leave Van Diemen's Land unless I get a pardon. Mr Cullen doesn't treat me like a convict. He treats me like a worker, he's kind. Mrs Cullen has a cook who feeds us well, and their girls are well mannered. Seeing them every day though makes me desperate for our boys.*

*The Government here starts a bank account for convicts. They put our pay in the account, and when we go to the Stores to get something that's not in our rations, it comes out of our account. When we are free, we get the money. Did you think I could ever think about being free, Sarah? I didn't. But I can think about being free. I can get a Ticket of Leave, and I can get a Pardon if I behave. And, Mr Cullen told me that convicts' wives or husbands can come to Van Diemen's Land as free settlers, and the Government will assign convicts to their wives or husbands, so they become the settler's problem.*

*I don't know how things are going with money, Sarah, but that would be amazing if you and the boys could come here. Settlers are given land grants, Sarah. Grants of land. When you get your first grant of land, you can get tents and other supplies from the Stores. You have to clear the land and build your own house, but what an adventure that would be.*

*The weather is good; it's hot this time of year, hotter than I've ever experienced, or could imagine, but the air is fresh, the animals and birds and plants and trees are strange and wonderful. The children run around in the sun with feet bare and not a lot of clothes to hinder their playing. Mr Cullen's girls look healthy and fit, Sarah. I'm well and fit too. My pale English skin is becoming like the leather I used to make shoes with.*

*I went up to Hobart Town on the Derwent estuary with Mr Cullen just the other day, because we needed supplies, and I saw Tedder again. He's working as a clerk in the Stores – seeing as his reading and writing and numbers work is very good. You remember*

*him, my mate on the Retribution. He's looking good now, but he told me on the quiet he's having trouble with one of the guards. The one on the Indefatigable that tormented us when he could, is giving Tedder a hard time. Even stole his stuff. But, he's dressed clean and tidy and keeping the books for the Stores. He's got his* own hut. He was very happy to see me. I introduced him to Mr Cullen, and they had a bit of a talk while I got some supplies together.

I don't know how long it will take for you to get my letter, Sarah. The boys must be growing, getting taller. I hope you are making enough money to send them to school. There is a small school in New Norfolk. Most of the children here don't go to school every day, they have too many tasks to carry out at home. All the children help with the farm, the gardens, the animals. There is a lot to do on each property to keep the families and the community fed. Some children have lessons given by their mothers or by convicts who can read and write.

I pray you are able to write to me. I pray that I will hear that you are well, and the boys are growing and are healthy.

Your loving husband, James.

# 15

# LONDON TO PORTSMOUTH

*The domestic services of an inn were overseen by a housekeeper, often the wife or female relation of the owner. Some inns were famous for their fine service and good food. Others were known for taking advantage of passengers by providing undercooked meat, soup too hot to drink, or meals served too late to be eaten before passengers had to hurry back onto the coach for the next stage of their journey.*

*http://englishhistoryauthors.blogspot.com.au/2016/12/coaching-inns-in-early-19th-century.html*

**May 1813**

'He will worry that I have cast him aside when he doesn't hear from me,' Sarah told her mother.

'Well, ye can't do nothin' 'bout it, Sarah. That's how long it takes for a letter to go to the other side of the world. Just think about how surprised he will be to see you all.' She wiped a tear from her cheek before Sarah saw it.

'It made me happy to read that he's settled with a family and not in chains getting beaten every day. I thought his life over there would be awful. I'm so relieved it isn't.'

'There's time yet, Sarah. You and I both know where James Jr gets his temper,' said her mother, nodding toward the eldest boy.

James caused Sarah concern. He was surly and spiteful and lost his temper at the smallest provocation. She'd thought telling him they were going to Van Diemen's Land to live with his father would improve things, but James Jr withdrew into himself whenever she mentioned her husband.

'I hope his father can sort him out when we get to Van Diemen's Land.'

'He might have to sort himself out on the ship goin' over,' said her mother. 'That's goin' to test the mettle of all of ye.' She wiped another tear, but this time Sarah saw.

'Oh, Mother. I will miss you terribly,' Sarah said drawing the woman toward her. 'I wouldn't have been able to manage on my own. You have been a great support.'

'Rubbish. That boarder helped with the boys, and you did a great job with the apprentice in the shop. But I will miss ye, and miss seeing the boys grow into men.'

She hugged her mother for some time, savouring the musty smell of her clothes and the feel of her weathered face on her own. The tears her mother shed reminded Sarah of the finality their parting would bring.

'Best get back to the sewin',' Sarah's mother scolded 'don't want some rotten thief runnin' off with ye money afore ye even set foot on the dirt over there.'

They sat in the small kitchen of Sarah's Spitalfields home, using the light from the fire to sew pound notes into the bodice of Sarah's travelling dress and the lining of her coat. Before they concealed each note Sarah checked that the boys weren't watching, she didn't want them knowing where the money she had saved for over a year and a half, was hidden.

Finished with their fiddly task, Sarah's mother kissed her daughter and grandsons and made her way home. She would see them off tomorrow and never set eyes on them again. The tears froze on her cheeks.

With her mother's help, Sarah and the boys loaded their trunks onto the cart her mother had borrowed. She locked the door for the last time, glanced up and down the street that had been home for twelve years, and entrusted the key to her mother for transfer to the landlord. The four travellers and Sarah's mother pushed the cart to the coach stop.

'Good thing the ships don't leave in winter, we'd never get this pushed through snow,' her mother complained.

'Where's ye husband, missus?' the coachman quizzed Sarah.

A quick look at the boys to indicate they keep silent, she explained that her husband was in the colonies and they were going to join him.

Seemingly satisfied, the coachman gave the boys their orders. 'You, the bigger one, help my attendant there,' he said pointing to a man loading luggage into the coach's boot. 'Get your own bags and load them where he tells you. Get your brothers to help.'

The coachman continued giving orders until all his passengers were accounted for and luggage stowed. 'We be leavin' in five minutes, say ye goodbyes.'

Holding her mother's hands in hers, Sarah said 'I will write all the time, Mother, I'll let you know how we settle in, and what the boys are doing. You must get the Reverend to read my letters to you, and to help you write back.'

It upset her that her mother was staying in London alone, but despite her efforts to cajole, bully, bribe, and pressure, the woman still refused to travel to Van Diemen's Land with them. The past year and a half without James and his income had been difficult; if not for this woman's help she and the boys would have ended up in the poor house. Sarah hugged her mother tightly for the last time.

'Be off with ye. I'll be fine, and so will ye and the boys. Goodbye boys look after yer Mama and be good on that bloody boat. It's a hell of a long way to the other side of the world.

'Sarah, here's a little present I have for ye. Think of me when ye use it.' She put a new bar of Pear's soap into her daughter's hand, then gave each grandson a hug and helped them climb into the coach.

Urging the horses to move, the coachman eased the coach away from London and away from their life. 'Regrets are for the lost,' Sarah thought as she watched her mother disappear. 'I will not be lost.'

Wondering how long they'd been travelling, Sarah looked at her father's fob watch which was hidden in a pocket inside her coat. It had been about two hours and James Jr, fidgeting with his hair and annoying his brothers, demanded to know how much longer their trip would take.

'Portsmouth is a good distance away, James. We have to stop at Guildford overnight, and won't be at the ship until mid-morning tomorrow.'

'That's too far and too long,' the eldest screamed.

'Don't speak to me like that,' Sarah growled. 'This is short compared to the months we will be on board the ship. You and your brothers will have to adjust.'

'I hate you, and I hate Papa, I wish they'd hanged him when they said they would, then we could've just lived our life without him. We wouldn't be leaving England.' He was sobbing between breaths.

Unaware that the three other passengers in the coach were watching the scene unfold, Sarah reached forward and slapped James' face. Five-year-old William pulled away, whimpering. This was the first time she had slapped any of them. James usually dispensed the physical punishments. 'Another thing I've had to do on my own.'

One of the gentlemen passengers intervened 'You are a very rude boy to your mother. She did right to slap your face, I'm sure your father would have whipped you for such insolence.'

His feet planted firmly on the coach floor, James folded his arms over his chest, clenched his jaw and stared with rage-filled eyes, out the window. To Sarah's annoyance, he sat, without moving, until the coachman pulled the horses up at one of the coaching inns dotted along the route.

'Time to get out and stretch your legs and get somethin' to eat,' he instructed.

While the coachman organised fresh horses, Sarah took her boys into the inn. James skulked along behind whilst William and John walked next to her. It was dark inside, but not gloomy, the windows were open to the late morning sunlight and the smell of freshly baked bread and simmering stews wafted through the air.

'What can I do fer ye, Missus?' asked a voice from behind the counter. It took Sarah by surprise; she'd been too busy taking in the sights of the tavern to look for service.

'Oh, thank you,' she stuttered. 'The boys and I need something to eat and drink, please, something light, we still have a way to travel today.'

'Sure ting, Missus find yerselves somewheres to sit, and we'll be right wit ye.'

The four travellers sat at the end of a long table, on benches: Sarah and John one side and James and William the other. The woman from behind the counter appeared carrying a platter with bread, cheese, and bacon, a pot of tea and some ale. Sarah shared the food between them, putting generous portions on each plate. John and William ate greedily, not only did the food fill their stomachs, but the ritual of dinner eased the boredom of the journey.

James scowled at his brothers and ignored his mother. He didn't attempt to eat, and Sarah didn't encourage him.

Sarah hadn't realised how hungry she was until the smell of the food reached her nostrils and made her mouth water. She allowed herself the luxury of sugar in her tea and poured each of the boys a small mug of ale. James didn't touch his. When it was time to move on, she wrapped the remains of dinner in her scarf, paid the innkeeper and strode out into the early afternoon with two boys by her side and one dragging along behind.

'I'm going to sit with the coachman,' James Jr informed her.

'Well that will depend on him, James, not on you. Is that alright, sir?'

'Yes, Missus. But don't understand why he'd wanna sit up here. As the day closes in, it's goin' to get mighty cold.

He'll freeze his arse off. Sorry, Missus,' he added tipping his hat.

The younger boys entertained themselves in the coach inventing games they could play on the floor; there was more space with James sitting outside. As she watched John and William play, Sarah wondered how long James Jr's behaviour would last, and how she should manage it.

'Guildford coming up,' called the coachman.

Sarah organised and tidied up the younger boys; she straightened their caps and breeches and brushed down their jackets, then fixed her own bonnet into position, tied it under her chin, and smoothed down her dress. Reaching up for the bag she'd stowed in the overhead rack, she and the boys were ready and accepted the help offered by the coachman's attendant. John and William stood with her as they waited for James to get down from the coachman's seat.

'Come along, James, the driver needs to get the horses sorted, and I am sure he would like to eat and get some sleep too,' Sarah encouraged.

'Thanks, Missus. I do need to get the horses in the stable afore the cold sets in. Get down, young James, and mind your mother.'

James climbed down and stood in defiance. 'I'm happy to sleep with the horses.'

'Well, you're not. You will come with me,' Sarah turned and walked towards the front door of the Guildford Inn. Two boys kept up, one took as long as he could.

James Jr gobbled the hot vegetable soup, freshly baked bread, cheese and potatoes they had for supper as if he hadn't eaten for days. Sarah watched with a wry smile. She had decided not to fight him: if he wanted to sit outside in the cold, he could, if he didn't want to eat, she wouldn't make him, if he didn't want to join in the games with his brothers, she would leave him be.

The innkeeper showed the four of them to a small, warm room at the top of the stairs. The fire was well alight, clean towels were on the beds, and there was fresh, warm water in the pitcher.

James Jr poured water into the bowl, splashed it on his face and on the floor, dried himself, took off his shoes and jacket and climbed into one of the beds.

'He didn't say goodnight,' complained John.

'He's too tired and cold from sitting with the coachman,' William said.

Eager to get into bed herself, Sarah took John and William to the water pitcher 'You two wash your face and hands and get into bed. We have an early start in the morning. We'll be at the ship before dinner.'

John was in bed snoring softly before William had finished taking off his shoes; he climbed in next to James who pretended to be asleep.

Sarah took out the new bar of transparent Pears soap her mother had given her. She held the bar up to the light from the fire, so she could see through it; she smelt it, put it against her cheek, and decided to use it sparingly on the voyage so she would have some left when they arrived in Van Diemen's Land. After tending to herself she crawled into the bed with John. Worrying about James Jr, the long journey ahead and how her husband would fret at not hearing from her, played on her mind and kept her awake. She got up, stoked the fire, pulled her coat around her shoulders, sat in the chair next to the hearth, and drifted into a fitful sleep.

. . .

For the morning journey to Portsmouth, James Jr again sat with the coachman.

'Get down and help yer ma with yer brothers,' the coachman ordered when they arrived at Portsmouth.

James looked at the older man without following the instructions.

'I told yer to get down and help. Now get down and help,' roared the driver into James's face. The boy clambered down and offered his hand to John. William helped his mother collect their belongings from inside the coach and the boot.

Handing a neatly crafted leather carry bag to James, Sarah said 'This is yours, you must look after it until we are settled on the ship. Don't lose it. It holds all the things you wanted to bring from home,' James snatched the bag from his mother without looking at her. She noticed the whites of his knuckles around the handle.

The attendant unloaded their trunk from the coach, dipped his hat to Sarah and waited politely for a tip. Furtively looking around to see if anyone was taking any special notice, she removed some notes from her purse and handed them to the coachman and his attendant.

They'd never been to the sea. The sights and sounds of Portsmouth assaulted their senses: waves lapping the shore, orders being shouted to sailors, traders calling out the virtues of their wares, people arguing, children running between water barrels and adults, dogs barking, and the distinct smell of the sea. Sarah pulled her youngest child in close and drew her other arm around the older two, holding them protectively.

'Now what do we do?' whined James Jr.

'We find someone to help us to the ship, James.' Sarah spoke quietly and calmly needing to reassure herself as much as the boys.

'What ship? They all look the same,' said James Jr, continuing his attack.

'Ours is called the *HM Brig Kangaroo*. So, I imagine we look for that name on the side of the ship.'

'That one up there says *Kangaroo,*' announced James, pointing to a ship further up the dock. 'How are we supposed to get the heavy trunk up there by ourselves?'

'We'll have to find someone to help.' Different scenarios whirled in Sarah's exhausted mind: 'I can't leave James here with the trunk I can't trust him to stay. I can't take the three of them with me to find help, because the trunk will be gone when we get back, and we can't carry it on our own.' She sat down on the offending trunk. William clambered up next to her.

'Are we going to stay here all day, then?' James badgered.

'No need for that, boy. I'll give you and your ma a hand to get to your ship. Which one is it?' The voice belonged to a marine dressed in a smart red uniform. He patted William on the head and smiled at Sarah.

'Thank you, sir, I am grateful, but I think it is too heavy for one man and a boy.'

The marine called to a sailor for help, and they led the way, carrying the trunk to the ship. Sarah and the boys tentatively stepped up the gangplank to the deck of *HM Brig Kangaroo.*

'It's got guns. Look, Mama. It's got guns. The ship's got guns. Do you think she'll need to use them?' James danced with excitement.

'I hope not,' Sarah breathed, exasperated.

'She's got guns alright, young man,' the marine explained 'she's an armed brig only four years old, with twelve guns, and on her way to New South Wales. Governor Macquarie wants a ship to run between Sydney and Hobart Town.'

'We are going to Van Diemen's Land,' James explained. 'Is that near Hobart Town?'

'Yes, young man. Hobart Town is where the government of Van Diemen's Land runs things from.'

The marine finished by saluting James and bowing slightly toward Sarah. 'Someone from the crew will be along soon to take you and your belongings to your quarters, mum.'

'Thank you for your help, sir.' Sarah went to open her purse, not sure if the marine expected payment for his assistance.

'No need for that, mum. It's part of the job.' He moved off, leaving them on the deck to wait for the promised help.

James Jr had come alive, he was running from Sarah to the side of the ship, dangling half his body over to get a closer look at the guns protruding from below, and back to Sarah. She didn't attempt to stop him. If he fell overboard, someone would get him. She closed her eyes.

'Missus, missus.'

Sarah's head shot up with a jolt and her eyes frantically darted around to count three boys. William was asleep, his head on her lap, John was watching James, who was still dancing around the guns.

'We's 'ere to take yer stuff to your quarters,' explained a sailor. 'Need to see yer ticket so we know where to take ye.'

Untying and removing her bonnet Sarah took out the four tickets she'd hidden there when they left Spitalfields.

Following the sailors and their trunk deep into the bowels of the ship where light and fresh air refused to linger, they finally reached what would be their home for the next few months. Sarah clasped her hands together in front, so the boys wouldn't see them trembling.

# 16

# THE TERROR OF TOOTHLESS

James Tedder's day started as any other. He'd been working at the Commissariat for two weeks, had arranged for all the supplies and furniture he needed, had a lock on the door, and hadn't set eyes on Toothless. The *Indefatigable* was still in port, he was going to get paper and pen and ink today and sit down after supper and write to his parents.

The oatmeal he bought from the Stores was the same as the oatmeal they ate on the *Indefatigable*, but he didn't have to add more water to make it go further. Sitting at his table, the one he bought from the Stores from his own pay, Tedder was allowing himself to feel a little accomplished. 'By the time I've served my seven years, I should have quite some money saved. I'll be able to start a business of my own, and maybe even go home to England,' he thought. Finishing his oatmeal and cup of tea, he washed the dishes, washed his face, combed his hair, reminding himself to get a mirror, locked the door, and bounced to work.

'Morning, Mr Williamson.'

'Morning Tedder. Got things set up in your hut?'

'Yes, sir. All setup. Good to have things that belong to me.'

'Well, they belong to you as long as you follow the rules, Tedder.'

'Yes, sir. That I will be doing.'

Tedder got to work setting up the account books and checking records to see which settlers would be supplying meat, maize, and wheat to the Stores over the coming week. He made sure the quills were ready, and that the ink bottles were at hand.

'Well, lookie 'ere, the convict's all brand-spankin' new in his clean clothes and rosy cheeks.'

Tedder stifled a scream before it had a chance to make its way out of his mouth and into Toothless' face.

'Good morning, Sir,' he managed to say without stumbling the words.

'I'm 'ere to collect some stuff, convict. Some stuff I need. And you 'member our arrangement, don't you?'

'What arrangement was that, sir?'

'Don't you go on bein' a clever dick, convict,' warned Toothless. 'I 'ave a list a friend made up for me, so you'll get everythin' on the list, and it'll come outta your bank account, not mine.'

Tedder had dreaded this day since Toothless attacked him a few weeks back. Each morning he checked to see if the *Indefatigable* was still in port, feeling stressed and anxious when he saw her rocking gently on the waves. When the *Indefatigable* left, Toothless would go with her, back to England, to torment some other poor souls. She was still here, so was Toothless. He had to come up with a plan, and quickly. He wasn't going to use his savings to pay for Toothless' indulgences, but he would have to pretend he was, facing the consequences of Toothless' wrath later.

Toothless shoved the list in front of Tedder. 'I'll wait while ye get my things, clever dick.'

Tedder moved around the shelves, and barrels and bins, looking at the list and collecting tea, sugar, molasses, salt beef, salt pork, oatmeal, rice, and cabbage. He knew Toothless would have received a full complement of supplies for his own use, courtesy of the Government, and that he would be selling these things to settlers and other guards. The injustice riled him as the items made their way into a potato sack.

'Well done, convict,' Toothless grinned as the supplies were put at his feet. 'I'll be back afore the *Indefatigable* sails to get some more, so me and me friends will have a good journey.'

He threw the sack over his shoulder, winked at Tedder, turned and shuffled out of the Store. Tedder released the breath he'd been holding.

Remembering Toothless and his cohort were unable to read and write, Tedder made up an IOU on a Commissariat inventory sheet. He listed the items Toothless had him secure, and the value. All he needed now was Toothless' name to put at the bottom, accompanied by an X, indicating his signature.

The bell over the superintendent's door sounded and Tedder finished work for the day. He helped Mr Williamson secure the building, bid him good evening, and turned to walk into town. His plan was to loiter around the guards' quarters to try and hear Toothless being referred to by his name. He didn't have to wait long, Toothless caught sight of Tedder before he had a chance to hide. He strode toward him, waving and smiling. Tedder felt sick.

'Roger, wait,' called one of the guards leaving the barracks. Toothless turned to see who called him; ignoring Tedder he walked towards the caller.

Tedder had a starting point; he would check the records tomorrow to see how many guards with the Christian name Roger had bought from the Commissariat.

Not quite hungry enough to go home and start cooking supper, Tedder walked to the edge of the estuary, found a dry patch of sand, and lay back to enjoy the last remnants of the day's spring sunshine. He watched the sun set, mesmerised by its display of colours as it shifted on the horizon.

Tedder walked to work without incident and helped Mr Williamson set up for a new day of trading. He went through the account book, looking for guards with the first name Roger. He found four. 'This is amazing record keeping,' he said, in awe of the meticulous detail attached to each record. Not only did the record show what was bought when, but it listed the ship the guard was embarked from. There was only one guard named Roger from the *Indefatigable*. Tedder allowed himself a wry smile. The last name was recorded as Bentley. Roger Bentley. Tedder wrote "Roger Bentley" at the foot of the Commissariat IOU he had prepared and put it in his pocket to produce when required. The first part of his plan completed, he still needed to work out how to get Toothless to put his 'X' on the document.

He didn't see Toothless for almost a week, this troubled him. Toothless had to sign the IOU or Tedder would lose his job when the stocktake was done and he couldn't explain the whereabouts of the goods. When Toothless came into the Commissariat a few minutes after opening one morning, Tedder faced the wall and grinned to himself.

'Hello there, convict. Nice lot of stuff you got for me t 'other week. Need more of it, have another list. Hurry up.' Toothless pushed the list toward Tedder, turned his back on him and lent against the counter, waiting. Tedder collected the items but quickly made up another IOU before returning with the goods.

'Good on yer convict,' Toothless encouraged 'good doin' business with yer.'

'Ah, before you go, sir,' Tedder stammered. 'I need you to sign the list of goods I've given you.'

'They's comin' outta your allowance, convict, not mine,' roared Toothless.

'I know, sir, but there has to be a record of what's been taken for the stock take, so the right person gets charged for the goods.' He put both pieces of paper in front of Toothless. 'This one is for today, and this one is for the other week. That's my name at the bottom of the page, and you need to sign to say you saw me take the stuff. Because you're the guard.'

Squirming as he watched Toothless processing the information, Tedder let out the breath he was holding when Toothless took the pen and put an "X" at the foot of each page. With a grunt, Toothless picked up his potato sack and walked away.

Tedder woke up sitting on wet sand, tied to a mooring post on the foreshore. A mooring post that would be half submerged when the tide came in. Shaking his head to clear his thoughts, he remembered getting ready for work, opening his door and stepping out into a drizzly, cool morning. Then that voice.

'Think ye smart, don't ye convict? Cos ye can read and write ye think ye better than the likes of us. Well, ye're not that smart, cos 'ere ye are, tied to a post, with the tide comin' in. I got a whippin' for those papers you had me sign, convict. But that's fine with me, not a weakling like you, I'll get over it. It'll be easier to get over it too, knowin' ye're still tied to this post when we sail outta here on the high tide. Look at ye all surprised like. *Indefatigable* heads back to England on the morrow convict, and we'll all be on 'er, and ye'll still be tied to this post. Ye'll never see England again.'

One last punch to his stomach, one last punch to his head, one last kick to his groin, and Toothless and his friends left Tedder to his fate.

His breathing ragged from the blows, Tedder tried in vain to loosen the ropes around his wrists, legs, and ankles. The water lapped at the soles of his shoes. He didn't remember what day it was. 'The only consolation is that *Indefatigable* wouldn't sail on a Sunday. It must be a workday. Mr Williamson will wonder where I am.' Tedder wriggled his hands trying to loosen the ropes. His legs were now under water, so struggling against the ropes around his ankles was futile. He appreciated the irony of his situation: Death had many opportunities to take him in the last two years, and it waited until he had a good job and some prospects for a future. He lowered his head to his chest and closed his eyes. 'I've heard drowning is an awful way to die.'

He prayed.

The water lapped at his waist. His legs were numb from the cold, his hands frozen. His fingers stuck to the rope he had tried to get off. The gentle waves sparkled and reflected the sun, as they danced around his body. His arms froze in position as the water level made its way up his chest. He was glad he hadn't had the chance to write to his mother, she would have read the news of a happy situation, and now he would die on the banks of an estuary 10,000 miles from home.

The water lapped at his chin. Tedder did not know how far the water reached at high tide but knew Toothless would not have tied him to a post that might not be fully submerged. He marvelled at how a man who can't read and write is clever in other ways. He moved his head from side to side to stop the water going up his nose. He didn't panic. The water covered his nose. He closed his eyes.


'Tedder, Tedder, Tedder! Jesus Christ Almighty, Tedder,' Mr Williamson roared in anguish. He threw his jacket and shoes on the ground, put his knife between his teeth, took a breath, and disappeared into the water that held Tedder prisoner. Mr Williamson couldn't see; his feet had stirred up the sand and clouded the water. Feeling his way, he found where Tedder's hands were tied to the post. Moving his own hands further up the rope, he started sawing back and forth with his knife. As the rope relented under the pressure, releasing its grip, Tedder's body slumped forward. Dropping his knife, Mr Williamson struggled to get Tedder to the surface. He dragged him, face down, to the water's edge. Once on the sand, he quickly rolled him over, slapping his face, turning his head, anything for a response. Tedder lay on the sand, motionless. Enraged by Tedder's predicament, Mr Williamson rolled him left to right yelling at him to wake up. 'You are a bloody idiot, Tedder. Why can't you just tell me when things go bad?' In desperation at the stupidity of Tedder's death, he thumped the lad hard on the chest. Tedder coughed, spewing water from his lungs.

Looking at Mr Williamson, he rasped 'Has *Indefatigable* sailed?'

# 17

# FRIENDSHIP

James Blay walked to the river's edge to get the boat ready for the trip to Hobart Town. The sun crept up behind Pulpit Rock smothering it in orange, yellow and ochre hues. As it spread across the sky, it brought with it the stifling heat of a new February day. It was taking Blay some time to get used to the heat, even though Mr Cullen told him Van Diemen's Land was cool compared to Sydney Town and Norfolk Island. He thought about his family in London in the depths of winter. 'I hope Sarah has enough money for coal for the fires and the boys are staying well. The children here are so healthy looking compared with London.'

'Blay,' called Mr Cullen from the verandah of the house 'come and help me with the stock. We'll have to load and be off quickly. It will be a hot one.'

Blay secured the boat and hurried up to help Mr Cullen load the handcart. They stacked bags of maize and wheat and the dried pork and beef the government stores had ordered, onto the cart. Blay lifted the handles to push the cart, while Mr Cullen guided it on the track.

'Go back to the stable and get your hat, Blay,' ordered Mr

Cullen. 'By the end of the day you'll be redder than the sky over there,' he said pointing to the well-advanced sunrise.

Picking up the oars, Blay allowed himself to relax, breathe deeply and take in the beauty of the Derwent River as they navigated their way to Hobart Town. He looked forward to seeing Tedder. 'Do you think James Tedder will still be working at the Stores, Mr Cullen?'

'Spose so. Unless he's been stealing. Then he'll be on the chain gang.'

Swatting flies away from his face, Blay let go of the oars in turn. 'As soon as the sun rises they ambush.' He pulled a small branch from a tree they sailed close to and used it as a weapon to ward of the flies' attack. 'I don't think Tedder would steal anything, Mr Cullen. I don't think he'd know how.'

'Well he must know how to break the law in some way, otherwise, he wouldn't be here.'

Blay worried about Tedder. 'He's young and trusting and can't see the evil lurking in the hearts of some. He'd die on a chain gang."

'Nothing you can do about it, Blay. Wait until we get to Hobart Town. Keep your eye out for snags in the river.'

In their eyes for the first part of the trip, the sun scolded them for getting in its way. The higher the sun rose in the sky, the more stifling its heat became.

'When we get around the bend up ahead, Blay, we'll stop rowing and put our shirts in the river and put them back on. We'll cool down. Get a drink from the river when we stop.

'We'll stay in Hobart this night, Blay. By the time we get unloaded and get the supplies to the Stores it will be too late to return on the Derwent in daylight. An early start again with the sun in our eyes some of the way on the morrow.'

Excited to see Hobart Town come into view, Blay jumped off the boat into the shallow waters of the Derwent estuary and pulled it to rest on the sand.

'Stay here and mind the cargo, Blay. Defend it with your life, if need be,' Cullen ordered.

Blay stood, feet astride, arms folded across his chest, as he watched Mr Cullen march up the beach into Hobart Town and the Government Stores. 'I hope Tedder is still working there. Be good to see him again.'

The grin was involuntary, Blay wouldn't have been able to stop it spreading across his face if he'd tried. Tedder was sitting on a wagon with Mr Cullen, heading to the water's edge to collect the cargo. He waved to Blay. Unfolding his arms, Blay raised them in the air, then clasped his hands behind his head. He paced back and forth trying to hide the joy he felt at seeing Tedder in one piece and still working at the Commissariat.

'Good to see you again, Blay,' Tedder said as he made his way down from the wagon. Making no attempt to hide his happiness, Blay stepped forward and hugged Tedder close to him. Tedder reciprocated the affection.

Mr Cullen cleared his throat. 'Good to see you are happy to see each other, but we have work to do. You can hug later.'

The three men unloaded the boat and stacked the supplies onto the wagon. Mr Cullen drove it back to the Commissariat. Tedder and Blay walked.

'What have you been doing to look so brown, Blay? You look like a piece of leather,' laughed Tedder

'I've been working on the Cullen farm. Mr Cullen has proved to be a fair master and I've learned lots of skills along the way. Nothing to help with shoemaking, mind,' answered Blay, with a smirk. 'He even let me write to Sarah. The letter went on the *Estramina* when she sailed back to Sydney. I'm happy you have stayed out of trouble, Tedder and are still working at the Stores.'

'I've had my tribulations. Toothless nearly succeeded in doing away with me.'

'The rotten guard on *Indefatigable* - the one who flogged me?'

'The very same. I wager he is the one who orchestrated that your boots go missing.'

Blay nodded in agreement.

'He nearly killed me after I'd been in the Commissariat a few weeks. Tied me to a mooring post when the tide was coming in. Then scuttled off back to England on *Indefatigable*. Mr Williamson, in charge of the Commissariat, saved my life, Blay. I'm lucky to be alive.'

'Jesus Christ, Tedder. My time at the Cullen farm has been quiet and peaceful compared to yours here in Hobart.'

The Government Stores building appeared as they turned into a well-furrowed road.

'We're here, Blay. I'll get my books to record Mr Cullen's supplies, and get another convict to help unload.'

Blay and Mr Cullen lent on the wagon. Perspiration slid from Blay's forehead into and burning his eyes. The drops he missed when running his hands over his face, found their way into his mouth, the salty taste making him even thirstier. 'Why is summer so hot, here?'

'You are staying in Hobart Town for the night, Sir?' Tedder asked Mr Cullen.

'Yes, it is too hot to return now and will be too dark when it's cooler. We'll leave at first light.'

'Mr Cullen, I would be honoured if you and Blay would

stay with me the night. I have accommodation and food to prepare. My quarters are modest but comfortable.'

'Yes, Tedder, that would be most kind. My friend Mr Hands, where I usually stay, is not in Hobart Town at present.'

Blay let out an audible sigh of relief. Cullen ignored him.

## 18

## SEA LEGS

*The voyage to Australia was long and monotonous, particularly in the early days of travel when a sailing ship could take up to four months to reach Australia. Living conditions were notoriously bad with poor sanitation, cramped quarters and rations that was not much better than what the convicts received. Only when the British government passed several passenger acts in the mid 19th century and set standards for sanitation, space and diet, did conditions improve.*

*By the beginning of the 19th century more ships carried paying passengers without convicts, but the comfort had not vastly improved. Passenger ships were generally divided into classes, so those who could afford to pay for first-class cabins could enjoy their own quarters, buy better food, take servants and section themselves off from poorer passengers. Second-class passengers were slightly worse off than first-class, although on some ships they shared rooms with up to 100 other passengers.*

*Passengers in the lowest class, known as steerage, lived in cramped shared spaces, with no privacy and hammocks instead of beds. It was not far removed from the convict accommodation, apart from the lack of bars and better levels of hygiene.*

*Illness was regular, with many diary entries mentioning the first death on board. In the more cramped sections illness spread quickly and although first-class passengers could be untouched "sea sickness affected people no matter what class". Theft was another problem, particularly food.*

*http://blogs.slv.vic.gov.au/family-matters/collections/salt-beef-tinned-carrots-and-haggis-the-19th-century-ships-diet/*

'Here ye go missus.' Sarah thanked the sailors for their help and thought it prudent to offer them a monetary token. 'Much obliged missus,' said the sailor who did all the talking. 'We'll see you on the voyage.' She watched them climb the stairs to the upper level of the ship.

'I guess we should find somewhere to sleep and to put our things,' she said to the boys. The smile that appeared on James Jr's face when he saw the *Kangaroo's* guns was still there. His recent sullen demeanour had been transformed into that of a boy full of life and happiness. Sarah looked at him often, expecting the smile to evaporate as quickly as it had appeared. William hadn't stopped whimpering with fatigue, and John's eyes darted around taking in all the new sights.

'James walk around for me, will you? See if you can spot four hammocks for us. They need to be close to each other.'

The eldest boy skipped off without having to be told again. Sarah watched as he walked around the edges of the space, weaving in and out of banks of hammocks looking for suitable accommodation. About halfway up the space he turned to her and raised his arms, beckoning.

Sitting John and William on the trunk with instructions not to move, Sarah shuffled through the throngs of people who, like her, were trying to get settled. Her head spun from watching James Jr to looking back at William and John.

'This is perfect, James. Well done,' she praised, as four vacant hammocks, two by two appeared. 'How are we going to get the trunk over here, and make sure we keep our beds do you think?' she asked James.

'You stay here, Mama, with the beds, mind them. I'll go back and William and John and me will drag the trunk up here.'

'That's a good plan, James, but John is too little to be much help, and William isn't as strong as you.' She watched the boy's chest puff out, just a little.

'I know that, Mama. Someone will see us struggling and offer to help, I'm sure. You'll see.'

Sarah nodded permission and James hurried back to his brothers. She watched as he gave them instructions. William and John were to be at one end of the trunk and James the other. He nodded at the two smaller boys and the three of them attempted to drag the trunk. It moved a little. They tried again. Sarah had to stop herself from running toward them to help; she let James take control.

James stood up very straight as a gentleman dressed in travelling clothes approached him. Sarah watched James nod politely, say thank you and shake the man's hand. Within minutes another two gentlemen had joined the first, and the trunk was effortlessly on its way to their new accommodation.

'Thank you so much, sir. Thank you for helping my eldest son get our trunk up here,' Sarah praised James Jr in front of the strangers.

'Not a problem, missus. You are welcome. You have a fine lad here. Good and strong.'

James beamed as he watched the helpers walk away. 'See, I told you, Mama. I told you someone would help.'

'Yes, indeed you did, James. Well seems like you have already started to become a man and the voyage hasn't begun yet.'

James Jr helped Sarah organise the bedding. 'Put the old blankets on the hammocks, James, and leave the pillows in the trunk until we go to bed.'

'That's not going to keep us warm,' complained her middle son.

'I know, William,' Sarah explained 'we have to take care of our belongings. Some people will have less and might be tempted to take our things without permission. These old blankets are just to let others know someone has claimed the hammocks. I will get the thicker blankets out when we go to bed.' She locked the trunk, put the key in her purse, and James Jr and William helped her push the trunk against the wall between two of the hammocks. 'Looks like this is home for the next few months, boys.'

'I'm hungry,' wailed John.

'Me too,' chimed in William.

'Are you hungry, James?' Sarah asked.

'Come to think of it, yes I am,' he grinned.

Sarah wasn't sure of the time. They hadn't had any dinner, arriving late in the morning and taking all this time to get organised.

'Oh my,' she exclaimed 'Your grandmother packed some food for us. It's in the trunk.'

Timber tables with benches along each side occupied the centre of the steerage deck, almost from one end to the other. She herded the three boys to the benches and hurried back to the hammocks. Her mother had packed bread, which Sarah knew would be hard by now, cheese and biscuits. She shared the food between the four of them, ensuring James Jr received the largest portions, knowing he would notice.

'The bread will be a bit hard, but it will fill your stomachs until supper.'

While she watched the boys eat, Sarah realised she had no idea where their food was to come from, how it was to be cooked, how she would wash clothes, or how she and the boys would bathe.

The jarring sound of a bell not unlike those used by town criers, penetrated the noise of chatter on the steerage deck. The sailor ringing the bell boomed as loudly as his device.

'Listen up everyone, all of ye. Only sayin' what I'm sayin' the one time. Ye all to come up to the upper deck. First Mate has instructions for ye on how things will be run on this *HM Brig Kangaroo,* on her journey to New South Wales.' Finished with his commands he turned and headed up to the top deck.

Sarah gathered the boys and hurried them up the stairs after the sailor. The other passengers followed her lead. She listened carefully as the First Mate bellowed the rules and regulations of the voyage. John and William fidgeted, James Jr moved over to the side and lent against one of the guns.


The First Mate read out a lengthy list: 'You won't steal from any other passengers. You will be flogged and put in a cell until we get to New South Wales if you steal, no matter your age - old, young, in between. The ship's captain is Lieutenant Charles Jeffreys and he won't stand for stealing. You'll keep the quarters clean; you'll make up a roster to share the workload around. When the fresh fruit and vegetables we have on board run out, you won't get any more until we dock for supplies and any repairs. Use drinking water wisely, we can only refill water barrels if it rains, or if we dock where it is available. You will be told when we are heading for a port. You'll do your own cooking with the rations you are given each day. You'll get meat, potatoes, rice, biscuits, and bread. When you are seasick – clean up the mess so the deck doesn't stink -wash bedding and clothes. If someone in your party becomes ill, notify the ship's surgeon at once. If you can't find the ship's surgeon, ask a sailor. You can come up to the outside deck for fresh air, but don't get in the way of any sailors doing their work. First Class passengers have priority, don't annoy them. Watch children carefully, if they go over-board that's usually the end of them. *HM Brig Kangaroo* is only four years old, so you steerage passengers are fortunate in that your quarters are quite new. This is her first voyage to New South Wales. She is staying there to sail between New South Wales and Van Diemen's Land. That is all.'

The First Mate moved away from the passengers who were grouped together on the upper deck. No opportunity for questions. Sarah hoped everyone was listening because there was a lot to remember.

The sailor with the bell rang it loudly from behind the group.

'You'll line up over there,' he said pointing to the forward part of the ship 'and get your supplies for supper. Every morn, before eight, someone from your party will line up to get food supplies for the day. If no one from your party collects supplies, you will go hungry. The ship sails in ten minutes.'

Sarah looked around for James, he hadn't moved from

his position next to the gun. She held the hands of William and John and moved to a place in the line to collect their rations for supper. 'If I'd known this was happening, I would have brought a basket.'

'Indeed,' said a woman's voice from behind. 'How many you cookin' for luvy?' Sarah was asked. '

'Four of us,' she replied.

'There's only me and my little boy,' she said pointing to a small child who clung to her side, 'so if you need help let me know,' offered the woman.

Sarah thanked the woman as she collected her supplies for supper, and with James Jr's help, carried them down the steps. Just as they reached the steerage deck, laden with supplies for supper, the ship lurched way from the Portsmouth dock. John lost his balance and fell onto his hands and knees. He screamed so loudly, the First Mate appeared at the top of the stairs wanting to know what was going on.

'Nothing, Sir. My little boy fell as the ship moved.'

'Better get used to it,' the First Mate grumbled stomping away.

Sarah handed the things she was carrying to William 'You and James take these to our hammocks. I'll have to carry John.'

The child was convulsing with sobs by the time Sarah had him in his hammock.

'My breeches are ripped,' he wailed. His knee was bleeding heavily.

'Yes, John, your breeches are ripped. We'll take them off, I'll have to repair them.'

Opening the trunk Sarah rummaged around the contents until she found the bundle of rags she was looking for. Pulling one out, she tore it into strips and wet it with water from one of the jugs placed on the tables. John screamed while she cleaned his wound.

'Shh, John,' she soothed 'keep still so I can clean your leg and put a bandage on it. He is very, very tired,' she said to James, 'I'll get him something to eat now, and put him to bed.'

While John snored softly in the hammock, his little body rocking gently with the movement of the *Kangaroo*, Sarah, William and James sat at one end of the long bench eating biscuits and dried beef.

'Do you think this is the food Papa would have eaten when he was sent away to New South Wales?' William asked his mother.

'I think we are probably eating a bit better than Papa and the others did on their voyage, William. But at least we know that he is alive and working for someone kind.'

Looking around the steerage deck at the other passengers, Sarah noticed they looked as tired as she felt. There were many children, like John, already asleep in the gently rocking hammocks. She hoped she would be able to make some friends on the journey, she was already feeling lonely, and really missed her mother.

Sarah and James Jr and William climbed the stairs to the upper deck to watch the shores of England disappear over the horizon. She wiped tears from her cheeks, careful not to let the boys see. As the ship moved into open waters the gentle rocking transformed into lurching. Struggling to keep their feet, Sarah and the children made their way down the stairs to the steerage deck.

'I think it's time we got some sleep, boys. This is our first day, it's been long and tiring.'

Taking the better-quality blankets from the trunk Sarah put them over her children. The ship moved with the waves like a wagon going up and down hills. She hoped they didn't get seasick. She washed her face, took off her boots and jacket, put her purse under her pillow, pulled the blanket up to her chin and went to sleep.

'Mama, Mama, Mama.' Sarah woke to the sound of a child screaming out for its mother. 'I wonder where the mother is?' she thought, half asleep.

'Mama wake up,' James shook her.

Sarah sat upright in the hammock, momentarily forgetting where she was. 'What's wrong?'

'John is screaming. Says he's hungry, and the other passengers are going upstairs to get their day's supplies.'

'The rules,' she said as she climbed out of the hammock. 'Where are my boots? James, get my purse from under the pillow and unlock the trunk. There's a basket in the bottom somewhere. John, stop crying. I'll get breakfast shortly.'

Sarah put on her bonnet, grabbed a shawl from the trunk, took the basket and made her way to the stairs. 'You stay here and wait for me,' she instructed the boys.

'You just made it, Missus,' scowled the bell ringing sailor as Sarah made her way to the supplies table.

'I'm sorry, I overslept. It won't happen again, Sir.' Sarah decided grovelling was probably a good way to keep on the right side of the crew, she might need their assistance again.

'Hmph. What's yer name?' the sailor asked.

'Sarah Blay.'

The sailor checked his passenger list 'There's you and three boys, here's your supplies for today: biscuits, dried pork, bread, cabbage, and potatoes. How you eat it and when is up to you.'

Thanking the sailor as he put the supplies into her

basket, Sarah gave a final slight curtsey and headed back down to her hungry children.

Working cooperatively, the steerage passengers shared cooking and eating areas. Those without children waited while families cooked and ate. They staggered breakfast, dinner, and supper to make mealtimes more equitable. Neither Sarah nor the boys had been seasick, but many passengers had. The women scrubbed the floors and tables with salt water and washed blankets and pillows to remove the stench of stale and fresh vomit.

'It will pass eventually,' one of the older women passengers told her.

Sarah had tasked James Jr with keeping track of the days. He did this with chalk, on the underside of the lid of the trunk. On the fourth day, John's grumpy behaviour had worsened, and he was complaining his knee was sore. It was bright red and swollen. Sarah touched his forehead; he had a fever. 'His knee is infected.' She sat him in his hammock and using a rag from the trunk, soaked it in seawater from one of the buckets, and placed it on his knee. It worried her that he didn't cry.

John wanted to know if his leg would be alright, 'Will it get better, Mama?'

'Of course, John,' Sarah soothed. Trying to convince them both.

John whimpered all night. He was hot, then cold. His leg hurt, he was thirsty. His head hurt. Sarah fretted.

In the morning, Sarah sent James Jr to find the ship's surgeon.

'There's nothing more I can do than you are doing now, Missus,' the surgeon told her. 'Keep it clean with the sea water and make sure he drinks.'

By the sixth day, John was delirious with fever, his leg was swollen and throbbing, he wasn't eating, and it was a struggle to get him to take water.

'Will I get the surgeon, again?' asked James as he watched Sarah fussing over his youngest brother.

'He said he can't do anything for him, James,' Sarah wiped her forehead with the back of her hands.

'He's useless anyway,' offered a woman's voice from behind, 'we need to make a potato poultice. Do you want me to help?'

'Yes, please,' Sarah pleaded, turning to face her saviour.

'I'm Mary Fogarty.'

'You were in the line with me on the first day,' Sarah remembered.

'Yes. Now let's get to work. We need clean rags and a potato.'

Mary cut the potato in half and sliced it thinly. She wrapped the slices in a clean rag Sarah had given her and tied it around John's knee. 'We'll put on a new one tonight, and a new one in the morning,' Mary explained. 'The infection should start drawing out by tomorrow. Make sure you have clean rags ready.'

Sarah impulsively hugged Mary, remembering how much she missed her mother, and how lonely she was. Mary returned the hug.

'He's not going to get better overnight, but we've done all we can,' Mary patted Sarah's hand and walked back to her seat at the table. Her little boy, whose name Sarah didn't know, stuck to his mother's side, following and sitting next to his mother.

. . .

John had another restless night and Sarah despaired he would not recover.

'Let's have a look at his knee,' Mary said after she had collected her day's supplies. 'Have you collected your day's supplies, Sarah?'

'No, I haven't yet. James, would you be able to take the basket and get our day's supplies, please?' she asked her eldest.

James Jr grabbed the basket and scurried up the stairs to the upper deck. 'He needs to feel important,' Sarah said as she watched him go.

Mary felt John's brow. 'I think his temperature has gone down a little.' She removed the night time poultice. Her little boy stood by her side.

Sarah gasped.

'See, it's working,' said Mary proudly. 'The rag is covered in the pus the potato is drawing out. Do you have any more potato and a rag?' she asked.

A new poultice wrapped around John's knee and a few spoons of water forced into his mouth saw the little boy ready to sleep.

Sarah sat next to Mary Fogarty at the table, to wash and cut potatoes. 'I can't thank you enough, Mrs Fogarty. You saved John's life.'

'I was glad to help, Sarah. He's out of the woods, but his knee still needs to be kept clean. If you need more rags, let me know. This is only the beginning of our journey.'

'May I inquire as to why you are going to New South Wales? My boys and I are going because my husband is there. He was sent on the *Indefatigable* last year. I got a letter from him saying he is assigned to a farmer in New Norfolk in Van Diemen's Land. He sounded happy enough. In his letter, he said if I could go, he might be assigned to me.'

Mary Fogarty's eyes filled up with tears. 'Oh, Mrs Blay. We have much in common. My husband, Thomas, was on *Indefatigable* last year. They sent him away for life for pick pocketing. My little Thomas here was only one year old when his father was taken away.'

Sarah smiled at Mary, 'I think we will be good friends, Mrs Fogarty.'

# 19

# THE FIRST FLEETER

*The **First Fleet** is the name given to the 11 ships that left England on 13 May 1787 to found the penal colony that became the first European settlement in Australia. The Fleet consisted of two Royal Navy vessels, three store ships, and six convict transports, carrying between 1,000 and 1,500 convicts, marines, seamen, civil officers and free people (accounts differ on the numbers), and a vast quantity of stores. From England, the Fleet sailed southwest to Rio de Janeiro, then east to Cape Town and via the Great Southern Ocean to Botany Bay, arriving over the period of 18 to 20 January 1788, taking 250 to 252 days from departure to final arrival.*

From : https://en.wikipedia.org/wiki/First_Fleet

'How do you come to be in Van Diemen's Land, Mr Cullen?' ventured James Tedder as he prepared their supper. He was most happy to have company and very happy to see Blay again.

'It's a very long story, Tedder, so I will make parts of it short or I'll still be tellin' the tale this time tomorrow. It's also a story that Blay here has been busting to know,' said Cullen, nodding at Blay.

'Transported in 1787, I was,' Cullen began. 'Don't look so shocked, most of the people you've seen in Hobart Town are either military, current convicts or settlers as they like to call us now. I left England 25 years ago.'

Tedder stared at Mr Cullen, disbelieving. 'So, there's hope that I could make a good life, or even go home to England?'

'If you've got family in England you might want to go back, otherwise, there's no point. You can make a good life here when your time is up, or if you get a Ticket of Leave before then.'

Blay interrupted, 'Mr Cullen told me about Tickets of Leave, Tedder. Even the likes of me, with a sentence of life, can get a Ticket of Leave. Means you can work for anyone you want and keep your money. And you get a land grant,' beamed Blay.

Tedder sat down with a thud at the little table. 'This is something I did not know about. How is it no one told me?'

'You would have found out soon enough, Tedder. Now, best get on with the supper. Blay and me are hungry, thirsty, hot, and tired.'

'Will you get on with your story, too?' Blay asked.

'Yes,' said Cullen with a smile.

'I got knicked for stealing with my then lady friend and sentenced to seven years in Africa. Thank God Africa got changed to New South Wales. We heard men didn't do so well in Africa. I'm not going to do a lot of talking about the almost year it took to get to New South Wales, it'll take too long. Most of us survived intact, but there was trouble on the *Scarborough*, the ship I was on. Some of the men were organising a mutiny, were going to take it over and sail back to England. It was folly from the start and doomed to fail. Captain Phillip got wind of it and took away our privileges for some time.'

Cullen stared out the window, onto the dirt streets as if he could see the *Scarborough* as she sailed towards the unknown land on the other side of the world. He settled into an easy rhythm of storytelling, seeming to enjoy the opportunity to share.

'I'm not going to tell you every little detail 'cos I can't remember them anyway.

'Spent some time on the hulks as did the two of you. Lucky to survive the squalor and deprivation. A couple of things went my way after being knicked: Africa was out of the picture and Captain Phillip was in charge of our sailing. I remember finally leaving England – it was May 1787. We didn't arrive in New South Wales till January 1788. It was a long way and a long time.'

Cullen remained silent for a few minutes. Neither Tedder nor Blay disturbed him.

'I see the *Scarborough* in my nightmares, we were stowed below like livestock: grown men, boys, lying in their own vomit and piss, shackled, shaking, some even crying. I wasn't going to waste my energy on crying or vomiting, I needed to survive.'

Shuddering at the memory, he continued. 'The daily routine was boring and predictable when the weather was calm. But when the squalls picked up we had to batten down the hatches and bear the stench from seasickness vomit and piss and shit. You know about the journey here, but you were lucky it only takes five months now, not ten like it took us.'

Tedder and Blay looked knowingly at each other.

'We were sent to work pretty quickly after landing in

Port Jackson. What a relief to walk on dry land, on a surface that didn't wobble under your feet. I was part of the group Captain Phillip thought low risk, probably because I was older than most of the others. He sent us to the edge of the bay to get on with the task of tree-felling and clearing the shoreline. I felt all the lashes you got on your second day, Blay. I came by twenty-five not long after we arrived cos the stupid, ignorant, overseer had no idea how to cut down trees and was putting us in danger. I told him how to do it properly and got whipped for my trouble. He was still wrong, but I kept my mouth shut after that.'

Cullen took a spoon of the vegetable soup Tedder had put in front of him, continuing his story between mouthfuls.

'We didn't have much. Most of the animals died on the voyage. The first building we had to put up was a storehouse for the provisions we took off the ship. But the black rats that travelled with us from England had eaten or ruined much of the supplies. Then they ran off into the bush and later ate the vegetables and wheat we planted. Lots of the convicts and the marines got sick with the scurvy and the flux.[1]

Then on top of that, a couple of days after we got off the ships, there was a God Almighty storm. The afternoon sky darkened, we couldn't stand up in the wind, and the pouring rain flooded the campsites. We missed a hit from a bolt of lightning, but it struck a tree, split it in half and killed five sheep who were hiding in a little shelter built for them under the tree. We felt surely doomed. It rained until well into the night. Next day after the storm, Captain Phillip, now called Governor Phillip called everyone to hear him speak. Most of what he said was all about him being in charge and the punishments for breaking the laws he made in the colony. But, the best part and the only part I remember in full was him saying that "through commitment, good behaviour, and strong endeavours, you might soon regain the advantages which you forfeited". [2] Most of us cheered. Most of us wanted to earn our freedom. That was the day I decided to work hard, to do my time, so I could earn my freedom.'

'When did you earn your freedom, Mr Cullen?' Tedder asked.

'On Norfolk Island, lad. I was sent there in March 1790 and emancipated in December 1791. I worked hard in the nearly two years from when I arrived 'til I got my freedom. I still remember the taste.'

Tedder marvelled at how this man had been isolated from his homeland for more than Tedder's whole life. He had trouble putting the picture together: this was a prison, he was a convict, Mr Cullen had been a convict, but hope appeared on the horizon.

'Life in Port Jackson was tough. Is there any bread, Tedder?'

# 20

# LAND HO

The boredom of the journey was telling on the boys. James Jr had tired of examining the guns each day and had been chastised many times for annoying the sailors in their work. The First Mate threatened to throw him in the brig. At the call of "Land Ho" James Jr, John and William disappeared to the upper deck.

'Mama, Mama,' James called down to Sarah 'we are nearly in port. Do you think we'll be able to get off?'

'We'll have to wait until the captain gives his instructions, James. Remain calm. We will all leave together if we are permitted.'

Amid a mass of people, Sarah made her way to the upper deck. She couldn't see the boys and could only move in small steps. Making her way through the throng she manoeuvred to a position on the port side of the ship and lent on the rails. She had seen nothing like it. The sea not only sparkled in the sunlight but danced around the ship, lapping at the hull, changing colour as it rose and fell. She took off her cap and let the warm sea air play with her hair.

The sun kissed her upturned face. Eyes closed, savouring the warm fresh air and sunshine, Sarah took deep breaths.

The First Mate's orders were repeated through sailors, 'Everyone to your quarters while we dock. Now.'

Carried along with the other passengers, Sarah moved to the steerage deck. She made her way to their hammocks and waited for the boys. William, holding John's hand, arrived with Mary Fogarty and little Thomas.

'Where is James Jr?' she asked.

'I lost him in the crowd, Mama,' explained William. 'But I kept hold tight of John's hand, so I wouldn't lose him.'

John complained, 'He squeezed my hand so tight, Mama, I thought it would be broken in pieces.'

Sarah patted his hand 'It will be alright, John.'

Eyes fixed on the stairs, Sarah waited for James Jr to appear. Her shoulders tensed as she fretted about him being in the brig. She couldn't go up and look for him without running the risk of being put in the brig herself. The orders were clear, and all passengers knew the First Mate was to be obeyed. John and William sat with her at the table waiting for permission to leave the *HM Brig Kangaroo*. The familiar noises of the ship banging against the dock, sailors yelling at each other, and orders being barked, filled the deck as the vessel was settled into port in Rio de Janeiro.

Sarah overheard Mary Fogarty express concern about the length of stay in Rio. 'I pray we are not here as long as we were in Madeira,' she said to herself. 'I want this tiresome journey to be finished.'

Sarah had found the stay in Madeira pleasant but agreed with Mary Fogarty that three weeks was too long. All the passengers wanted to be on their way after a few days, but Lieutenant Jeffreys had other plans. 'It also adds to the cost,' Sarah complained to Mary, 'we have to supplement our rations by buying extra food on shore. And I'm sure the traders put up their prices when a ship comes in. Have you heard how long we will be in Rio de Janeiro, Mary?'

'No. Not too long, I hope. Has James returned?'

'No,' Sarah said with an irritated tone.

'I'm sure he'll be fine, Sarah. He's probably helping up on deck.'

Sarah wasn't convinced. She knew James had a habit of getting in the way of the crew. 'If he just stays with the guns and out of the way, he'll be alright,' she mumbled.

A sailor appeared at the top of the stairs and rang the bell twice. The noise reverberated on the deck, William and John covered their ears.

'First Mate says you have permission to leave the ship. Some of you are goin' to be with convicts in New South Wales, but the likes of the crooks here in Rio will make your head spin. Keep your valuables very close, don't trust anyone, and sleep on the ship.'

'Sir,' Sarah called out. The sailor turned.

'Have you seen my eldest son, James? I haven't sighted him since the *land ho* call was made.'

'He's probably in the brig missus. First Mate warned him over and over.'

'Thank you,' Sarah blushed with embarrassment. She waited while the other passengers in steerage gathered bonnets, caps and hats, children, and money, and made their way to shore.

'Why are we waiting?' whined John.

'It will be easier to find James when everyone has left.'

Herding the boys in front of her, the three made their way to the upper deck.

'James, James, James Jr,' called Sarah as she and John

JANEEN ANN O'CONNELL

and William walked around in circles. Panic set in when she had walked the entire deck three times, with no response.

The First Mate stepped out of the Captain's cabin, 'Why are you not on shore with the other passengers?'

Taking a deep breath to keep the tears at bay, Sarah explained, 'I can't find my eldest son, James.'

'Oh, yes, that one. He's a handful, isn't he? Gets underfoot and yelled at. But sometimes he's quite useful. Says he wants to be a sailor.'

Sarah didn't believe for one minute that James Jr wanted to be a sailor. Like his father, he knew how to manipulate people to his will.

'Could you check the brig for me, please, sir?' Sarah asked.

'He's not in the brig. But I'll check to ease your mind.'

Sarah waited; the warm sea breeze and kissing sunshine were wasted on her this time.

'He's not in the brig,' assured the First Mate. 'I'll get the crew to keep an eye out for him while they go about their tasks. I hope for his sake, Missus that he isn't ashore somewhere on his own. This is not a safe place for women on their own, or children on their own.'

Sarah could hold the panic down no longer; her legs went from under her.

'Here Missus, you all right?' fussed the First Mate. 'Get your Ma some water,' he ordered William. Sarah drank thankfully. It didn't stop the panic but helped her calm a little.

'Take your Ma back to your quarters, boy,' William was ordered. 'If someone on the crew finds him, we'll send him to you, with a kick up the backside for good measure.'

'What if you don't find him on the ship?' Sarah cried.

'Well, he'll be in trouble somewhere, then.'

# 21

# THE THIRD DAY

Mary Fogarty had befriended an older woman, Elizabeth Richardson, whose son, also on *Indefatigable,* was the only family she had left. 'We'll take William and John ashore today if you like, Sarah,' Mrs Richardson offered. Mary and I will keep an eye on them.'

'Thank you. They will enjoy the change.'

Sarah watched John, holding Mrs Richardson's hand, skip up the stairs. 'Not a worry in the world.' William was more aware of James' disappearance and fretted along with his mother. He walked next to little Thomas Fogarty.

'Three days. Where can he be?' Sarah had several scenarios running around in her head, each one competing to be the worst. She made her way to the upper deck to get some air. In the early afternoon light, Rio de Janeiro looked peaceful and welcoming. Its beaches were blessed with beautiful bright yellow sand that seemed to pull away and run back as the sea lapped against it. She could hear laughter, music, and happy chatter drifting over the tops of the city's buildings. Sarah lent over the rail of the ship and cried, again.

'Still no sign of him, Missus,' offered a sailor standing behind.

'Thank you for trying, sir.' Sarah knew the sailors were looking for James in their spare time both on the ship and ashore.

'I think he'll be alright, Missus. He's an inventive lad and knows how to get out of scrapes.'

Sarah smiled at the sailor's attempt to improve her mood.

'Why don't you go ashore, Missus? If you keep your wits about you, it's a beautiful city. Nothing like London. It's clean,' he grinned, showing a number of gaps in his mouth where teeth had been.

'Perhaps tomorrow,' Sarah turned her back on the sailor and closed her eyes. Listening to the water lap against the hull of the ship, not wanting to go back down to steerage, she found something to sit on and waited for William and John.

'They behaved well,' Mary Fogarty told Sarah. 'John does get excited though.'

'Yes, but I suppose at this time it is better than fretting like William.' Sarah looked at the middle boy, standing with his arms folded and his head down. It was almost as if he was punishing himself.

'William,' she called 'come here for a minute and sit next to me.'

Obeying his mother, William sat down, still with his head down and arms folded.

'When was the last time you saw James? You are not in any trouble,' she reassured. 'I am trying to put together a picture in my mind about where he went and what he did.'

William squirmed but didn't answer.

'Please William, if you know something you must tell me. Can't you see how worried I am?'

'He made me promise not to tell. He said he'd lock me in the brig and throw the key overboard if I told you, or anyone.'

Taking a very deep breath to calm her nerves and to keep her voice steady, Sarah pressed the boy for more information 'No one is going to throw you in the brig, William. Tell me what you know.'

'When we got the *land, ho* call the other day and we all went onto the deck, James hid up on the bow of the ship. He said he was going ashore to have an adventure.'

Sarah closed her eyes, held her breath for a few seconds and thanked William for telling her. 'Nothing for it,' she thought, 'I'll have to go ashore and look for him. 'Did he say where he was going to go?'

'No, just that he wanted to have an adventure. Because he was sick of being on the ship.' William's eyes focused on the floor.

'I need help,' Sarah said out loud.

'Everything alright, Missus?' asked the sailor who had spoken to her earlier.

'Are you allowed to go ashore?' she asked

'Yes, Missus. We get rostered on duty and off duty. Off-duty we can go ashore.'

'Are you off duty, now?'

'What is it you need, Missus?'

'I think my son, James has gone ashore. His brother said he was looking for an adventure.'

'The little shit. Oops, sorry Missus.'

'You are right, he is a little shit. And when I get hold of him he will get the biggest whipping of his life,' Sarah gritted her teeth and clenched her fists as if getting ready for battle. 'Do you know of any sailors who would be good enough to come ashore with me to help me search for James?' she asked.

'I'll go with you Missus. I was about to go anyways. Me name's Thomas.'

'Pleased to meet you Thomas,' said Sarah with a slight curtsey. 'I am Sarah Blay. I'll get someone to watch the other two and get my hat. I won't be long.'

On her return, the sailor was waiting, ready to help her onto the dock.

'Where will we start?' Sarah asked Thomas as they made their way into the city.

'Boys are attracted to the carnival and circus people,' he said, looking to see Sarah's reaction. There was a slight frown.

'James would be one of those boys,' she said.


Sarah walked close to Thomas; the throngs of people, the music, the pushing, and shoving made her head spin. She didn't want to get lost while looking for her lost son.

Thomas wlked through the crowds with ease, he took long strides, and people moved out of his way. Tall, with a physique that proved he worked hard, and a creamy colour to his skin that set him apart from white English faces, Sarah wondered where he was originally from.

'We'll begin with some of the circus people,' he said to Sarah, his voice raised to be heard over the din.

She followed as they moved from the music, laughter, yelling and talking to even louder music, interspersed with cheers from crowds of people.

Telling Sarah to wait for him at one of the taverns in the

circus quarter, Thomas explained, 'It's not appropriate for a lady to go where I will be going, Missus,' he said when she resisted his instruction.

Sarah waited as asked, bemused by the exciting atmosphere, of smells and sights that included foods she had never seen before, and cooking aromas that made her mouth water. She saw people dressed in an amazing array of colours and fabrics, women showing their legs, men calling out to passers-by, tempting them with samples of foods she could not identify; she lost track of time.

'He's not here, Missus,' Thomas said in Sarah's ear. She jumped with fright. So entranced by the sights of Rio de Janeiro she hadn't noticed his return.

'They haven't seen him. Probably just as well, cos they'd sell him to the slavers as quick as a wink,' Thomas said. 'Oh, I'm sorry, Missus. Don't fret. I'm sure we'll find him. He's most likely with the carnival folk learning how to hustle good honest people out of their money. It'll be dark in less than an hour, Missus. We should go back to the *Kangaroo* and start looking again on the morrow.'

Sarah wanted to keep looking, but knew Thomas was right. If James had survived three nights in this town on his own wits, he would survive another. She nodded to Thomas, and walked again through the throngs, to the safety of the ship.

While preparing supper, Sarah told Mrs Richardson of her search, careful to leave out things that would alarm John, who was listening to every word.

'Happy to watch the boys again for you on the morrow, Sarah,' offered Mary Fogarty.

'Thank you. I don't know what I'd do without you.'

. . .

Thomas collected Sarah from steerage at eight the next morning. 'I have to be back to start work at noon,' he explained. Putting on her hat and boots, Sarah followed Thomas back into the city.

The sights and sounds of Rio didn't intrigue her as much today, she and Thomas had limited time, and much ground to cover.

Sarah stood back as Thomas approached people he seemed to know – both men and women – of different skin colours, with different hairstyles, but all wearing what seemed to be the trademark clothing of Rio – bright colours, bare skin showing, and big white, flashy smiles. He shook his head after each conversation.

Looking at the sun's angle in the sky Thomas said, 'It's getting close to midday, Missus. I'm going to have to go back to the ship. I'll get whipped if I'm not at my station for the start of my shift. I don't think it's a good idea for you to say here on your own.'

Sarah fidgeted with the buttons on her jacket and straightened her hat. 'I can't leave with a whole afternoon still ahead. I must keep looking.'

'I have one more person to seek who might be helpful,' said Thomas, 'follow me.'

They moved deeper into the carnival district. Sarah noticed some of the men staring at her menacingly. Her skin crawled. She had to almost run to keep up with Thomas as he took his long strides. He planted her next to an old woman who was selling small colourful birds in tiny cages.

'Wait here, with this woman, don't move.'

She had never seen birds like this, the reds and yellows of their chest and feathers were breathtaking.

'This is my contact, he thinks he knows where James is,' Thomas said, bringing Sarah back from the adulation of the birds.

She swallowed hard, nodded, and followed him.

The contact took them even deeper into the dark heart of the city. The smells were not as fresh and vibrant, nor were the colours. She couldn't hear the street music. The contact held up his hand indicating they should stop.

'What is it?' Sarah asked.

'Sshh,' ordered the man.

Sarah heard whimpering. 'Is that a dog?' she whispered to Thomas.

'No Missus. Sounds to me like children.' Thomas put his index finger over the middle of his mouth. Sarah listened as intently as the men with her.

The man Thomas had referred to as his contact, signalled at them to wait. He tip-toed down a lane, stopping at what looked to Sarah to be a grate in the roadway. He squatted and put his hand through the grate. Indicating that Thomas should come, but Sarah should stay, the man removed a knife from his belt and scraped around the edges of the grate to loosen it. As Thomas arrived the man pointed down – Sarah couldn't hear what was being said – her heart was beating so fast she thought it would jump out of her chest. Thomas nodded grimly. He and the other man loosened the grate enough to lift it onto the road. Thomas lay down, lowering the top half of his body into the hole in the road. Sarah could hear him now, grunting and cursing. He got up onto his knees and pulled a child through the hole. The child's clothes were torn and ragged, he was filthy. He turned toward her. She fainted.

Sarah gasped as water was thrown onto her face.

Thomas helped her to sit up. James looking down at her, had old tears staining his face.

Through intermittent sobs, he coughed 'I'm sorry, Mama.'

Sarah didn't answer him.

Turning to Thomas she asked if he could help her to stand. 'Is he alright?' she said quietly in Thomas' ear. He nodded.

'I have to leave now. I have to be back on the ship by noon,' Thomas exclaimed.

'Thank you so much for your help, Thomas. I will see to myself and James returning, we will walk more slowly than you and will hold you up. You go on ahead. I will be careful.' Sarah watched the sailor sprint along the lane and out into the market toward the *HM Brig Kangaroo*.

'Thank you to you too, sir,' Sarah said to Thomas' contact. 'Here is something for your trouble,' she put two shillings into his open hand. The grin scared her a little, but she straightened her back, took James by the hand, and half dragged, half pushed him towards the market.


Relieved to be back on the ship in one piece and with her purse still tucked into her bodice, Sarah knew she had to deal with James.

'James, James, you're back,' squealed John with delight 'but you stink, and you are really, really, dirty. Where did you go? Where have you been? What did you do?'

'Time for that later, John,' Sarah scolded. 'William, get some water organised for a bath for your brother.'

Sarah left the two older boys to organise the bath. She sat at the table, put her head in her hands and cried until she thought every ounce of water in her body had seeped out through her eyes.

Mrs Richardson patted her back, trying to be a comfort. 'What happened to him?'

'I don't know, I haven't asked him. We found him in a hole in the road. I could hear him whimpering, I thought I was hearing a dog.' Sarah got up from the table, thanked Mrs Richardson for all her help, and limped over to the bath to supervise.

'Mrs Blay.' roared the First Mate as he jumped down the stairs to the steerage deck. 'Please come over here so we can speak.'

Sarah left James soaking in the bath, picked up his filthy clothes, and deposited them on top of the trunk on her way to speak to the First Mate.

'Thomas told me where you found the lad. He was very lucky. About to be sold to the slavers and sent to God knows where apparently. No need to spell it out, Missus, but I don't want that lad on deck on his own, and I don't want him leaving the ship on his own. He's to be with you all the time until we get to New South Wales. Then I don't give a damn what he does.'

The First Mate turned and hurried back up the stairs, not waiting for a response, not looking back. The rules were laid out. She understood.

'Now you are clean and have had some food, James, you will sit here with me, and tell me what happened and why you left the ship alone.' Sarah made a space for James to sit next to her on top of the trunk in their quarters.

After a few deep breaths, the boy relayed his story. 'I

wanted an adventure. It's been getting boring on the ship, I heard the sailors talking about Rio de Janeiro and it sounded wonderful. I got lost and was looking for a way back to the ship when this old lady with no teeth said she'd help me. She pushed me along and shoved me into the arms of a big black man. He grinned at me, his teeth were huge. I just stood there, staring up at him. He had a big red hat on his head that looked like one of those black hats the toffs wear at home, but it didn't have a brim, but it had a tassel waving from the top. And he wore a long dress with long sleeves. I just kept staring at him. He picked me up and threw me through a doorway, then I was pushed down a really, really dark stairway until I landed at the bottom where there were lots of other boys and girls. That's it, Mama. Then you found me. I don't know how long I was there, but we didn't get any food or water, and most of the others cried all the time.' James wiped his eyes and looked at his mother.

Looking at her son's face through eyes that had not been closed in three days, eyes full of grit and dust, and sore from salt filled tears, Sarah said 'You will not leave the steerage deck without my permission. You will not, go anywhere, without my permission, or without me. Do you understand?'

James rocked back and forth, kept his head down, his hands clenched by his sides and mumbled, 'Yes, Mama.'

'If you disobey, the First Mate will put you in the brig for the rest of the voyage. Go to bed.' Sarah left James to get himself organised and went to comfort John and tend to William. 'I should whip him, but taking away his freedom, and the threat of the brig should be enough.'

22
━━━━━━

# NORFOLK ISLAND

*The last fatal voyage of the* **Sirius** *was commenced from Sydney on March 6, 1790. She was despatched, in command of Captain Hunter, to Norfolk Island, with Major Ross and two companies of marines and about 200 convicts, and arrived off the island on the 16th of that month. The anchorage as by no means a good one but the passengers were safely landed by means of surfboats. The Sirius remained off the settlement awaiting an opportunity to land her stores, but on March 19 she was carried by the currents on to the reef, where she shortly afterwards went to pieces.*

From:
The Sydney Morning Herald (NSW: 1842-1954), Wednesday 6 September 1905, page 8 (trove.nla.gov.au)

*From 1788 to 1814 Norfolk Island existed as an extension of the penal settlement in New South Wales but by the early 1800s the Island was no longer needed as a penal colony as one had been set up in Van Diemen's Land. Although the settlers were reluctant to*

165

*move from Norfolk Island, the settlement was steadily reduced over the years. Rough seas and suitable landing sites posed difficulties in supplying provisions and communications. By 1810 the population had decreased to 117 and in 1813 plans were put in place for the abandonment of the Island. It was finally deserted in February 1814.*

(State Archives and Records Authority of New South Wales.)

'Next part of the story picks up on Norfolk Island,' continued Cullen after they'd finished the soup and had some rice, dried beef, and green beans. 'You heard of that place?' he asked.

Tedder revealed he had no knowledge of the Island. He was eager to learn more. Blay agreed.

'Governor Phillip was in a pickle. More convicts were coming from England and he barely had enough food and supplies for those of us already in place. We were on rations. He picked some of us to go to Norfolk Island to get out of his hair. He told us we were to grow our own food and look after ourselves. He expected we'd have surplus that we'd send back to Port Jackson. Don't know how he worked out who would go, 'cos he still needed farmers in Port Jackson, but my bit of farming experience got me aboard the *HMS Sirius*. We left Port Jackson on 7th March 1790 and saw the coast of Norfolk Island on 16th March that year. There's no place to land there, *HMS Sirius* went into Cascade Bay and all the women convicts and their children got off as did the men convicts, including me. But we had to walk to the other side of the island to Sydney Town. The rest couldn't get off because the winds picked up. Captain Hunter sailed her around the Island to Sydney Bay and *Sirius* got herself smashed up on the reef. God kept playin' his tricks on us, but we beat Him again, 'cos all lives and most of the supplies were saved.'

'Would you like some tea, Mr Cullen, Blay?' Tedder asked.

'My story boring you, Tedder?' asked Mr Cullen.

Tedder was horrified. 'No, Mr Cullen. You've had a long day travelling in the heat, and we've just eaten. I suddenly realised I hadn't offered you a drink.'

Embarrassed Tedder made the tea for his guests.

'What happened on Norfolk Island, Mr Cullen? When did your sentence finish? How did you come about land to farm?' Did you find a wife? Did you have children? Tedder's pent-up questions poured out.

'Steady on Tedder' Cullen reprimanded 'I'll tell my story in my own time. Blay already knows the answer to most of your questions.' Cullen looked at Blay, whose head wobbled as he struggled to stay awake.

Tedder sat quietly, waiting.


'I've been trying to remember the early days on Norfolk Island. Seems a long time ago now,' Cullen continued. 'We slept around a fire in the outside that first night on the Island. The crew of the *Sirius* slept in the few tents that were up. We had no shoes – hadn't had for some time - but we all had our blanket and the bucket we left Port Jackson with. By Jesus, I remember how cold it was. We were all wet, our clothes, right through to our bones. It'd been raining when we got off the *Sirius* and we walked in the rain from one side of the Island to the other. They lit a big fire of pine scraps to try and stop us from getting chills and dying. We curled up in our blankets on the ground, huddled near the fire and slept – mainly from exhaustion - it had been a very tiring journey.

'There was plenty of timber on the Island and we cut it down and built houses to live in. It was stirring to have a roof, windows, a floor, and a door. The windows had no bars, (or glass) the door had no lock to lock us in unless we put it on ourselves. I remember the first night in my little hut. I cried myself to sleep; I felt like a man again, not like a prisoner – like someone else's property – although technically I still was the property of New South Wales.

'Sydney Town grew and grew, with streets and small wooden huts. It grew faster than Hobart Town has. The Island's commandant, Major Ross got everyone busy – even the crew of the *Sirius* who had no way of getting off the Island until another ship came – were set to work. Major Ross had some plans for all of us; we were to produce as much of our own food as possible, so the Government didn't have to feed us. To keep ourselves on our own little farms. We had a community baker, but we only had bread on Sundays and Wednesdays. On Mondays and Thursdays, we had rice and Saturdays we had pease. Tuesdays and Fridays, we had porridge of Indian corn mixed with oatmeal. But you know what? The food was only part of it – most of us knew this Norfolk Island and the way Major Ross was running it, would see us build our future as free men. Every time I looked up into the night sky, a sky full to the brim with stars winking at me with the promise of the future a man needs; I had hope that life would get better.

'I did well for myself. I kept my head down, worked hard and just over a year after getting to Norfolk Island, I had twenty-five rods, [1] cleared on a Sydney Town lot.' [2]

Blay asked, 'Did you live alone in those early days, Mr Cullen?'

'I lived with a lass called Anne Coombes. She was on the First Fleet too and sent to Norfolk Island same time as me. Lt Governor Ross wanted convicts to marry and work together, so we could support ourselves. I liked Anne but didn't want to marry her.

'We built the house together. She looked after the house garden and the house we lived in and I did the farming. But she left me after a couple of years, went off and married someone else. She wanted to get hitched, but I didn't see the point. I was no spring chicken then and neither was she. I was happy just living under the same roof. So, I was on my own for a couple of years.'

Mr Cullen's story astonished Tedder. While he was still a convict, he farmed his own land, kept his own animals, built his own house, and lived with a woman of his choosing. This certainly wasn't the hell hole of a prison Tedder had been expecting.

'So, after your seven years' sentence was finished, what happened then, Mr Cullen?'

'Didn't make any difference to my life on Norfolk Island, Tedder. I had a Ticket of Leave, with land grants, so I was free except I couldn't go back to England. Didn't want to do that anyway. When my sentence finished I got a Certificate of Freedom, and that was that. My life kept going the same way. Only change was that because I was free, the government could hand over convicts to me to keep track of and to get working. The first one they gave me was Elizabeth. Poor little mite was pregnant when she arrived. I was supposed to get her to work looking after the place so she could earn her keep. Young Irish girl, only 21 when she got here. She worked hard, had worked in some lord's house in Dublin and charged with knicking some jewellery from him so got transported for seven years. She said she was framed.

Anyway, the baby, a boy, died not long after he was born. She took it pretty hard but got on with her lot. We started living together as a married couple after about a year. She'll tell you her story when she's ready.'

Tedder found it more and more difficult to come to terms with the story Mr Cullen was telling him. These people were convicts, like him, but they lived normal farming lives. 'Sounds as if their lives were better than they had in England and Ireland.' His heart filled with hope, the hope that comes from the realisation that the terror you thought was coming to swallow you up, got side-tracked and went to find someone else.

# 23

# TRANSPORTED AGAIN

*By 1803, the Secretary of State, <u>Lord Hobart</u>, called for the removal of part of the Norfolk Island military establishment, settlers and convicts to <u>Van Diemen's Land</u>, due to its great expense and the difficulties of communication between Norfolk Island and Sydney. This was achieved more slowly than anticipated, due to reluctance of settlers to uproot themselves from the land they had struggled to tame, and compensation claims for loss of stock.*

*https://en.wikipedia.org/wiki/History_of_Norfolk_Island*

Tedder asked, 'If you were so happy and content and built a good life on Norfolk Island, Mr Cullen, why did you come to live in this place you call New Norfolk?'

Cullen ran his gnarled hand through his grey, thinning hair. Tedder wondered how old he was.

'Ah, Tedder. What a good question. As free as many of us were, we were still subjects of the Crown, and the Crown, in its wisdom, said Norfolk Island was costing too much to operate and decided to shut it down. Some of the settlers wrote to Governor Bligh – we wanted to stay on Norfolk Island and support ourselves – many of us, especially me, were too old to start again. We had a good life and didn't want to leave it. Didn't matter. We got our marching orders.'

Cullen stopped speaking, staring up the River Derwent as if he were trying to find the happiness he had cherished on Norfolk Island.

'You know what, Tedder, Blay? Before we had to start getting ready to leave our island home, I had 16 acres in grain, 36 as pasture. I had one male and six female sheep, one male and nine female goats, twenty-eight male and twenty female hogs, and I had 150 bushels of maize in hand.[1] Does that sound like success to you?'

Neither Blay nor Tedder knew if Mr Cullen expected an answer, so they both nodded that he did sound successful, wanting the older man to keep telling his story.

'Heartbreaking thing is that they burnt everything we left behind, just in case the French took a fancy to it. All that work.'

Tedder saw tears form in Cullen's eyes.

'Sounds to me like you were a very successful farmer and landholder, Mr Cullen. In England, you would have been remarkably high and mighty with that much land and stock.'

'Hmm, that I would, Tedder. Got paid for the land and stock they took from me on Norfolk and got 65 acres here in New Norfolk. But, I had to start all over again. A man my age, I was 65 when I had to begin another farm here in Van Diemen's Land. But, there are a lot of things I have made room for in my life, and regret isn't one of them.'

·  ·  ·

Tedder noticed a melancholy change in Cullen's bearing, he seemed to shrink a little and his eyes became dull and heavy. He didn't know how Cullen's eyes were "heavy" but that was the only word he could find that described Cullen's look.

'Only good thing about the move to New Norfolk,' continued Cullen, 'was that we weren't alone. All our friends from Norfolk Island came here too, and we made sure we set up our farms next to each other, like on the island. Government gave us more land than we had on Norfolk Island, but we had to find it, clear it, and build our houses on it. What Blay sees on our farm now took more than two years to establish. This coming spring, Robert and I are going to start construction of a grand mansion that Elizabeth will be the mistress of.'

He smiled to himself.

## 24

# SYDNEY

*At length on 10 January 1814, His Majesty's colonial armed Brig
Kangaroo commanded by Lieutenant Charles Jeffreys of the
Royal Navy arrived at Sydney after a passage of seven months
and eight days from England.*
*Macquarie required Jeffreys to explain the delays on the voyage.
Jeffreys' account stated that he was at Madeira from 21 June to 3
July 1813 in consequence of H.M.S. Inconstant, under whose
orders he was, having gone there.*
*Then he was at Rio de Janeiro from 20 August to 20 September
for refreshments and to get the brig caulked in every part of her
upper works, they having proved leaky in consequence of her
having been built of green wood. After 45 days' passage from Rio
to the Cape of Good Hope on account of heavy weather, he was at
the latter place from 3 to 13 November replenishing water and
getting refreshments which the women passengers stood in great
need of, and to refit the rigging which had suffered damage in the
foul weather. He also reported only two deaths on the voyage,*
*both* children not 18 months old.'

From https://espace.library.uq.edu.au/

**12 January 1814**

Like the other passengers, Sarah Blay and her three sons packed their belongings in readiness to leave the *HM Brig Kangaroo* and walk once more on a surface that didn't move. The *Kangaroo* had berthed two days earlier, but the steerage passengers were the last to leave.

The First Mate appeared on the steps that lead to the upper deck. 'Some of you are going to Hobart Town in Van Diemen's Land,' he announced 'don't bother packing up your stuff if that's you. We will sail for Van Diemen's Land on the morrow.'

'Can we leave the ship at all, Mama?' asked John.

'I hope so,' said Sarah 'It's suffocating down here.' I'll have to go up and see.'

Leaving the boys in steerage with Mary Fogarty and little Thomas, and Elizabeth Richardson, Sarah lifted her skirts and hurried up the steps to catch the First Mate.

'Are you alright, Missus?' asked a familiar voice.

'Thomas, thank goodness. The First Mate told us the ship is going to Hobart Town tomorrow. We have to get out of steerage to get some air, it's hotter than hell down there.'

Taking a step back at the lady's brazen response, Thomas told her the passengers could go to the upper deck, but not ashore. 'It's a very quick turnaround, Missus, and the Captain isn't goin' to wait for anyone runnin' late in Sydney.'

Sarah bit her lower lip and folded her arms across her chest. 'Very well, Thomas, thank you.' She went down the stairs to collect the boys. 'At least we'll get some air and to see the sky.'

'Why is it so hot?' wailed John.

'I don't know. The seasons are upside down because we

are on the other side of the world, it is summer here. But why it is so hot, I don't know.' Sarah took a handkerchief from her purse and waved it over her face to create a breeze. 'Let's find somewhere out of the sun to sit,' she encouraged the boys.

Physically and emotionally exhausted, Sarah found the long travelling time had worn her patience. 'It's seven months since we left England. It didn't take James that long to get to Van Diemen's Land. I need to find my feet and get the boys settled.' Sarah's inner demons challenged her decision to uproot the boys and take them to an unknown country and future. Her head dropped onto her chest and her eyes closed. John drew in close and put his head on Sarah's shoulder. William lay on the deck under the rig, hands under his head, staring at the cloudless, bright blue sky. James Jr moved away from his mother and brothers. Leaning over the edge of the ship, positioned between two of the *HM Brig Kangaroo's* guns, he watched with indifference at the people moving about on the dirt roads of Sydney.

## 25
___

# EXPANSION

James Tedder rose before his house guests, eager to see them properly fed and prepared for their return journey to New Norfolk. Putting on his boots and coat, carrying the bucket to fetch water from the town water barrels, Tedder crept through the little hut.

'No need for stealth, Tedder,' said Cullen. 'I'm awake and I'm sure Blay is or will be soon.' He chuckled.

'Just fetching some water for the oatmeal and tea.' Tedder closed the door, stepping out into the crisp autumn morning. The rising sun filled the horizon with broken rays of orange and red; the promise of a good day. Tedder waited in line at the barrels. Convicts started work at seven in the morning, most were queued early for the water necessary to prepare breakfast.

Mr Cullen and Blay were washing their faces at the edge of the Derwent estuary when Tedder put the kettle on the fire to boil. He straightened the beds and put his mugs, plates, and spoons on the table, ready to share his rations with his old friend Blay, and his new friend, Mr Cullen.

'Good of you to put us up, Tedder,' said Mr Cullen as they stepped inside, 'and to share your rations with us.'

As much as he enjoyed his privacy, Tedder was pleased to have the company. He missed James Blay's encouragement and support. 'I'll just have to be more careful with my rations over the next week,' he said quietly while stirring the oatmeal.

Breakfast was disturbed by a banging on Tedder's door. The visitor didn't wait to be invited, he opened the door and stepped into Tedder's hut. The abrupt intrusion reminded Tedder of his station in life; he was a convict at the behest of others.

'Lieutenant Governor Major Geils wants to see Mr Cullen,' announced the marine behind the banging.

'What, now?' Cullen demanded.

'I'm sorry, Mr Cullen. I'll wait outside while you finish eating and accompany you to the Lieutenant Governor's quarters.'

'Mr Cullen, good to see you again, sir. I trust you are keeping well, and that things are sorted in New Norfolk. Please, sit down.'

Eager to get the conversation started, Cullen sat on the offered chair, with Geils' desk between them. 'Yes, indeed on all accounts, Major Geils. How can I be of service, today?'

'We are establishing a Government Store at New Norfolk. The population is growing and until a road is constructed, settlers are required, as you know, to travel the Derwent to collect supplies. We'll build a new store and send larger boats up the river with supplies for the Store and collect the meat and maize and wheat the settlers sell to the Government. It will be a more efficient process. Do you agree?'

'Yes, Major Geils, it sounds like a grand plan.'

'Good, you will oversee the Store. You'll need to start organising its construction as soon as possible. I'd like it ready before winter sets in.'[1]

As a convict, Cullen obeyed orders without question. On the one occasion, he did question, he was whipped. But he hadn't been a convict for a long time, and now didn't like being told what to do.

'Thank you for your consideration, Major Geils, but I will not have the time to oversee the Government stores and work on my farm. So, I will decline your offer.'

'Yes, it is an extra load, Mr Cullen. But you will be provided with experienced, trustworthy convicts to assist with the running of the establishment. And you will be paid a stipend.'

Cullen quickly weighed up the advantages of having a Government Store in New Norfolk, and of being able to run it efficiently with the alternative of not having one at all, or having a fool with no idea, running it. 'Do you know the convicts who will be assisting?' he asked Major Geils.

'The first one we'll send to you is young Tedder. I believe you stayed in his hut last night. If you agree with my proposal, Tedder will be sent to you in two weeks to begin work. Mr Williamson, who oversees the Hobart Town stores, wants Tedder to teach the job to his replacement.'

Standing, ready to leave, Cullen put forward his hand 'You have an arrangement, Major Geils.'

'Good. Thank you, Mr Cullen. Please send Tedder when you get back to his hut.'


James Blay smiled most of the way back to New Norfolk. He took pleasure in the breeze lifting off the surface of the Derwent and even enjoyed the silence Mr Cullen made him endure. Tedder was going to New Norfolk. A friendship rekindled. The good news about Tedder being assigned to work in the stores at New Norfolk overshadowed the sadness that swept over Blay when again there was no word from Sarah. Ships had sailed from England in the long almost two years since he'd arrived in Van Diemen's Land, and docked in Hobart Town, all without word from his wife. He fretted that she had remarried, that his boys would be calling someone else their Papa.

# 26

# ENDLESS DELAYS

Sarah sat in the rented room in Sydney where she and the boys had been compelled to stay until a ship was ready to sail to Hobart Town. It pained them all to look at the *HM Brig Kangaroo* at dock each day with no word of if, or when, she would sail. They'd been removed from the brig the morning they thought they were leaving. Governor Macquarie gave no explanation.

Looking at herself in the small mirror nailed to the wall above the wash basin brought tears. 'I look so old. James will not recognise me,' she said to the mirror. The seven-month journey to New South Wales, and now the six months waiting in Sydney had worn her out. Managing James Jr's behaviour and ensuring William didn't copy his older brother used up her reserves of energy. She was also running out of money.

'James, William,' Sarah called from the open window into the street, 'come up to the room for your lessons, please.'

Sarah gave the boys lessons during the day. It kept them all occupied. She hoped her husband would be pleased that the children's education continued. It was something he had always been concerned about. John sat between his older brothers at the little table and watched them running their fingers across words on the page. He listened while they read the words aloud to their mother. When they picked up quills and copied letters onto paper, John mimicked the process.

Engrossed in their work, a bang at the door caused John to scream and Sarah and the older boys to jump.

'Sorry to scare you Missus,' the reassuring voice of Thomas penetrated the sound of John's screams.

'Thomas, it is good to see you. What is happening?'

'*Kangaroo* sails on Sunday, [1] Missus. Eight in the forenoon.'

'Thank you, Thomas. Will we board Saturday?'

'Yes. I'll get one of the sailors to come up in the afternoon to help you with the trunk. Good day to you, Missus.'

Sarah's sigh was more audible to the boys than she planned. 'Close your books, boys. You can go out and play in Sydney for the last time. We'll pack in the morning. James, William, don't take your eyes off John.'


While the children played outside, Sarah unpicked a small section of the hem of the travelling dress she kept in the trunk. She managed her money wisely and hadn't used the secret supply. It had been difficult to budget for the nearly six months they'd been in Sydney. 'When we get to Hobart Town, it will be nearly one-year and a half since we left London.' She put one crown she'd withdrawn from the hem into her purse and hid it under her bonnet on the bed. Four pounds remained securely fastened in the hem of her dress.

Packing didn't take long, Sarah had kept most of their

things in the trunk, each day looking hopefully out at the *HM Brig Kangaroo*, wondering if that day would see them board and sail to Hobart Town. She hadn't answered James' letter. There was no point, it wouldn't have reached him before she arrived. Getting it out periodically to re-read the story of how life was better than he expected, gave her strength.

As promised, Thomas provided someone to help Sarah and the boys with their trunk. There weren't as many free settlers on board the ship for this voyage, so steerage wasn't cramped, but she did carry convicts. Sarah had reservations about travelling on a transport vessel, and the irony didn't escape her. She told herself that her James wasn't really a convict, he made a silly mistake.

James Jr was animated about the *HM Brig Kangaroo's* passengers who were not on board by choice. 'Mama, we are going to be sailing the way Papa did. I'll have to talk to some of the convicts to see if they know anything about Van Diemen's Land.'

'No, James, you won't. We are not allowed to talk to the convicts or mix with them. You'll stay with me and your brothers.'

James Jr glared so spitefully at Sarah that he momentarily intimidated her. 'Help your brothers unpack the trunk.'

The closer the *Kangaroo* got to Hobart Town, the sullener James Jr became. Sarah asked the boys if they were looking forward to finally completing their journey and seeing their father.

'I don't remember what Papa looks like,' said now five-year-old, John.'

'Don't be so stupid,' remonstrated James 'how could you forget what he looks like? I won't forget that he left us, and that's why we've been on this shit of a ship for so long.'

For the second time since they left their home in Spital-fields, Sarah slapped James Jr's cheek. He didn't react. He didn't move, yell, or put his hand to his face. Instead, he put on his malicious glare and directed it at Sarah.

# 27

# ANOTHER NEW JOB

James Tedder said goodbye to Mr Williamson, thanked him again for saving his life, and for treating him like a person, and not the property of the New South Wales Government.

'It's all right, Tedder. You've done a good job. Your efficiency will be missed.'

Walking slowly to his hut Tedder noticed the changes to Hobart Town. Roads were being constructed, buildings looked more permanent and there were more settlers arriving with each ship. He stoked the fire, made supper, and opened the book Mr Williamson had given him as a departure gift – "Sense and Sensibility", by someone called Jane Austen. Tedder had never heard of her, but it had been so long since he had something other than stock lists to read, he was grateful for anything. Mr Williamson told him that he ordered supplies from London, including books, fabric for his wife to make their clothes and furnishings, and newspapers and household items.

Enjoying the experience of reading for pleasure, Tedder stayed up until the fire was almost out. He re-stoked it, put the book in his travelling bag, and settled into his cot for the last time.

'Tedder, James Tedder. Answer the fucking door.' Tedder thought he was dreaming and turned over to dismiss the noise.

'I'll break it down if you don't answer it, and you'll pay for repairs.'

'Shit, I'm not dreaming.' Tedder jumped out of bed and opened the door to a marine whose face was as red as his uniform.

'Must be wonderful to have the luxury of sleeping and not working, Tedder. You are still a convict, are you not? You were the last time I checked.'

'Yes, sir. I'm sorry.'

'Get your stuff, you've got five minutes. A boat is heading up the Derwent to New Norfolk and you will be on it.'

'Yes, sir, right away.'

'In that five minutes, you have to make time to see a Mrs Blay. She's staying at the inn, arrived on the *HM Brig Kangaroo* yesterday. Apparently, her husband is a friend of yours?'

'Mrs Blay? Mrs James Blay?' asked Tedder

'I don't know all her personal details, Tedder. Get moving. Time's wasting.'

This wasn't the departure Tedder had planned. He had no time for breakfast, to tidy up the hut or to wash. He threw his meagre belongings in a bag, put on his boots and cap, and took one last look at the small room that had been home for two years.

Sarah was waiting for him outside the inn. He hardly recognised her, she had aged and looked very drawn and tired. 'Mrs Blay. I am delighted to see you. What a surprise this is. Your husband will be thrilled. He told me only two weeks ago, that he thought you had remarried and given up on him.'

'Hello, James,' Sarah said. 'You look so well, so "normal". We left London in May last year. Two weeks after I received my James' letter. I had already planned to follow him, but his letter convinced me it was what we should do. We have been sailing the seas or waiting on land all this time.'

Tedder thought she was going to cry. 'What a trial, Mrs Blay. Are the boys alright?'

'Yes, thank you, they are well. I believe you are going to the Cullen Farm today?'

'I am, I start a new position working in the stores there. Mr Cullen, Blay's master is also going to be overseeing my work. He is a good man. Blay and I are both fortunate with the assignments we were allotted.'

Sarah's voice dropped, and Tedder noticed a hint of despair. 'Would you please give this letter to my husband? I want to let him know we are here. Do you think this Mr Cullen will allow him to see us? I don't know what to do next. We must find somewhere permanent to live. James' letter said he was on the Cullen Farm, but I didn't know it was nearly a day's journey from Hobart Town.' Sarah wrung her hands and pulled at the ribbon which held her bonnet in place.

'Mr Cullen is a fair man, Mrs Blay. I'm sure he will let your husband see you.'

Tedder touched his cap and wished Sarah a good day. He tucked the letter into his pocket, and with renewed vigour, hurried to the estuary to sail to New Norfolk.

. . .

James Blay sat on the ground under one of the large trees that seemed to hug the Cullen farmhouse. His hands shook as he unfolded the scrap of paper his wife had given Tedder.

"*My dear James.*

*I worry that you have spent many months thinking I had forsaken you for another, when in truth, the boys and I left London in May 1813 on the Kangaroo – two weeks after I received your letter. The journey from London to Sydney took seven months and eight days. We arrived in Sydney on 14 January this year [1814] and lived in a rented room, waiting for a ship to sail to Hobart Town. The Kangaroo was the first ship available; she left Sydney on 21 August last. It has been a long, tiresome voyage, James. Seeing you will have made the effort worthwhile.*

*I pray you are well.*

*Your wife, Sarah*"

No longer able to control his emotions, Blay let the tears roll down his face and his sobs, heard from the house, brought Mrs Cullen outside. She looked quizzically at her husband.

Cullen explained the situation to Elizabeth, 'Blay here has a note from his wife. She is in Hobart Town. Travelled more than a year to get here. He is crying with happiness, aren't you Blay?'

Blay managed to nod in agreement.

'And who might this be?' Elizabeth Cullen queried, looking at James Tedder.

'This is Tedder. He is going to work in the Government Stores here in New Norfolk. He's starting tomorrow. His name is James too – far too many James. So, we'll be calling him Tedder.'

'But there is no store yet, Mr Cullen,' observed Elizabeth

'The boat brought up some supplies, which included Tedder, here. He'll catalogue the haul and we'll store it in a large tent while the storehouse is built.'

Elizabeth moved her head in the direction of Blay. Indicating to her husband that something would need to be done with him.

'Blay will go to Hobart Town day after tomorrow, Elizabeth. He can collect some personal items for you from the store.'

James Blay's sobs grew more intense. 'I will be able to see my wife and sons?'

'Yes, Blay. We will speak more about it when you have recovered yourself. In the meantime, please show Tedder to his quarters.'

Tedder helped Blay to his feet, and with his arm around the shoulders of his friend, walked with him to the stable where Blay had his sleeping quarters.

With the sobs receding, Blay managed to ask Tedder how Sarah looked.

'Very tired, I must admit. She has been travelling for a year, managing trials and tribulations and three boys. You said in Woolwich that she was a strong woman. I think you underestimated her strength.'

'Did you see the boys?'

'No there was no time. I foolishly overslept and had but five minutes to pack, see your wife and get on the boat. She did not have them with her when we met. I imagine they were in her accommodation. Perhaps still sleeping.'

'I can't believe she is here. I thought she had given me up for dead.'

'It seems your letter swayed her, Blay. Perhaps she

thought there was opportunity to be had, better than in London.'

'Perhaps. It is of no consequence though, is it? Sarah and the boys are here.'

'That makes things more awkward, James. Now that Blay's wife and three sons are here, and he is assigned to us,' Elizabeth commented while she helped Cook prepare dinner.

'At least Tedder will be occupied. He seems capable enough,' said Cullen.

'What are you considering, James?'

'Blay will continue to work for us for now. Mrs Blay and her children can stay in the sandstone cottage until she gets settled elsewhere. She will apply to have Blay assigned to her as is the Governor's preferred arrangement. We will then get another convict assignee to help Robert and I build the new house.'

'I'll get the girls. Sit down, James. We will consider the options later. Cook, please fetch Blay and Tedder for dinner.'

Tedder could smell the food long before he was near the kitchen door. 'I am quite hungry, Blay. I haven't eaten today. Didn't allow time for breakfast.'

'The Cullens have an amazing cook. She's an assigned convict too. Supply of food has improved greatly since we arrived, Tedder, and Cook doesn't waste anything. She is from Dublin, as was Mrs Cullen.'

The two convicts left their boots at the door and Tedder hung his coat on the hooks near the entrance to the kitchen. He stopped and took a quick breath as he stepped into the warm room. There were three girls sitting on one side of the table, Mr Cullen at one end and Mrs

Cullen, the other. There were two places set opposite the girls. Tedder followed Blay's lead and sat at one of the places.

'Thank you, Mr and Mrs Cullen. This is most welcome and most unexpected.'

'Hmmph,' said Cullen. 'We are multiplying. You will earn your keep, Tedder, don't worry about that. First thing tomorrow, you can put up the big tent they provided to use as the Store.'

'Who is the new one?' asked the girl sitting in the middle.

'This is James Tedder, Catherine,' answered Mrs Cullen. 'He will be working with Papa helping to build and run a store here in New Norfolk.'

'Why is everyone called James?' the youngest, Betsy wanted to know.

'Seems it's a popular name, Betsy,' answered Cullen.

'Like my name is the same as Mama's?'

'Yes. Families use the same names to show respect.'

James Bryan Cullen introduced his daughters to Tedder. 'This is Sophia, the eldest, next is Catherine and the youngest is Elizabeth, but she is called Betsy so not to confuse her with my wife.'

'I'm very pleased to meet you all,' said Tedder, acknowledging each girl with a nod in her direction. 'How old are you all?'

'I'm 14, Sophia is 15 and Betsy is 9,' answered Catherine.

'Thank you, Miss Catherine.'

Although she wasn't the eldest, Catherine had an air of authority that Tedder found endearing. She reminded him of his sister, Esther.

'Why does Blay look so sad? Why are you sad, Blay?' asked Sophia.

'It is none of your worry, Sophia,' remonstrated Elizabeth Cullen.

Blay was touched by the girl's concern. He had been eating with the Cullens for two years and they had become a substitute family for him. 'My wife and sons are in Hobart Town, Miss Sophia. Your Papa says I can see them the day after tomorrow. I am sad because it has taken my poor wife more than one year to get here. Tedder says she looks tired.'

'Oh, but that is good news. Blay. You should not be sad. Think how happy you will be to see your wife and sons. Are they coming here? Will we meet them?'

'Those are things that still need to be sorted, Sophia,' her father interrupted 'eat your supper and stop bothering Blay and Tedder.'

## 28

# REUNITED

James Cullen stood in the kitchen watching Cook get organised for the day. She was a small woman, short and tiny built. Her hands moved deftly, and she hummed while she worked. He realised he didn't even know her name, to him and the children, she was always "Cook". Elizabeth handled the convict domestics, she made sure they were fed and clothed and put in a good day's work. "Cook" didn't need handling.

'I've got some fresh eggs and bread ready for you, sir,' she said, without turning around.

'Thank you, Cook.'

James Cullen sat down to eat, mulling over the upheaval the new arrivals would undoubtedly bring. James Blay was a good enough worker, but Cullen thought a family being nearby might distract him. 'We will see. After all, he is still a convict.'

Robert Bishop knocked on the kitchen door, took off his boots, didn't wait for a response, and let himself in.

'Good morning, James. Smells good, Cook. Is there enough for me?'

James thought he saw a coy smile from Cook as she looked at Robert.

'Of course, Mr Bishop, there is always enough to share with you. Sit down.'

'Thank you for taking Blay into Hobart Town, Robert,' said Cullen. It was an awkward position to be in, me not having the time to go myself.'

'I just hope he holds it together when he sees his family, James. What is his wife going to do?'

'Elizabeth and I have decided she can stay here until she gets herself set up. Elizabeth will offer her work as a domestic. No doubt Blay will be assigned to her when she has a land grant. Until then, he'll continue to work for us.' Cullen mopped up the yolk from his eggs with a piece of bread and followed it with a gulp of sweet, hot, tea.

Blay knocked on the kitchen door and waited for an invitation to enter. He and Tedder acknowledged everyone in the room and sat down to breakfast. Cullen noticed how agitated Blay was. His hands shook, and he had random cuts on his face from shaving carelessly. His hair was trimmed but it wasn't straight. His jacket was brushed clean.

'You look dapper this morning, Blay,' Cullen commented.

'Thank you, sir, I want to look respectable for Sarah. I want to look like a husband, not a convict. And I want to look like a father. No offence, sir.'

'None taken. Your hands will need to stop shaking before you get to Hobart Town, though. She'll think you're sick.'

Blay put his hands on his lap and clasped them together. He took deep breaths, closed his eyes and willed his hands to be still.

'Get on with your breakfast, Blay. We have to be on the

river and get going,' Robert Bishop instructed, 'or we won't do the round trip in daylight.'

Sarah read the letter from her husband again, making sure she had the day and time correct. The boys slept, she would leave them to wake on their own, this was going to be a busy day. James would arrive around ten in the morning. His letter said he would be leaving New Norfolk at seven, as soon as the sun rose. She was relieved to read that the Cullens had agreed to let her and the boys stay at their farm until she was settled, but mindful that this imposition was very generous and wondered if there would be a price to pay later.

Sarah took her best travelling dress out of the trunk, the one whose hem she and her mother had sewn the money into; she wanted to look her best for her husband and the Cullen family. Before putting it on, she went outside to collect fresh water from the barrels. She used the water to fill up the bowl on the sideboard in the room. James was awake, but still lying in bed. 'Turn away, James, I want to wash before you all get up.' She waited while he turned his back to her. She quickly washed her face and upper body, put on her petticoat, and reached across for her dress. 'I've finished, James.' She didn't wait for a response or an action but sat down in front of the small mirror to brush her hair.

'You look nice, Mama,' John's small voice broke the morning silence. She smiled at the boy, his little face looked older in the diffused light of the room.

'We have all aged one year since we left London. I wonder if I have changed that much.'

With the boys dressed for the day, Sarah thought about breakfast. She had used all the money she kept under her bonnet and in her personal bag for the extra cost of living in Sydney for six months. She hadn't budgeted for such an expense when she announced to her mother that she had enough saved to leave for Van Diemen's Land. 'I'll have to get a crown out of my hem for breakfast.'

While the boys were washing, and brushing their hair, Sarah sat on the edge of the bed and picked up the hem of her dress. She turned it over and moved her fingers along to feel the raised stitching that indicated her secret hiding place, eyes watching the children. The tips of her fingers felt broken threads, her pulse quickened, she blinked continuously, her palms becoming hot and clammy. Forcing herself to look, Sarah saw that the stitches had been cut and the hem pushed up. She was confronted with an empty space where four pounds had been hidden safely for more than a year.

## 29

## A FAMILY REUNION

Blay shivered most of the way from New Norfolk to Hobart Town. He wasn't particularly cold, but the goose bumps on his flesh and the constant movement of his arms and legs gave the appearance of impending disaster. Robert Bishop ignored him.

Bishop ordered Blay to tie up the wherry securely. 'You will be here, ready to return to New Norfolk in one hour. That is enough time for your wife to report to Lieutenant Governor Colonel Davey and inform him of her proposed living situations.'

'Thank you, Mr Bishop, we will be here.' James Blay nodded respectfully to Robert Bishop, put his hands in his pockets to try to stop them shaking, and made his way to the makeshift accommodation house he knew Sarah to be in.

She had been staring out the window since nine in the morning, so she wouldn't miss him. She swallowed hard, straightened her bonnet, lifted her skirt a little, and ran on the muddy streets of Hobart Town into the arms of her husband. James and Sarah Blay spent the first few minutes holding each other, she was crying loudly, he quietly.

'Papa, Papa,' William ran to Blay.

John stood back a little not quite sure if this man, seemingly taller than when he left England, certainly with a different tinge to his skin, was really his father.

Blay got down on his knees and put out his arms towards the two sons who had run to meet him. John and William buried themselves in the embrace. Sarah scanned the area for James Jr.

'Where is James Jr?' asked Blay.

'He was with us in the room,' Sarah replied. 'William, go and see if James is still there, please.' William skipped off, jumping in the puddles he found along the way.

'He's not there, Mama. His bag and coat and hat are gone.'

Blay turned to his wife, 'What is going on? Where is he? We have a deadline. Mr Bishop said we have an hour, and you have to report your intentions to Colonel Davey.'

Sarah had been managing on her own for three years, the last year travelling from one side of the world to the other. She collapsed into the arms of her husband and sobbed. Between sobs, Blay learned that James Jr had been difficult to manage. Sarah didn't tell her husband about Rio de Janeiro, that would take too long, and she didn't have the energy or the will.

'Wipe your eyes, Sarah. Straighten your bonnet and go to see Colonel Davey. Tell him you are staying with the Cullens at New Norfolk. Take William and John with you, he might be predisposed to work more quickly with two fidgeting boys in his vicinity. I'll look for James Jr.'

· · ·

Blay started in the room where his wife and sons had spent the last three nights. William was right, there was no sign of James or his bag. Blay walked slowly through the door into the street, noticing footprints in the mud. The unmistakable mark of Sarah's boots, followed by two sets of smaller boots, going in the same direction. A larger, but not adult size of boot prints made their way through the mud towards the *HM Brig Kangaroo* docked in the Derwent estuary.

'Permission to come aboard,' Blay said to the sailor at the end of the gangplank. The sailor put his arm out to stop Blay's progress and wanted to know his reason for boarding the ship.

'I have reason to believe my son has come on board.'

'There's only been one boy come on board,' said the sailor, 'and he's the son of the cook.'

'Have you seen this boy before today?' asked Blay. 'Are you sure he's the son of the cook? Because my son is devious and would have lied convincingly. He has been on this ship before and knows it well, he might be planning to stow away.'

'You get over there, off this gangplank. I'm pulling it up. I'll speak to the cook.' The sailor hauled up the gangplank and left Blay waiting on the dock.

'Mr Bishop,' Blay called out when he saw his travelling companion walking towards the wherry which was tied up further down the dock. Bishop turned and waved. Blay signalled with his arm that Bishop should come to him. Blay started walking in Bishop's direction, repeatedly looking over his shoulder at the ship. The two met between the large vessel and the small boat.

'Why are you summoning me, Blay? I gave you an hour and it is almost time.'

'My wife is with Colonel Davey, Mr Bishop sir, with two

of the boys. The other boy is missing. I have it in my mind that he is attempting to stow away on the *Kangaroo*. A sailor is looking for him.'

'This isn't good, Blay. The boy is trouble and we haven't even made it back to New Norfolk. If he isn't found when the ship's bell is rung for half through the hour next, you and I will return to New Norfolk and Mrs Blay will stay here looking for her son. Need I remind you of your obligation to Mr Cullen?'

Blay shook his head. 'I can only pray, sir that the sailor finds the boy.'

Sarah, William, and John found Blay waiting on the dock. 'I have reported to Colonel Davey. Will we get our things from the room? Where is James?' Sarah asked

'I think he is trying to stow away on the *Kangaroo*, I followed boot prints from the room. A sailor is searching for him. If he isn't found when the ship's bell is rung next, you will have to stay, and I will return to New Norfolk.'

Neither of them said anything else. Anxiety sucked away the air between them.

'Is this your brat?' called the sailor to Blay. He was holding a struggling boy whose arms had been tied behind his back.

Blay moved closer to the edge of the dock. His heart both jumped and sank. 'Yes, sir, that is my boy.'

The sailor pushed James Jr into the arms of another, and the gangplank was lowered. James Jr was dragged down to the dock, his bag thrown after him. As soon as he and his bag were on Victoria Dock, the gangplank was raised. 'Don't wanta see that brat anywhere near this brig again.'

Sarah did not speak to her son.

The happiness turned to anxiety, turned to relief,

exploded from Blay 'What is the meaning of this? What were you doing? Your Mama was terrified.'

'I don't care. I want to go back to England. I hate it here. I hate you, I hate Mama. I'll live with Grandmama and look after her. I'm not staying in this shit hole.'

Blay clipped the back of his son's head. Sarah jumped, John gasped, and William took a step back. From a distance, Mr Bishop watched the drama unfold.

'After all your mother has been through to bring you here,' Blay said.

James Jr roared at his father, 'I said I don't care. I didn't want to come. I want to go home.'

'How would you have managed when they found you on the ship? How would you have paid your way? How would you live if you got back to England?' Blay demanded of his son.

Sarah gulped and put her hand over her mouth. She was suspicious that James Jr had taken the money from the hem of her dress but hadn't pursued the thought. 'I might know the answer to that,' she said to her husband, explaining about the missing money.

Blay turned on his son, 'You are a rotten little thief and a liar. And when we get to New Norfolk you will be whipped for stealing from your Mama and your brothers.'

'You can't whip me,' James Jr hissed. 'You are a liar and a thief who should have been hanged. We are here, in this awful place, because of YOU.'

The truth of his son's allegations shook Blay's confidence. He didn't know what to do. Looking at Sarah for guidance, he saw a mother's face filled with horror, disappointment, and sadness.

Leaving James Jr's hands tied behind his back, Blay told William to pick up his older brother's bag. Indicating that

Sarah, John, and William should follow, he pushed his eldest son along the dock towards the wherry that would take them all to New Norfolk.

'Mr Bishop, this is my eldest son, James Jr. He is not to be untied no matter how much he complains.' He introduced Sarah and the other two boys to Mr Bishop, got them settled in the wherry, and pushed James Jr back along the dock towards the rented room the family had been staying in.

Robert Bishop followed. Blay would need help carrying the trunk and dealing with this brat.


Avoiding eye contact with her eldest son, Sarah sat in the wherry and enjoyed the passing scenery and bird life along the Derwent. John was especially interested in the eels and fish he could see beneath the surface of the water. She had to pull him away from the edge of the boat a few times.

William seemed more enamoured with the animals on the shoreline. He was fascinated with the different creatures. 'What's that in front of that one, Papa?'

'That's her baby, William. They are pademelons, they carry their babies in pouches on their bellies. The babies jump in and out as they want.'

'Are they any of these creatures on the farm, Papa? Will we see more of these? I've never seen anything like it in my life.'

Blay smiled at William, and at Sarah. At least two of the children were happy to see him and to be on the River Derwent, making their way to the Cullen Farm. 'Yes, there are pademelons on the farm.'

. . .

Longing for her husband's embrace, Sarah watched him rowing the boat along the river. His skin was a different colour, it had a glow she hadn't seen on him in London. His hair was longer and lighter. His body more developed than when he was a shoemaker. The muscles in his arms moved through the sleeves of his shirt. She had watched earlier when he removed his jacket, feeling as if she was seeing him for the first time. His back was broader than she remembered. She crossed her legs to soften the ache she felt between them.

Blay didn't turn to look at Sarah while he was rowing, but he knew she was looking at him. 'She has been through so much, especially with James Jr. She's lost weight, seems shorter, if that's possible, and her hair is greying. The spark is missing from her eyes, I'll have to bring it back somehow. Tonight, perhaps, when we are alone?' He pulled his jacket over his lap to hide his anticipated excitement and kept the oars moving.

## 30

# NEW FRIENDS

'You have to untie me sometime,' James Jr spat at his father. Blay ignored him while he helped Sarah, John, and William out of the boat. He and Mr Bishop unloaded the trunk and set it under a tree.

Mr Bishop ordered James Jr out of the boat. The child argued that his brothers were helped, and they didn't have their hands tied behind their back. Mr Bishop took off his cap, wiped his forehead with the back of his hand, returned his cap to its rightful position, and glared at the boy. 'I said, get out of the fucking boat.' Bishop's voice was raised in such anger that John cried.

James Jr struggled to hold his balance, he moved to the side of the boat closest to the small dock, turned around, manoeuvred his backside to sit on the timbers, swung his legs out of the wherry, got to his knees, and then to his feet. His eyes emanated hatred and rage as he looked at each adult in turn. He left most of the hatred for his father.

'I'll let Mr Cullen know we are here,' said Bishop. Looking accusingly at Sarah, he continued, 'Although he's probably heard all the yelling anyway.'

Blay and Roger Gavin, another convict assigned to the Cullens, carried the trunk to the small cottage that Sarah and the boys would use.

'What's with the lad with his hands tied?' Gavin asked Blay.

'My eldest son. Been giving Mrs Blay some grief. Can't be trusted.'

They put the trunk inside, Gavin tipped his cap to Sarah and went on to continue his work.

The boys followed their parents into the cottage. When they were alone, James Jr flew into a rage, demanding to know why his father hadn't defended him in front of Bishop. 'You just stood there and watched while he made me struggle to get out of that boat. You didn't step in and help me, you just watched.'

Blay was in no mind to explain to his eldest that as a convict, he had no right to interfere with Mr Bishop's decisions, even if they involved his own son. 'You have done the wrong thing, James. You have shown no regret, and you have displayed rudeness and insolence to your elders. The ropes will be removed, but you will be confined to this cottage to help your mother get settled. If you disobey, you will be whipped for insolence and disobedience.'

'You can't whip me for taking the money, though, can you? I was right, you are a thief, so you can't punish me for being one too. As soon as I get a chance, I am leaving this shit hole.'


About to knock on the cottage door, Elizabeth Cullen heard the discourse between Blay and a child. Bishop had said the eldest was trouble and Blay had tied the boy's hands. Listening to him speak to his father, she wondered if they had done the sensible thing, offering to have Mrs Blay and her boys on the farm. She retraced her steps back to the main house.

'Thought you were going to the cottage, Missus,' said Cook when Elizabeth stepped back into the kitchen.

'Yes, I'll go in a minute.' She sat at the table worrying about the insolence she heard from the child. 'Blay will step up and punish him, I'm sure. Otherwise, I'll get Bishop to do it.'

Picking up her skirt, Elizabeth again left the kitchen and walked towards the cottage. This time there was low murmuring conversation between Mr and Mrs Blay. She knocked on the door.

Blay bowed slightly to Elizabeth, inviting her in. He introduced Sarah, John, William, and then James. The eldest child's face was still tomato red and he was breathing heavily. He had his arms in front of him and was massaging his wrists.

Elizabeth could see the stress on Blay's face and his wife looked extremely tired and embarrassed. 'But then again, I've never seen her before, she might always look like that.' The youngest boy was quite pretty. His hair was long, fair, and wavy, and his complexion still looked English. The middle boy seemed short for his age, with an air of indifference about him; his hair was shorter, more appropriate for his age, and quite a lot darker. She noticed he had his father's eyes. The eldest had the look of lightning strikes and an aura of thunder. 'I don't think I will let this one near the girls for a while. I don't' think I can trust him not to hurt them.'

Elizabeth welcomed Sarah and the boys to the Cullen Farm, and to New Norfolk.

## 31

#### DUBLIN TO NEW NORFOLK

'I'm very honoured to meet you, Mrs Cullen.' Sarah bent her knee slightly.

'And I you, Mrs Blay. Your husband has worked hard the months he has been with us. My husband, James is very pleased with his efforts.'

'When I said goodbye to him, it was with the fear that he would live and die brutally, in an open-air prison at the ends of the earth.'

'Oh, some do, Mrs Blay. Some do. The incorrigible, the belligerent, the downright lazy, they're the ones who don't do so well. But your husband was fortunate to be assigned to James Bryan Cullen, as I was, many years ago.'

Sarah's eyes widened in disbelief 'You were also a convict, Mrs Cullen?'

'Yes. It was the best thing that could have happened to me. No way, if I'd stayed in Dublin, that I'd be respectfully married to a landowner, with a nice house, and plans to build a great mansion, and with three healthy children.'

Sarah looked around for somewhere to sit. The six children were playing in the garden and the house paddock.

The Cullen girls had taken charge of her boys and were busy showing them the wonders of this new place. 'May I sit?'

'Of course, Mrs Blay. Please, we'll rest over here under the ghost gum.'

Sarah worked out at once why it was called a "ghost gum". 'The bark is almost white, it must shimmer in the moonlight.' She had noticed the tree on arrival, but now, sitting under it was overwhelmed with a feeling of insignificance. 'It is a magnificent tree, Mrs Cullen. I'm amazed at its grandeur.'

'Yes, we built the house near it to get the summer shade. But we've since learned that these types of trees, gum trees, lose their branches from time to time. They drop off when it's been very windy. The new house will be built further away from the reaches of falling tree branches. James doesn't want to chop it down, so we'll work around it. But, I imagine you asking to sit down, is a consequence of me revealing my convict past. You seemed shocked by my disclosure.'

Sarah looked around the property before speaking, taking in the signs of success. 'Mrs Cullen, I thought my husband obtaining a position with you and Mr Cullen was an amazingly good outcome of transportation, but I find myself in awe of people who were sent to the other side of the world so long ago, and who have succeeded.' She pushed an unruly curl off her face.

'Well, New South Wales was primarily a prison, Mrs Blay. However, those of us who were disposed to work hard and finish our sentences, have stayed to build a much better life than we could ever have back home. My life in Dublin was not pleasant. I was charged with stealing a gold watch and a pair of silver buckles from my employer, James

Dogherty[1] (sic). The bastard had his way with me many times. I was a kitchen maid in his grand house, and at his disposal. It was work there and submit, or to the poorhouse. He lined us all up in his parlour and didn't like the way I looked at him, so said I was the one who took his things. Old Franny took them, but I carried the blame. Found guilty and sentenced to seven years.'

Sarah felt deeply sorry for the wife of her husband's boss. 'It must have been horrific for you. How old were you?'

'I was 21 years when sentenced and 22 when I got to New South Wales in 1796. It wasn't so bad. There were lots of us Irish girls on *Marquis Cornwallis* and if we were prepared to give a little something of ourselves if you know what I mean, we got extra rations and a chance to sleep in a cabin.'

Inadvertently catching her breath at Elizabeth Cullen's revelation, Sarah found it difficult to visualise this woman as a poor Irish girl guilty of stealing from her employer and being sentenced to seven years' transportation. Nor did she imagine Mrs Cullen, who Sarah thought was around her own age, would give herself to sailors to gain an advantage. 'Please, Mrs Cullen, do not feel obliged to tell me your history. It is your business only.'

'This is New Norfolk, Mrs Blay. All of us here are from Norfolk Island. All of us know each other's stories, that's what brought us together, and keeps us together. Nothing I say is a secret.'

'After hearing about your past situation, your prosperity is even more astonishing, Mrs Cullen. How was it you were sent to this Norfolk Island you mentioned?'

'Another strange decision, Mrs Blay. I was one of fourteen Irish girls sent on to Norfolk Island from Sydney Cove, with a spinning wheel. They assumed we, being Irish, would know how to use it to spin flax. I didn't protest. I didn't like the look of Sydney Cove. But I had never used a spinning wheel. My mother could barely feed us, least of all have money to buy a piece of luxury like a spinning wheel. But I pretended I knew and was sent on to Norfolk Island.

'I was assigned to James and I looked after the house and garden until the baby was born. Don't look so shocked, Mrs Blay. The sailor who gave me a bed and extra rations on *Marquis Cornwallis* left me with a keepsake that I thought would be with me for some time. I named him William, but he died a few months after birth. That was the hardest part of all the things that happened. I'm sure you understand. James and I had a son together while I was still a convict; we named him Stephen[2]. But like my William, he was not meant for this world, or for Norfolk Island, and he died before his first birthday. James was distraught. We had three daughters after that. I don't think James has recovered from losing his one and only son. A man can't pass on land grants to daughters.'

Sarah reached out and hugged Elizabeth Cullen. She half expected her to pull away, but she submitted to the embrace. 'I am so sad for you and your husband, Mrs Cullen.'

'It was a long time ago, Mrs Blay. As you can see, we have three healthy daughters. If I'd stayed in Dublin, I don't think I would have survived. The master would have caused me to be with child and I would have been sent to the poorhouse where the child and I would probably both have died. Being charged with stealing from him and being transported, even though I've lost two sons, was the best thing I could have done. I live my life with no room for regrets, Mrs Blay. And I hope you and your husband can say the same, in time.'

.   .   .

Even though the boys were in bed, Sarah wasn't sure they were asleep. She ached for her husband's touch and indicated to him with the turn of her head, that they should go outside. She flung her arms around his neck and welcomed his warm lips as they met hers. His manhood sprung up quickly and she felt the moistness between her legs that had not been there for two years.

'Where can we go? She implored.

'We can go to my quarters in the stable, I'll ask Tedder to leave us for a little while.'

It took Tedder a few seconds to realise why Blay wanted the space. He tumbled out of his cot, put on his boots, breeches, and jacket, and hurried to the horse's stall; nodding in Sarah's direction.

She blushed, she wasn't sure if it was embarrassment or the aching need she felt.

As Blay's nakedness was revealed to her she became even more aroused. 'I don't ever remember feeling like this before. Perhaps it's because it's been so long.'

Instead of just lifting up her dress, the way she did in her previous life, she took it off and lay on the cot in her petticoats. Blay's body was firm, muscled and the colour of golden sand. He helped her remove her petticoat, kissing her face, squeezing, and kissing her breasts, rubbing himself on her stomach. She arched her back as his manhood penetrated her for the first time in two years. It hurt a little, but she was determined not to let the moment be spoiled. Her legs went around his back as his thrusting increased, and her arms went around his shoulders – she felt bumps on his skin – lots of bumps on his skin, like stripes. 'I'll ask later.' She wanted to scream with pleasure but bit her lip so no one would hear her. Blay grunted and moaned with each movement of their bodies. A feeling she had never had, in their eleven years of marriage, overtook her, she moaned with delight as her body convulsed a little and the pleasure reached a climax. Blay slumped on top of her, panting and sweating.


Tedder waited in the horse's stall. He knew Blay and Sarah were trying to be quiet, but the sounds of lust, love, and joy aroused feelings in him that were long ago stifled. He pictured Bagram Simeon, on his knees in the coach, unbuttoning Tedder's breeches, fondling his manhood and as soon as it became firm and upright, putting it in his mouth and licking and sucking. He saw the evil old man looking up at him, from his position on the floor of the coach, waiting for James to be satisfied. He felt sick and shivered at the memory of being expected to do the same to Simeon. He had not been with a woman, ever. He hoped that when he found someone, his lovemaking would not be tainted by the memory of Bagram Simeon. He wanted it to be like James and Sarah Blay sounded.

# 32

# NEW NORFOLK, NEW LIFE

The boys were up at sunrise, badgering Sarah about break-fast. She hadn't spoken to her husband or Mrs Cullen about the arrangements for meals assuming she would be expected to provide for her own family. She looked around the cottage, noticing the details she missed yesterday. The two rooms were well proportioned, the bedroom had two double beds, a dresser with a pitcher and bowl and chest of drawers, and a square, knitted woollen rug. 'Some of the boys clothes will have to stay in the trunk.' The kitchen had a large fireplace that dominated most of the wall it sat against. Hanging from the cradle over the fire was a kettle large enough to keep hot water in for most of the day. Placed neatly on the hearth was a large cast iron pot, and a frying pan. A large table sat in the centre of the room with two benches either side. Plenty of room for the five of them. 'Room for us all. Hopefully, James can join us,' she said aloud. There were rocking chairs either side of the fireplace. A sideboard held crockery and cutlery. 'What a lovely little home.'

'What's for breakfast, Mama?' asked John. He looked hopefully at Sarah, waiting for an answer he could be excited about.

'I don't know. I'll have to ask Papa about where the food is.'

'There's food in the cupboards. There's eggs and bread and there's milk over there in that pitcher,' James Jr informed her. 'We looked around last night when you and Papa went to the stable.'

She turned bright red and covered it by reaching over the fire to get the kettle. She sent James outside to fill the kettle with water while she stoked the fire. The other two boys helped with the eggs and bread. 'Where is Papa? Is he coming for breakfast? asked John.

'I don't know, John. He might be working already.'

'But he hasn't had any breakfast. He'll be hungry working without breakfast.' John seemed distressed about his father's meal plans.

'He might have had breakfast in the main house, John,' Sarah explained. 'Especially if he has to start work early.'

With John apparently satisfied with the explanation. Sarah helped James with the kettle. It would take some time to boil and she really wanted a cup of tea. In future she would leave it over the hot coals.

'Are we going to school?' William wanted to know.

Sarah had some organising to do. She would speak to Mrs Cullen about school, about food requirements, and the arrangements her husband had with Mr Cullen for work. She wanted to know how she could eventually obtain her own land to farm and build a house.

There was no sign of Blay during or after their breakfast. Sarah had the boys wash, dress, and pull up the beds.

Catherine Cullen knocked on the door of the cottage, 'Mama said to come to the house, Mrs Blay, so you can talk about what is to be done.' She skipped off not waiting for a reply.

'I'm going to the main house, boys. Unpack your clothes from the trunk, put them in piles on the beds – one pile each – and we'll put them away when I come back. Find your own special things and put them away in the drawers.'

Elizabeth Cullen greeted Sarah, 'Good morning, Mrs Blay. I trust you and the children found the cottage adequate?'

'Thank you, Mrs Cullen. It is lovely. I cannot thank you enough.'

Elizabeth nodded. She asked Cook to make Sarah a cup of tea, as they settled at the kitchen table. The tea was served in mismatched china teacups and saucers, the teapot had a broken lid, but the spout and handle were intact. It matched one of the saucers. Elizabeth noticed Sarah looking at the china 'We don't have access to much here, Mrs Blay. We must make do. The china is from the belongings of one of the free settlers who died early in her years here. She brought them over from England with her, along with all her fine clothes and furniture. Her husband sold it all when she died and he went back to England.'

Sarah was delighted to drink her tea from a china cup, no matter where it came from or how mismatched it was. 'It's delightful, Mrs Cullen. It is tea, in a china cup, I will enjoy it.'

Cook noticed the two women were about the same age, although Mrs Blay's long travels had given her a more seasoned appearance. They seemed to get along and were chatting amicably when that awful child, the eldest one, came to the kitchen door.

'What is it, James?' Sarah asked.

'What are we to do while you are in here talking?'

Elizabeth and Cook stared at Sarah waiting for her to respond to the insolence.

'Mrs Cullen, Cook,' said Sarah. 'Please excuse me.'

Sarah left the kitchen and led James outside, she stood over him, her hands on her hips and feet slightly apart, looking down on him, with the intention to intimidate.

'Don't you dare interrupt me like that. These people have been kind enough to give us somewhere to live. You will show respect,' she hissed. Her hand went up in front of his face just as James was about to respond. 'I don't want you to speak. Go and sit over there under that tree and wait until I am ready to discuss our plans for today and every other day.'

James watched his mother return to the kitchen. He kept going over the injustice of being dragged to the other side of the world against his will, of his father being the cause of them leaving their home, of leaving England, of his plans to leave this place. He hated his mother for bringing him here.

'I apologise for the interruption, Mrs Cullen,' Sarah said, finishing her cup of tea.

'All is well, Mrs Blay?'

'I hope so. He is a concern to me and my husband, he changed when his father was convicted and sentenced to transportation. Now he is always angry, he is cruel to his brothers, disobedient and insolent – the latter you just witnessed.'

Elizabeth patted Sarah's hand in reassurance. They spent the next hour going over the living arrangements for Sarah, the boys, and Blay. Blay would eat breakfast and dinner in the main house with the Cullens, Tedder and Roger Gavin. He would eat supper with his wife and children and stay in the cottage with them each evening. Sarah would be required to open an account at the Government Stores for her supplies, and to settle the account at the end of each month. Elizabeth assured Sarah that Tedder would organise the paperwork for her. Sarah would also be required to offer some assistance in the Cullen household to go towards her and her sons' keep.

'I suggest, Mrs Blay, that you start a vegetable garden, it will give the boys something productive to do as well as provide sustenance. You should perhaps get some chickens and a goat for milk. The boys can also help Cook. And they can assist Roger Gavin, whose main task is maintaining the gardens around the house.'

'May I inquire as to where the school is, Mrs Cullen?'

'We don't have a school building in New Norfolk, Mrs Blay. Some women educate their children at home for part of the day, and some teachers set up classes in their own houses. I have no reading or writing, so am unable to do that with my children. Mr Cullen says girls don't need a formal education. He has our daughters kept busy doing their chores around the farm, both in the gardens and inside learning to sew and cook. Sophia is to be married in January next year when she has reached 16. She is marrying William Rayner Jr. His father was on *Scarborough* in the Second Fleet, and William Jr was born on Norfolk Island same as our girls. You look shocked, Mrs Blay. I did say to you that all of us here in New Norfolk had a shared history.'

'I think I will be shocked for some time about how many of your friends started a new life from a heartbreaking beginning, Mrs Cullen. But even though my husband is a convict still, he and I want the boys to continue their education. James Jr is eleven and will spend another year with schooling. John hasn't started yet, and William had been going to school for two years when we left London. I will have them doing lessons in the mornings after their early chores.'

Sarah asked if Elizabeth would like her to teach the girls too. Mrs Cullen argued that Catherine and Sophia were now past it, but the youngest Betsy could join if Mr Cullen agreed.


Sarah's life took on the semblance of normality in this place, where her husband was a convict and indentured to work for another man. She and the boys established a large vegetable garden at the rear of the house where the sun shone from the north and kissed the new shoots as they peeped up from the fertile soil. The goat provided milk most days, and the six chooks laid enough eggs for weekly requirements. She made the cottage a home and spent each night in the arms of her husband, repeating the passion and joy from their first encounter in New Norfolk.

James Jr seemed to have come to terms with his lot and had reigned in his anger, although on occasion Sarah did see it simmering beneath the surface. She had traded vegetables and eggs for books with some of the other settlers and allocated two hours each morning and one each afternoon, to educate her sons and sometimes, Miss Elizabeth Cullen.

33
___

# TEDDER'S NEW LIFE

James Tedder sat down for dinner with the Cullen family, Blay and Roger Gavin. He looked sheepishly at Catherine Cullen, sitting opposite. She kicked him under the table and laughed aloud as he jumped and spilled peas on the floor. Commenting on how bright red his face became, Catherine scolded him and said he'd have to eat the peas anyway.

'I know, Miss Catherine, thank you.'

'Leave him alone, Catherine,' Elizabeth Cullen chastised. 'He'll be hungry and wanting to eat.'

'Tedder,' said Mr Cullen across the table, 'the stores are quiet today, you'll lock the door after dinner and help with the house construction this afternoon. We have some heavy timbers to lift.'

Blay walked to the cottage he was renting from the Cullens to have supper with his wife and boys. 'Have you had an opportunity to notice how smitten Tedder is with Miss Catherine?' he asked Sarah.

'Yes, I noticed the first day. He is quite taken with her.

She is a forthright young woman, a lot like her mother. Tedder would be thinking marriage don't you think? Especially with Sophia now living with her new husband.'

Supper in the main house finished, Tedder made the usual acknowledgements and walked towards the stable where he and Roger Gavin had their quarters. 'James, James,' came a whisper from the tree line separating the house from the livestock paddocks. His heart quickening to match his footsteps Tedder made his way toward the whisper.

Catherine threw her arms around his neck and tempted him to kiss her. He had been waiting for this moment for months and was now hesitant and wary. 'What if someone finds us?'

Brushing his concerns aside, she said, 'I told mother I was going to see Sophia. Sophia will lie for me if she's asked. She's heavy with child and can't be bothered with my games as she calls them. We will be fine.'

'Have you done this before?'

'No, you will have to show me.'

'I can't show you. I haven't done it before either.'

Catherine giggled. 'Well then, we'll have to show each other, won't we?'

'What will happen if you become with child? Your father will have me flogged.'

She put her finger to his lips to stop him speaking and lifted her face toward him. He caressed her neck and kissed her with a passion he had never before felt. She stirred feelings in him that were demonstrated in the sudden erection of his manhood. Lifting her skirts she pulled him between her legs. She giggled again. He wondered if she was unsure. They lay on the damp ground between the trees, with the irrigation barrier hiding them from the main house. He put his hand up her skirt and caressed her mound, not knowing what to do next. She took his finger and guided it inside her. He groaned, she put her head back and moaned. She was wet and warm; he moved his finger up and down, not wanting to hurt her, but not wanting to stop. Using one hand, she undid his breeches, pulled out his manhood and squeezed it between her fingers. She pulled him towards her, lifting her skirts up around her breasts and revealing what made her a woman. Tedder positioned himself on top of Catherine, and she guided his manhood into her. He thrust up and down, and she moved her body with him. She squealed very quietly and told Tedder he had broken her maidenhead.

'Be gentle now,' she said. 'It is hurting a little, but Sophia told me that is to be expected.'

Tedder lay on his back next to Catherine panting, all energy spent. She smiled at him. 'We'll have to do this again,' she teased.

'Yes, we will, Catherine, but I fear I should ask your father for your hand in marriage. I don't' want to be flogged.'

Helping Catherine up he assisted with straightening her hair and skirts. She gently kissed him on the lips and made her way back to the main house. Watching her leave, he realised that he had not given Simeon a thought. He smiled.

Tedder slept fitfully, he relived the joyous time he had spent with Catherine over and over. His manhood reacted every time he remembered.

'Tedder,' said Mr Cullen over breakfast. 'You will close the Stores at dinner today. I need you to help Blay and Gavin and me with heavy timbers again, for the new house.

Tedder waited for an opportunity to speak to Mr Cullen when Blay and Roger Gavin could not hear. 'Mr Cullen, I would like to speak to you sir, after supper this evening, if I may?'

Cullen pushed his hat back away from his eyes and glared at Tedder. He didn't say anything.

'Thank you, sir,' said Tedder hopefully. 'I won't keep you long.'


Over supper, Catherine smiled at Tedder and rubbed her foot against his leg under the table, instead of kicking him.


'Mr Cullen, I know she is still fifteen, but I ask permission to marry Catherine when she reaches the age of sixteen.'

'Yes, we've been watching the two of you. But, you are a convict, Tedder. It is not only my consent you will seek, but the Lieutenant Governor, Thomas Davey, will have to give permission too. How long until your sentence is completed?'

Tedder fidgeted with the buttons on his jacket. 'I was sentenced in October 1810, sir, but we were told our sentence commenced when we arrived in New South Wales, not when the judge banged his gavel on the bench.'

'So, you arrived in 1812, and it is now 1815. My figuring is that you have four years still to go. I'll have to talk to Elizabeth. She is more responsible for the girls. Goodnight, Tedder.'

Tedder bade Mr Cullen goodnight and turned towards the stables. He would not see Catherine this evening. She whispered to him when she brought water in the afternoon, that she was feeling sore and would rest. He worried he had hurt her, but she reassured him that Sophia said it was quite normal. 'I will see her tomorrow and tell her I have asked her father about our marriage.'

He could feel the tension in the kitchen when he arrived for breakfast.

'Don't sit down Tedder,' Mr Cullen ordered. 'You will close the Stores at dinner today, as yesterday, and help with the construction of the new house. I will send word around New Norfolk that the Stores are open from breakfast until dinner while the weather is still good. When winter sets in our construction will slow, and you will return to the Stores. Come into the parlour for a moment, please, Tedder.'

Straightening his hair, and pulling at his breeches so they sat correctly, Tedder looked worryingly at Blay and followed Mr Cullen into the parlour. Catherine and Mrs Cullen were seated on the chaise. He nodded, acknowledging each woman in turn.

Without offering him a seat, Mr Cullen spoke, 'Catherine says she is interested to marry you, Tedder. However, Mrs Cullen and I insist she waits until she is sixteen. You will be able to marry her in August next year. That is if you get permission from the Lieutenant Governor. That's all, go and open the Stores.'

Tedder hummed all morning. He greeted his customers with a huge grin and went out of his way to accommodate all requests.

## 34

## THE NEW APPRENTICE

**1815**

'He is twelve years old, Sarah. It's time he went to work. In England, he would have been working at least two years already.'

Sarah wanted to scream in her husband's face that they weren't in England anymore and things that applied there, didn't here. But she knew her husband was right, especially about James Jr. In the two years they had lived in New Norfolk he had not settled well. He hadn't caused any trouble since stealing the money, but he was unkind to the Cullen girls and cruel to his brothers, especially John. Mr William McCormack was willing to take him on, so he should go to Hobart Town.

James Jr packed his things in the same bag he had brought from England two years earlier. Hiding beneath the vulnerable child exterior was an angry boy who was looking forward to getting away from his parents and the farm they were living on. He wasn't a farmer and didn't ever want to be. His plans to travel home to England were thwarted when news arrived of his Grandmama's passing. There was no one left there for him. He'd have to wait now until he had saved enough money, had a trade, and could make his own way. Then he would go home.

Sarah Blay hugged her eldest son, 'Mind Mr McCormack's instructions and you will soon have a trade like Papa. We will come to see you and you can visit your brothers and us.'

James Jr wasn't interested in seeing any of them very often, but he knew to play the part. He hugged his mother and said his goodbyes to his brothers. He thanked the Cullens for the accommodation, tipped his hat to Catherine especially, and climbed into the small boat he and his father would take to Hobart Town.

'When will we see James again?' asked John.

'It will be some time, he has to get settled and start learning his trade before he will have time to come and see us.' Sarah was proud of her eldest at this moment, but the pride was tinged with some relief that she would be free of his trying behaviour.

Blay delivered his eldest son to his new master, Mr William McCormack in Hobart Town. He was struck by the easygoing nature of the employer, and although pleased that James Jr was apprenticed to a shoemaker, Blay felt the ache of disappointment that it wasn't him teaching the trade to his son.

'Thank you, Mr McCormack, for taking on my boy. He is fortunate to get an apprenticeship in Van Diemen's Land.'

'Yes, Mr Blay, there are not many opportunities yet, but these will increase as free settlers arrive. I believe you were also a shoemaker in London?'

'Yes, sir, long before I made errors of judgement that had me sent to this place,' Blay explained.

'Your boy will be looked after, Mr Blay. If he follows instructions and minds his manners, we will get along. Say goodbye to your father, young James, he must return to New Norfolk.'

James Jr approached his father with his hand outstretched indicating a handshake was preferable to any displays of emotion.

Blay shook his son's hand and patted him on the head. He wiped his eyes many times on the walk down to the river.

# 35

# PADEMELONS

TASMANIAN PADEMELON, THYLOGALE BILLARDIERI

*The pademelon is a stocky animal with a relatively short tail and legs to aid its movement through dense vegetation. It ranges in colour from dark-brown to grey-brown above and has a red-brown belly. Males, which are considerably larger than females, have a muscular chest and forearms, and reach up to 12 kg in weight and 1 - 1.2 m in overall length, including the tail. Females average 3.9 kg in weight.*
*The unusual common name, pademelon, is of Aboriginal derivation. It is also sometimes referred to as the rufous wallaby.*

*Pademelons are solitary and nocturnal, spending the hours of daylight in thick vegetation. Rainforest and wet forest is the preferred habitat, although wet gullies in dry open eucalypt forest are also used. Such habitat next to cleared areas where feeding can occur is especially favoured. After dusk, the animals move onto such open areas to feed, but rarely stray more than 100 metres from the security of the forest edge.*
*The species is abundant and widespread throughout the state of*

*Tasmania. It is commonly seen around many of the state's national parks.*

www.parks.tas.gov.au

James Blay wept on and off from Hobart Town to New Norfolk. He had no regard for people's opinions of him on this day, four years of frustration finally found a release. The last year hadn't been so bad, with Sarah and the boys with him, but when it came down to it, he was still a convict. And because of that, his sons would not learn his trade from him. 'A stranger is teaching my son my trade.'

Sarah saw him coming and ran down to the water's edge, panting, face streaked with the marks of wiped away tears. 'William is missing.'

'What?'

'Betsy Cullen saw him chasing some pademelons earlier. No one has seen him since.'

'How long ago was that?' asked Blay.

'Just after dinner. It will be dark soon, James, and it is getting cold at night.'

Blay took off his hat and pushed his hair back. Putting his hat back where it belonged, he looked worryingly at Sarah. 'Who is looking for him?'

'Mr Cullen sent Roger and Tedder in the direction Betsy pointed, and Robert Bishop has gone a different way. It will be dark, soon, James.'

'I know, you said that. Show me which way Roger Gavin and Tedder went.'

The Cullen's kitchen held Sarah, Cook, Elizabeth Cullen, Catherine, Betsy, and John in its comforting embrace. John was whimpering. Sarah scolded him, 'Stop crying about it, John. That isn't helping.'

Taking John's hand Cook led him to the fire, 'You can help me prepare supper, John.' The child wiped his eyes, sat on a rocking chair, and picked peas out of pods.

Sarah watched out the kitchen door while the men traipsed back from their search. William was not with them.

'He will be cold tonight,' she said to Blay. 'Can't you keep looking?'

'How do you expect us to do that, Mrs Blay?' Mr Cullen asked. 'We won't be able to see. I'm not risking anyone else going missing. We'll continue at first light. He's a resourceful boy, he should find some shelter under trees and in some undergrowth.'

'Maybe a pademelon will keep him warm,' offered John.


Sarah sat up all night by the fire, worrying about her sons. This was James Jr's first night away from her – apart from the time he disappeared in Rio de Janeiro - and William had never been away.

Blay went to bed, he'd had an emotional day delivering his eldest to the shoemaker in Hobart Town, and then searching for the middle boy. Despite the anxiety, he felt over William's disappearance, he slept for a few hours.


Announcing himself, Robert Bishop knocked on the cottage door at daybreak. Sarah had dozed off at some point, her neck aching from her head lolling around on her chest. Her mouth was dry, and she was sure she looked as dishevelled as she felt.

Bishop opened the door and poked his head into the

warm room. 'Come to get Blay, Missus. We'll get started in a few minutes, it's near on daybreak.'

On hearing Bishop's knock, Blay jumped out of bed, splashed water on his face, and put on his boots and jacket. 'I'm ready, Mr Bishop. Let's be on our way.' He kissed Sarah on the head and closed the door behind him.

There was nothing to be done, Sarah would have to wait for any news. She kept herself busy during the day with the vegetable garden, John, and other chores around the cottage. Mrs Cullen brought her some biscuits and tea mid-morning and took John to the house on the promise he could help Cook.

The search party returned on sunset; William wasn't with them. Sarah fell to her knees when she saw the group walking across the home paddock, heads bowed.

'We'll find him tomorrow, Missus,' reassured Robert Bishop. 'There's more folks from around who will be coming to help with the search.'

Mrs Cullen had Cook prepare supper for the Blays, and Catherine and Betsy delivered it to the cottage. Sarah left it to her husband to show gratitude, she was numb with anguish.

'This is the second night. It's been so cold,' Sarah whispered to her husband as he held her to him in bed. 'If we don't find William, James Jr will be lost forever. He will not forgive me for bringing them here.'

'Not finding William won't make a difference, Sarah,' Blay replied. 'James Jr will not forgive either of us, no matter what comes his or our way.'

Blay held his wife until he recognised the sounds of sleep. He got up and sat in the rocking chair by the fire, stabbing at it every few minutes, annoying it with the poker until it retaliated with aggressive orange flames.

Washed and organised before Robert Bishop knocked on his door, Blay left the cottage, to again search for his middle son.

Catherine Cullen relayed the message to Sarah that she and John should come to the main house. Cook had breakfast plated and ready, but Sarah had no appetite. She watched John devour the eggs and bread.

'There's been talk of some natives in the area, Sarah,' Mrs Cullen began. 'Not meaning to alarm you, but we don't know what we are dealing with. They have been no trouble around our farm, but some others have had livestock killed with the natives' spears and other weapons. If your William has wandered into their terrain, he may have met with an untimely end. Mr Cullen thought you should be prepared.'

Sarah hadn't considered that William may be hurt or killed at the hand of natives. She folded her arms on the table and rested her head. She didn't want Mrs Cullen to see the colour wash out of her face.

The morning wore on into another afternoon, Sarah's fears fuelled her imagination, she was certain William was probably lost down a cliff somewhere or killed by natives. She put her hand over her mouth and ran outside, the vomit would not be stifled.

. . .

'Mama are you alright?' William was standing near the kitchen door, as if afraid to enter the house. On seeing his mother's plight, he moved towards her and offered his arms as comfort. Sarah held on to her son while she called to Mrs Cullen.

'Oh, my! Where did you come from, young William? Do you know the whole of New Norfolk is looking for you? Come inside, you look dirty and tired, Elizabeth Cullen said.

Cook prepared some food and drinks while William told his story. He was still telling it when the men returned from their search. The kitchen of the temporary Cullen house was full, and Cook fussed about, making sure everyone had food and drinks. John was at her side following orders and looking after visitors

On seeing his middle son safe, James Blay made a promise to God that he would go to church every Sunday. As part of his indenture to the Cullens, he was required to attend church, but he had managed to avoid it quite often.

'I saw a lot of pademelons, more than I'd ever seen, they were all together, with joeys in their pouches,' William began. 'We only ever see one or two, but they were all eating together. I just wanted to see a joey jump in the pouch. I started walking to them. When they saw me they jumped away, so I followed. I got lost. I didn't know the way back and it was getting dark. I started to cry. I sat down under a big tree and tried to keep warm.

'A black man and two boys came up and poked me with a big stick, they jumped back when I yelled that it hurt. I was really frightened. I mean, I knew they were in the bush, but we hadn't seen any, had we? One of the boys put out his hand, he had berries. I didn't know if he meant me to take them, but I took one. They all laughed at me. The boy put all the berries in his mouth at once. He went into the bush and came back with some more that he offered to me. This time I took as many as I could hold and pushed them all into my mouth; they were really sweet. I said thank you. They nodded at me. One boy used his hands to tell me to follow them. I didn't know if I should go with them, but it was cold, and I only had my jacket and the tree, so I went with them.

'They took me to their camp. The mothers and grand-mothers were cooking, and the fathers and grandfathers were singing, they all stopped when they saw me. Some of them didn't look happy that I was there. The father and boys who found me got their mother to give me some food, I don't know what it was, but it tasted good. They put me in their hut, they'd made it from branches and leaves, and it was warm and cosy. I went to sleep.

'I knew you'd be worried about me, Mama, so I asked them if they could show me the way home. Of course, they didn't understand, and I didn't understand them. I got a stick and drew the Cullen farm in the sand. The father who found me nodded. He pointed to the sun and waved his arm across the sky. They left me in their camp with the mothers and grandmothers and small children and disappeared into the bush. They were gone all day, they brought back huge lizards and snakes they'd killed. The mothers and grandmothers started getting the food ready. But Mama, there was a man in one of the huts, he was coughing and coughing and moaning, he sounded really sick. They crushed up some leaves from a bush and put them in a bowl like thing with water and made it hot over the fire, they made him breathe in the smoke from the leaves.

'The next morning, the sick man sounded much better, he wasn't coughing as much and was walking around. The father and sons who found me brought me back. They've gone back to their camp now.'

Sarah hugged her son and took him home to his own bed.

## 36

## FAMILY MATTERS

**1816**

Elizabeth Cullen looked across the kitchen table at her husband. This morning he looked all of his 76 years and although he appeared fit and healthy she wondered if he wasn't hiding something from her. Most people were surprised to learn James was 32 years older than her, his appearance belied his age. Sarah Blay had commented on how James had a straight back, had well-defined muscles and how strong he looked. But Elizabeth noticed he didn't appear as strong, he lost his breath when lifting bags of maize and wheat and was in bed much earlier than he used to be.

'The new house is coming on nicely, James. How long do you think it will be until it's finished?'

'It's taking longer than I wanted, but the priority is the farm, so we can eat.'

'Are you sure you're not doing too much? After all, you are Superintendent of the Stores as well.'

'The Stores aren't a concern, Tedder is quite competent

and trustworthy. All I must do is sign off on his paperwork. But if Blay gets his Ticket of Leave and a land grant I'll have to apply for another convict labourer, otherwise, your house won't be finished before I die.'

Elizabeth decided to leave the conversation for now. She didn't want James to know she was anxious about his health. Their age difference had bothered him since his 70th birthday, although he had said on the day that he wouldn't have lived this long if he'd stayed in London, nor been as healthy, and happy. She was glad she and the girls and this farm made him happy. She knew he had no regrets about taking up with her or for the life he had left behind in England, but she was allowed to worry.

'What are you thinking about?' James asked.

'I was imagining us living in the mansion you are building. About how amazing it is that I have gone from being a worthless kitchen maid in a rich man's house in Dublin, to be the mistress of my own house in Van Diemen's Land.'

James Cullen stood up from the kitchen table, leaned over and kissed Elizabeth's forehead. 'This is what I have wanted for you since that first day on Norfolk Island when they sent you to me - pregnant, swollen belly, pale skin, matted, lice-ridden hair, sores on your arms - and a beautiful smile. I loved you from that moment.'

Catherine strode into the kitchen with a bucket of goat's milk as her father left. Elizabeth wiped her cheeks. 'Are you alright, Mama? What has upset you?'

'Nothing has upset me, Catherine. Far from it, I am quite happy. I am a little sad to be losing another daughter in a few months, though.'

'You won't lose me, Mama. But, Mama, I was wondering where Teddy and I will live when we are married. Because while Teddy is a convict, he has to stay with Papa. Will you ask the Blays to leave the cottage?'

'Who is "Teddy"?'

'Oh, that's what I call my James, Mama. They are all named James, but Papa is the only one called by that. I'm not going to call my James James because that's Papa's name, and I'm not going to call him Tedder. I told him I'm calling him Teddy,' she beamed at her mother.

Elizabeth smiled at her daughter's reasoning. She had thought about the living arrangements for her middle daughter. James Tedder was a convict and although he had the Lieutenant Governor's permission to marry Catherine, he would be obliged to stay assigned to her husband. 'Papa and I will talk about it and see what is to be done.'

# 37

# ORDERS

Sarah Blay read the letter Robert Bishop had brought back from Hobart Town. 'It's from Mrs McCormack,' she said to her husband, 'says William McCormack has died, so in consequence James Jr no longer has employment as an apprentice shoemaker.'

'What are we to do with the boy then?' asked Blay, not expecting an answer. Sarah didn't give one.

'There is more, James. It appears Mr McCormack has left a land grant to James Jr. She read the solicitor's letter:

*"Know all men by these presents that J.G.H. Cummings Esquire of Hobarttown Van Diemens Land being professional since the decease of the within named William McCormack of all that allotment of ground granted by thus within Indenture or lease and that for and in consideration of twenty seven pounds, six shillings sterling hast bargained sold and assigned and did by those presents bargain, sell assign transfer and set over unto James Blay Junior of Hobarttown all my rights title and interest in and to the ? allotment of ground to have and hold the same for the rest residue and remainder of the term to course and ? for*

*progress or causing to be paid the usual quit rent of five shillings*
*and sixpence.*

    *Signed Geo H Cummings....*

    *February 1816"*[1]

Blay took the letter from Sarah and read it. 'The boy has a land grant? How is that possible?'

James Jr could be smarmy and sweet and polite when he wanted to use people, Sarah imagined her eldest son discovering the soft side of Mr McCormack's character and playing to it. 'He can be pleasant when he sees some gain for himself,' she said.

'He must have been very pleasant to the McCormack's to be left a land grant. We will have to send for him to see what is to happen next.'

James Jr sauntered into the cottage with an air of superiority that riled Sarah and caused John and William to step back from him. He didn't reciprocate his mother's embrace, nor did he greet his brothers or his father. Sitting down he pulled the lease document relating to the land out of his bag and spread it on the table.

'The land is in Hobart Town. Even though Mr McCormack left it to me, I can't take possession of it on my own, I need you, Mother to come to Hobart Town and sign some legal documents that describe how the land is mine, and you will manage it until I become of age. So, you will move to Hobart Town and build a house on my land and we will farm it. I don't know what will happen to you, Father. You might have to stay here at the Cullen farm because, after all, you are a convict.'

Blay clenched his fists at his side. He wanted to hit the

boy, but didn't have to think about striking his son for longer than a second or two, Sarah walked over to James Jr, teeth clenched, and face burning red.

'You don't speak to your father like that. I will slap you like I did in the coach on our way to Portsmouth. You are not grown enough for that to be impossible, you are only thirteen.'

'Thirteen with a land grant. That's something you don't have. I'm going to work that land and make money and go back to England to get away from this place and all of you.' He stormed out of the cottage.

'Why didn't you tell him you do have land, Sarah? Blay asked.

'He is a stranger to me. I don't want to share our good news with him. Anyway, we are happy in New Norfolk and his land is in Hobart Town.' Sarah was shaken by her son's attitude and judging by the looks on their faces, so were William and John.

'Do we have to move from here, Mama?'

'We will be leaving the Cullen farm, William, but not New Norfolk. We have some land to establish our own farm. I got a land grant, enough for us to grow our own food. We will be able to take our animals and we'll take some of the plants and vegetables to grow them in our own garden. Papa will put up a big tent for us to live in while he and John and you build us a new house. The Government will give Papa his own grant of land when he is a free man.'

'What about James Jr?' asked William.

'He has his life in Hobart Town, William, and he will find work until he is old enough to take possession of his own land.'

.   .   .

Sarah and her husband held hands and walked to the Cullen house together. Sarah had the documents she'd received from the Lieutenant Governor outlining her land lease and assigning her convict husband to her to manage and keep in food, clothing, and shelter. The Cullen family had just finished supper and were settling in for their evening activities. Betsy's head was bent over a book she bought from the Stores. Each time a ship arrived in Hobart Town it brought civilised things from London, including books, china, clothing, haberdashery, and newspapers - whose news was no longer *news* - by the time they arrived. Sarah encouraged Betsy to read as often as she could. Catherine and Tedder sat on the front verandah, holding hands and staring at each other.

Blay and his wife approached the kitchen door. 'Good evening Mr Cullen, Elizabeth. My husband I and I have some things to share if you are able to sit with us for a while.'

'Of course, Sarah, come in, we'll go into the parlour. James, light the candles, please,' Elizabeth Cullen directed her husband.

Blay had never been in the parlour of the Cullen house, he hadn't been past the kitchen. He stood near the door, waiting to be invited to sit down by his boss or Mrs Cullen. It caused him to remember the way he treated his apprentice in Spitalfields. The boy would wait to be invited to sit down for dinner and seemed out of place amid Blay family life. He regretted not being kinder to the lad.

Elizabeth Cullen showed Sarah to a seat and plonked in her favourite chair by the empty fireplace. James Cullen sat in the chair opposite his wife's. Blay remained by the door.

'Come in, Blay and sit by your wife,' said Elizabeth.

'Thank you, Mrs Cullen.'

'I'm glad you are both here,' said Elizabeth 'James and I had something we wanted to discuss with you. But you should tell us what is on your minds first.'

Sarah told the Cullens about James Jr's inheritance, and their decision to let him find another apprenticeship or work in Hobart Town until he was of the age to take on the bequeathed land.

'We are happy in New Norfolk and have no desire to live in Hobart Town,' Sarah explained. 'You know the Lieutenant Governor has approved the lease of land to me, however, you might not be happy to hear that my husband has been reassigned to me.'

Blay interjected, 'But, Mr Cullen, I will continue to work on your new house until you have another convict assigned to you. Sarah and William and John will live on her acres in a tent and get the vegetable gardens and stock pens organised. I will work on a house for my family in my own time until you get help.' Blay took a deep breath, he'd been dreading this moment for a few days.

'Thank you, Blay, that is appreciated,' Mr Cullen acknowledged. 'This has come at an opportune time, Sarah. Elizabeth and I were fretting over the accommodation arrangements for Catherine and Tedder once they are married in August. We were, at this meeting, going to give you notice to vacate the cottage in time for Catherine's wedding, but that is no longer necessary. There are convicts arriving in their hundreds every few months, I am sure the Lieutenant Governor will find someone suitable for us before too long.'

# 38

## BUSH MEDICINE

'Papa says the big house won't be finished in time for our wedding celebration, Teddy.'

'That does not concern me, Catherine,' Tedder comforted, 'we will marry in the same church your parents were married in and return to this farm for the celebration. It matters not if the new, big house is finished. Your father and I and Blay, and Roger Gavin and Robert Bishop can't work any faster. It will be done when it is done. I know your father wants it finished, and sometimes I wonder if he is concerned he will die before it is completed. But running the farm and the Stores consumes time.'

He caressed Catherine's face and neck with his lips, while his hand disappeared up her skirts. They had become adept at finding secluded places for their trysts, but Tedder had a feeling that Mrs Cullen knew about their meetings. Being a convict, he had few rights, and if Mrs Cullen took it upon herself to have them followed, he could be flogged and sent to a chain gang. 'Does it not worry you what would happen if we are caught at this activity, Catherine?'

Catherine giggled 'Oh, Teddy, don't be silly, we won't get

caught. And anyway, if we do, I'll beg Papa to be kind to you. I am his favourite daughter, after all.'

Her smile and her cheerful disposition kept him drawn to her. She seemed wiser than her fifteen years, and when she was lying under him on a warm bed of straw, or fresh green grass, or his canvas cot, she felt like a woman.

When they were both spent, Tedder helped Catherine up and straightened her skirts. 'Turn around, I'll brush the straw from the back of your dress and your hair.'

'Oh, Teddy, won't it be lovely when we are in the cottage and we can do this every morning and every night without worrying if we are caught?'

'Yes, my dear, I am counting the days. I love you.'

'Do you ever regret leaving London, Teddy? Do you regret the events that led to you becoming a convict here in Van Diemen's Land?'

Tedder held Catherine to him 'There is no room for regret in this happy life.'

Her mouth found his and she held the kiss until his breathing quickened. Smoothing back his hair, she made a quick grab for his manhood, and ran laughing out of the stables, back to the main house. 'You best get off to work, Teddy, before Papa comes looking for you,' she called over her shoulder.

Catherine crept around the outside of the house, to avoid being seen. Her parents would be up in a short while, but Cook would already be busy in the kitchen, and her sister Betsy sometimes woke up early to read the books Mrs Blay lent her. So annoying.

'Where have you been?' Betsy badgered when Catherine opened the door to their room.

'I've been to the outhouse if that's alright with you.'

'I don't believe you, you've been with Tedder. Papa will have him flogged if he catches you.'

Catherine took a long, deep breath and let it out slowly. It wasn't a good idea to antagonise her sister, she was their mother's favourite, and their mother wielded lots of power in the house. 'I went to the outhouse, Betsy, and now I'm washing up for breakfast.'

The girls made their way to the kitchen, the smell of frying bacon wafted through the house; Cook was already serving it, and homemade bread and fried eggs when they walked in. 'Where are Mama and Papa?' Catherine asked Cook. Their parents were always up before everyone else in the house, and their father was usually finished eating and leaving to work when the girls arrived.

'Your Papa is not well this morning, Catherine. Your Mama is with him. Here, you can take in this tea and bread for him before you sit down.'

Catherine held the tray in two hands and knocked her parents' door with her foot. 'Come in,' her mother responded.

'I can't Mama, I'm holding a tray.'

Elizabeth Cullen opened the door for her middle daughter. Catherine gasped at the sight of her father in his bed. 'What is wrong, Papa?'

'Papa is not feeling well this morning, Catherine, he's staying in bed for a while. When Robert Bishop arrives in the kitchen for breakfast, please come and let me know. Thank you for the tea.'

Dismissed, Catherine blew a kiss to her father and left the room, holding on to the tears until she was out of sight.

'Mr Bishop, Mama said to go to Papa's room immediately, please.' Catherine gave Robert Bishop his instruction as soon as he walked into the kitchen, then slouched on the chair next to her sister. 'I'm no longer hungry, Cook, thank you.'

'What's wrong?' Betsy demanded. 'Catherine, what's wrong with Papa?'

'I don't know. I took in the tea and Mama said to get Mr Bishop. Papa was in bed and he was a funny colour. He smiled at me but didn't lift his head.' Both girls cried.

'Why are you cryin'?' Cook demanded. 'You don't know what's goin' on, so don't waste your energy on tears, you might need that energy for later on to help your Mama.'

'Oh Teddy, Papa is sick and in bed,' Catherine blurted when Tedder and Roger Gavin arrived for their breakfast. Tedder sat heavily on a chair as Robert Bishop returned to the kitchen, he spoke to Cook and ignored everyone else in the room.

'I have to go to Hobart Town to get the surgeon, make sure Mr Cullen has plenty of sweet tea to drink – even if it means no one else gets any sugar. And Mrs Cullen will need to be reminded to eat and drink,' he turned to the girls 'You help Cook and your mother. I'll be back with the surgeon as soon as possible. Tedder, come with me, two pairs of rowing hands are better than one.'

Her daughters pestered until Elizabeth Cullen gave in and left the bedroom to get something to eat and drink and to wash her face. 'Cook, I knew he was hiding something. I knew he wasn't quite well, but at his age, I didn't want to think about it.'

'He'll be alright, Mrs Cullen, he's as strong a man as I have ever seen, no matter his age. Whatever it is, he'll get over it,' assured Cook.

Elizabeth smiled at the woman's confidence. 'I pray you

are right, Cook. Girls, why are you sitting here in the kitchen? Go about your jobs, there are animals to tend to and gardens to mind.' Catherine and Betsy jumped at their mother's orders and hurried outside to do their chores.

Jobs finished, Catherine and Betsy crept back into the kitchen. 'Go and get your mother, please, Miss Catherine,' Cook said, 'there are visitors in the parlour.'

'Visitors? How can we entertain visitors today?' Catherine demanded to know.

'They are not here to be entertained Miss Catherine, they are here to support your parents. The families who were on Norfolk Island with you and are now here in New Norfolk, have sent someone to see what support they can be.'

'How did they find out Papa was sick? He'll be furious.'

'All it would take is for Mr Bishop to tell one person on his way to the boat,' explained Cook. 'You know how close everyone is. Been through a lot together, builds a bond you can't get any other way. Now, please get your mother.'

Elizabeth Cullen put her hand on her husband's forehead, it was burning hot to touch, he was still sweating, but complained of being cold. And the cough she had heard over the past days was getting worse. He asked for a heat bundle to put on his right side to ease the pain there. She left James in Catherine's care and washed her face, tidied her hair and put on a dress suitable to greet the visitors.

All the gentlemen visitors stood when she walked in. Each had their cap in their hands and a worried expression.

'Good morning, gentlemen, thank you so much for visiting.'

The group included close friends from Norfolk Island, people who had faced the same challenges, disappointments, and successes as the Cullens: James Triffitt Sr, Denis

McCarty, and Abraham Hands. Their son in law William Rayner Jnr, and James Blay were there too.

'We are grateful you have all come to see us, but James will be fine; we are waiting for Robert Bishop and Tedder to bring back the surgeon,' said Elizabeth to the group.

'We've come to let you know, Elizabeth,' began James Triffitt, 'that each one of us will spare a convict labourer to help with the farm and the building of your new house until James is well enough to continue.'

Grateful for their generosity, Elizabeth sat in one of the mismatched armchairs she had bought when that woman, what was her name? went back to England. Looking at James early in the morning, she had not only worried about him but how the work on the farm would be organised and be done. 'Thank you. You are all wonderful to make this offer. We'll see what the surgeon says about James' health, and I will have Tedder or Mr Bishop keep you informed. Please stay a little longer, Cook will bring you some refreshments.'

Elizabeth stood up, bowed her head slightly to the worried group, and went into the kitchen. 'Cook, I know you are busy, but get Betsy and Catherine to help you – please get some refreshments together for our visitors.'

James coughed and had difficulty getting his breath. Elizabeth put extra pillows under his head to try and help. He was still complaining he was cold, so she put more wood on the fire, and got a blanket from one of the girls' beds. She sat on the chair next to the bed, and held his hand, praying quietly, something she hadn't done for a very long time.

Catherine knocked once on her parents' bedroom door but didn't wait for a response. 'Mama, Mr Bishop and Teddy are back with the Surgeon.'

. . .

'I think he has pleurisy, Mrs Cullen. He has the symptoms: a dry cough, fever and chills and a pain on one side of his chest. I will treat him with leeches to draw out the excess blood and get his humours balanced. Do you have native bees, here Mrs Cullen?'

'Yes doctor, we have hives, the girls look after them.'

'We will need fresh honey to soothe his throat from the coughing and to ease the infection on his lung. You will also have to get leeches collected from the river.'

Elizabeth watched the doctor performing his treatments, she would have to continue the regime when he returned to Hobart Town in the morning. The honey helped James Cullen's throat. Cook put it in his tea instead of sugar. The next day would indicate if the leeches were doing their job.


James Cullen's coughing could be heard all over the house, he coughed most of the night, and Elizabeth stayed with him, offering honey tea and cool rags when he was hot, and blankets when he was cold.

The surgeon left by first light. Robert Bishop took him back to Hobart Town on the Derwent River. Tedder stayed to continue with his work in the Stores and on the new Cullen house. Elizabeth and the girls stayed by Cullen's side, the leeches had been removed, and his chest was covered with little welts where the creatures had penetrated his skin and sucked his blood. The surgeon assured Elizabeth James would recover if she followed his instructions with the leeches and honey.

Cook knocked quietly on the bedroom door and waited to be invited in. 'Mrs Cullen, Sarah Blay and her son, William are here. Mrs Blay asked to see you.'

'I am not entertaining a social caller, Cook. Tell her to come back another time. James is worsening as the morning progresses.'

'Mrs Cullen, she says the boy has something important to say regarding Mr Cullen's health.'

Elizabeth greeted Sarah and William who were waiting in the parlour.

Sarah Blay didn't wait for Elizabeth to finish the pleasantries. 'Mrs Cullen, William has some information about the natives who had him when he was missing. He has been sneaking off and meeting with one of the native boys, they have become firm friends, apparently. William said he could ask his friend about the remedies they use on their sick.'

Elizabeth Cullen put her hand up to stop Sarah, but she was ignored.

'William said when he was staying at the camp, a man was coughing and moaning constantly, and the natives crushed up leaves with water and heated up the concoction and made the man breath it in. William says he was up the next day and his coughing had eased significantly. I think it is worth finding out what they use, Mrs Cullen because it doesn't sound to me as if the surgeon's remedies are making much of a difference.'

Reaching for the arms of her favoured chair, Elizabeth sat down and put her head in her hands, she could hear her husband coughing and struggling to breathe. 'Alright Sarah, William, it can't do any harm if it's only leaves. Please see what you can do.' She pulled herself up from the chair and left the room.

Two days after their first visit regarding James Cullen's health, Sarah Blay and William returned to the Cullen farm.

James Cullen's coughing could be heard outside the house, he sounded to Sarah as if he was trying to ward off the death rattles, each bout of coughing was followed by the distressing sound of him trying to get a breath. 'I hope and pray this works, William. I don't think the poor man has much time.'

Under William Blay's instruction, Cook crushed up the leaves from the bush the native boy had given him. [1] She added enough water to cover the leaves and put it on the fire to boil. 'My word, that's a strong smell William, are you sure this is what they did?'

'Yes, Cook. And when I showed my friend Mr Cullen's symptoms, he knew exactly which bush to pick the leaves from, and he showed me how to make the steam. Mr Cullen has to breathe it in, you should take the bowl to his room, and put it on the fire in there. It needs to steam a lot, it needs to fill the room for him to breath it in. When it stops smelling, we need to make more.'

Elizabeth stayed with her husband while the room filled with the smell of the leaves. It wasn't unpleasant, and Elizabeth felt the clearing effect on her own breathing. She put her head on the pillow next to her husband, and her hand on his chest to make sure he was still taking in air, and therefore, alive. After about twenty minutes Elizabeth noticed the ferocity of James' coughing ease, he was still coughing, but not with the same intensity. She hurried to the door, opened it and called out to Cook to make another batch of the leaves as quickly as possible, and to keep the supply constant.

Cook and Elizabeth took it in turns to doze off during the night. Cook had crushed all the leaves the native had given

William and divided them into lots for water to be added when needed.

By sunrise, James Bryan Cullen had stopped the incessant coughing and was sleeping relatively peacefully, with an intermittent much less dramatic cough, disturbing him.

Elizabeth Cullen helped her husband freshen up, she had Cook bring in a bowl and pitcher with warm water, she sat him up with pillows supporting his back and head, washed his face, arms and chest, and ran a wet cloth through his hair.

'I'm sorry, Elizabeth, you are too young to be looking after an old man. I'm sorry.' The rasp in James' voice a legacy of the incessant coughing.

'We look after each other, James. You took me in when I was a silly, pregnant, kitchen maid from Dublin. The second-best thing to happen to me was being transported, the best day of my life was when I was assigned to you on Norfolk Island. You saved me, so I will look after you whenever the need arises. Besides, you are very robust for any man of any age, and you will recover just fine. Now drink some more honey tea.'


Although exhausted James did feel better, the cough had calmed down, his throat was soothed, the pain in his side wasn't as strong as it had been a few days ago, and the fever and chills had gone. Not remembering much of the previous two days, James asked Elizabeth what the surgeon did to help him recover.

'The surgeon did nothing useful, James. He arrived from Hobart Town, said he thought you had pleurisy, ordered leeches to balance your "humours" and honey for your throat. He ate well, slept well in our home and ordered

Robert Bishop to take him back to Hobart Town when he had finished breakfast the next morning. It was William Blay who saved you, James. You will remember well when he disappeared and spent time with the natives?' She didn't wait for a response. 'He befriended one of the boys and had been sneaking off to meet with his native friend. It was fortunate for us that he did. William told Sarah he remembered a young native man being sick when he was there, and they steamed leaves all night and in the morning the man seemed much better. So, William met with his friend and got a supply of leaves – we steamed batches all night - and day. We've run out of the leaves, so William is trying to get some more, the native boy told him you would have to breathe the steam for a few days. I am just happy it is not an offensive smell.'

'I've heard stories about native medicines, Elizabeth, but dismissed them, thinking how could savages know more about modern healing than we do? Seems they do,' James said pensively. 'Seems they do.'

'Good morning, Mr Cullen, we are all most pleased that you are out of your sick bed and looking better,' Tedder said to James Cullen as Elizabeth helped him into the kitchen for breakfast.

'Thank you, Tedder. I trust the Stores have kept functioning, and the new house is still being built?'

Tedder smiled and nodded, 'Yes sir, everything is functioning as it should, and Catherine and I are counting the days until we are married.'

'And when is that supposed to be happening, Tedder?'

Tedder stopped smiling and swallowed hard.

'I'm teasing, Tedder,' said Cullen. 'Catherine reminds me

every morning how many days there are left. I am pleased she is not with child before the event. I have been successful in obtaining another grant of land, Tedder. You will work it for me after the wedding.'

Tedder was never sure how to take his boss 'I am going to be his son in law, but still a convict, that is going to be an interesting combination at times.'

'Papa, why do you tease my Teddy so?' Catherine chastised her father as she put her arms around his neck and kissed him on the forehead. 'We must do something for William Blay, Papa, and for the native boy whose leaves saved you.'

# 39

# WEDDING DAY

**19 August 1816**

'Keep still, Catherine, stop fidgeting or I'll poke you with a pin, on purpose.'

'Oh. Mama, I am so happy. Teddy is such a gentle man. I know he is ten years older, but that doesn't seem to matter when we are,' she stopped herself from saying *sleeping together* but her mother's wry smile indicated she knew.

'Yes, he is a good man, Catherine, and the ten years matter little. Papa is thirty-two years older than me and that has made no difference. The wonderful life I had on Norfolk Island and the wonderful life I have here in Van Diemen's Land is all to him. I don't think a younger man would have had the ability to achieve all your father has.'

Catherine kept still while her mother made some adjustments to the wedding dress; the dress her mother wore seven years earlier, when she and Papa were finally, after being pestered for years from Reverend Robert Knopwood, married by him. Sophia had worn the dress when she married William Rayner Jr in January last year. 'At least Teddy and I are not marrying in the middle of a horrible summer like Sophia did. The dress will be more comfortable,' Catherine told her mother.

Tedder stayed at the Blay's the night before the wedding. They had built a small home with four rooms on Sarah's land lease, and Blay was farming it successfully. Their middle son, William was a great help and Tedder thought it odd that the son of a London shoemaker should have a born talent for farming.

Thanks to William's friendship with the native boy, the Blay farm was not targeted by natives when others lost sheep and goats. Sarah didn't have help in the kitchen as Elizabeth Cullen did, but Tedder was impressed with how efficiently she ran the house, vegetable garden, and how great her meals were. 'You are a wonderful cook, Sarah.'

'Why, thank you, Tedder. I must admit having my own kitchen is something I never dreamed would happen. In Spitalfields, we rented a two-room house that was very cold in winter, and in summer,' she said laughing. 'Never thought I would own my own four-roomed house on ten acres. We have space for all of us to sit at the table for meals Tedder, and I have privacy. I know it isn't as grand as the one Mr Cullen is building for his wife, or even as grand as the one they live in now, but I am very happy to have it.'

'Do you have any regrets about what happened to Blay, and you coming here?'

'No. I have no regrets, Tedder. I have sadness. Sadness at leaving my mother, and her dying alone, sadness at James Jr hating being here, but no regrets. Do you have any, Tedder? Regrets?'

'Like you Sarah I have great sadness, but no regrets.'

'What are you sad about, Tedder?'

'Leaving my parents, my brothers, Henry and William, and my sister, Esther. I did write to them to tell them I am happy and even though I'm a convict I have found love and am gainfully employed. My father was heartbroken when I was arrested, it shamed him, he is a respected businessman and belongs to the Guild. I thought I had my life worked out in London, but I was a naive little boy who believed that an evil old man would give me 500 pounds if I let him use me as a plaything. I think Father was more distressed at how stupid I was than about what the old man did to me. Catherine and I have spoken about a trip to England when I gain my Certificate of Freedom and we have saved enough, but Mr Cullen has suggested I open a flour mill in Hobart Town when my sentence is complete. We have a lot to consider.'

Mr Cullen bought new clothes for Tedder: he had a new jacket, breeches, shirt, and cap and they weren't convict issue, they were real clothes. Tedder looked in the mirror Sarah Blay had placed on the sideboard in the kitchen. He was happy with the person who looked back. His hair was cut a good length, thanks again to Sarah Blay. His face, clean-shaven, had a tinge of light brown to it that had never existed in London, and his eyes had the life restored to them. Today he was marrying Catherine, a young, fiery, mischievous, yet loving girl who was going to be his for the rest of his life. 'Mother would like her,' he said to Sarah.

. . .

Tedder walked back to the Cullen Farm with Blay, Sarah, John, and William. The brilliant August sunshine reinforced the joy he was trying to contain for dignity's sake. Although the air held the cutting cold of mid-winter, the cloudless blue sky promised a day free of rain and icy winds. Winter in New Norfolk could sometimes be as harsh as London winters, although the snow rarely settled on the ground long enough to cause accessibility issues.

Mr Cullen greeted the group as they approached the worksite that was a half-built two storey mansion. 'You look dashing, Tedder. Glad to see the clothes fit you well enough. Dressed up as you are, it's easier to see you as the son of a respected London Guild member.' Turning to Sarah and Blay he added, 'It's a pleasure to see you, Sarah, I trust you have been well, and you too, Blay, you look fit.'

Tedder offered his hand to Mr Cullen, who shook it heartily. 'My daughter could do no better than the man she has chosen to wed,' he said.

'Thank you, sir. I will treat her well and look after her.'

'Reverend Knopwood is here, he arrived yesterday and stayed over. We are fortunate to have such a day at our disposal, we can have the ceremony in the garden.' Mr Cullen walked toward the house at the call of his wife.

'Good day to you, Tedder, Mrs Blay, Mr Blay, lads. A beautiful day for a wedding,' Reverend Knopwood made small talk with the groom and his friends while they waited for Catherine.

When Catherine Cullen walked toward him, James Tedder swallowed hard. He used the back of his hand to wipe his eyes hoping no one would see the tears of joy and misinterpret them for sadness. She smiled widely at him, filling him with confidence and hope, he returned the smile, hoping it would accurately reflect the happiness this day brought him.

Although Catherine's dress wasn't new, Tedder thought no other woman would have been able to wear it as beautifully as she. The low-cut front showed off her ivory skin and just enough of her beautifully formed breasts to tease. Her already small waist was accentuated as the dress highlighted her hips. The pink and gold colour of the fabric complemented her English / Irish blonde, red hair and the small posy of native, pink flowers she held gave her an air of innocence. Tedder grinned as he thought of the innocence they had shared.

Helping her undo the buttons at the back of her dress already had Tedder's manhood reacting. Catherine put her hand behind her searching for the rigidity that she knew would be there. He groaned, her dress fell to the floor. She turned to face him, her smile inviting his lips to touch hers.

'We can do this as often as we want,' she said softly 'and I want to do it now, Teddy.' She pulled her petticoats over her head and stood, her body quivering as he gently touched her face, neck, and breasts. They had made love many times, but always hiding out of view, secretly, in a hurry, he had never seen her complete nakedness. She giggled as she undid the buttons on his breeches 'It is difficult, James, with your manhood so large and stiff.'

He dropped his breeches to the floor and stepped out of them, she told him to raise his arms and she lifted off his shirt. She stood back to look at him, and the sound of her laughter filled their small bedroom. He was embarrassed and tried to cover himself with his hands. 'No, Teddy, don't do that. I'm laughing because you still have your boots on.'

The first experience as husband and wife in their own bed, in their own room, was over quickly. The second and subsequent times over the course of their wedding night were thoughtful, gentle and slow.

'I'm staying in bed a little while longer, Teddy. You go to the house to get your breakfast and I'll see you at dinner.'

Tedder dressed in his work clothing, kissed his wife and closed the door to the cottage as he left, smiling broadly and whistling a tune he made up as he walked along the well-trodden path to the main house.

'Good morning, Tedder,' Elizabeth Cullen acknowledged as he appeared in the kitchen. 'Mr Cullen wants to see you in the parlour before you sit down to eat.' The order wasn't unusual, but Tedder wondered what his master and new father in law wanted with him the day after his marriage to Catherine.

'Come in and sit down, Tedder. Why are you looking so concerned? Do you expect a punishment of some description?'

'No, Sir, this is my first meeting with you after my marriage to Catherine, I'm not sure if it as convict or son in law that you wish to see me.'

'Sit down, relax. Mrs Cullen and I do not see you as a convict to be ordered around and owned, however, you are just that until you gain a Ticket of Leave or your sentence expires. While I live and breathe you will be assigned here, and we will treat you as the husband of our middle daughter.' He smiled at Tedder, something he didn't do often.

'I want you to take over the management of the construction of the new house. It is in confidence that I tell you that the rate of building is too slow, and I fear I will die before it is finished. I promised Elizabeth a fine home and I will keep that promise with assistance from you.'

Tedder stood, offered his hand to Mr Cullen, and shook it vigorously, 'I will be honoured to oversee the continuing construction of your new home, Mr Cullen.' Returning to the kitchen, he nodded to Mrs Cullen, sat down and looked forward to the hearty breakfast Cook would put in front of him.

## 40

# FREEDOM

**1817**

'What does that mean, James, a Ticket of Leave?' Sarah Blay questioned her husband when she read the letter he had received from Lieutenant Governor Sorell.

'It means, Sarah, that I can travel over Van Diemen's Land, that I can work, apart from on this farm. I can even start making shoes again. It means, that as long as I behave, I will no longer be a convict. The Ticket holds until I get a pardon, or until my sentence expires. I'm working towards a pardon,' he said pulling her close to him and wrapping his arms around her shoulders. 'Do you have any regrets following me to this place, Sarah?'

'Tedder and I discussed this on his wedding day. No, I have no regrets, James. Do you?'

'In the beginning, I had many: when I was thrown into Newgate Gaol, the terrible time on the prison hulk, the journey here on the *Indefatigable*, getting flogged. But this life, this life with you, and John and William, this life that we have James Bryan Cullen to thank for. I regret none of it now.'

'Your father must know I've been granted an Absolute Pardon, Catherine. Surely, Lt Governor Sorell would have informed him, after all, I am assigned to him.'

James and Catherine Tedder had just finished supper and were sitting at the kitchen table in the little cottage. He had read the letter to Catherine.

'It will mean I get my own grant of land, we can have a home of our own, we can build a wonderful life for the child you carry. But I can't let your father down, he has been so good to me, and us. I'll continue to manage the construction of his new house; it's not far from complete, it should only be a few months until it's ready to live in.'

'Congratulations, Tedder. Your time is up, and the rest of your life begins,' Mr Cullen patted Tedder on the back, shook his hand and walked beside him towards the new house building site.

'Thank you, sir. I will continue to manage the construction of the house, and when I get my land grant, I'll work on it in the afternoons, and your house in the mornings. If that is acceptable to you.'

'It doesn't matter if it's acceptable to me, Tedder. You are free to make your own decisions. Being a free man again will change the way you interact with everyone in Van Diemen's Land. I see from the newspaper that Blay has a Ticket of Leave again. Let's hope this time he manages to keep it. I'm certain he didn't tell Sarah he had the first Ticket of Leave, she would have told my Elizabeth of the news.'

'What happened last time, Mr Cullen. I didn't like to ask.'

'He was insolent to James Jordan. Lucky, he wasn't flogged. Jordan wanted to know why Sarah Blay's livestock had never been pilfered or driven off by the natives and Blay told him to mind his own fucking business. We all know it's because of young William's friendship with a native boy. Don't know why Blay didn't just say that. Anyway, Jordan reported him to the Lt Governor, and Ticket of Leave, gone. He might take better care of this one,' Cullen added with a chuckle.

## 41

# THE GEORGIAN MANSION

*This is the Heritage listed house, in April 2018. Two hundred years after construction.*

**1818**

'Papa is so happy, Teddy. Thank you, the house he wanted to build for Mama since the early days on Norfolk Island, is finished.'

James Tedder's chest puffed out just a little as his wife draped him with praise. He had worked harder as a free man than he had as a convict. Sitting in his chair by the fire in the kitchen, he recounted his achievements since the pardon: land grants, contracts to sell meat to the Government Stores, the completion of the Cullen house and the birth of a beautiful baby girl, Margaret.

'Now that your father's grand house is finished, Catherine, I think it's time we tried our luck in Hobart Town. I want to consider setting up a mill to grind wheat.'

Catherine and her husband stood in the kitchen of the small cottage that had been their home for two years. Sophia and her husband William Rayner Jnr and their two daughters were already living in Hobart, she and Teddy were leaving, and her youngest sister, Betsy would be married in a few years. 'It's hard to leave, Teddy, I've lived here for nine years. I've never been away from Papa and Mama. It's sad that Papa's new house is finished when we are all leaving home.'

'We are not going back to England, Catherine, you will see them often. Your father will have reason to go to Hobart to conduct business with the Government and your mother will accompany him. Denis McCarty has finished the road between New Norfolk and Hobart Town, so with bullocks or horses, it won't take as long as the river journey does. Come along, let's get the rest of the bags onto the cart, while it's still daylight,' he teased.

'Goodbye Mama, Papa, I will miss you.' Catherine couldn't hold back the tears when she hugged her mother and cried openly when she saw her father wipe his eyes. 'I'll get Teddy to write as soon as we are settled, he has rented a house for us in Murray Street, so you can come and visit.'

'Look after this little baby girl, Catherine,' Elizabeth Cullen said as she kissed the infant on the head. 'Yours and Sophia's children are the beginning of a new dynasty on this side of the world.'

'You are right, Mrs Cullen,' Tedder said. 'I hadn't thought of my parents' line continuing through my daughter, but the family connections are flourishing, far away from where they began in England.'

Tedder offered his hand to Mr Cullen, 'Thank you,' he said to his father-in-law.

Cullen took his hand warmly and lent in to speak. 'Look after my daughter and granddaughter, Tedder, and thank you for all your help since you came here, especially with the new house. I will miss you.'

'My time as a convict in Van Diemen's Land was nothing as I expected. I thank you for the new skills I learned, for treating me with kindness and respect, and having faith in me.'

Tedder hugged Mrs Cullen, kissed Betsy on the cheek, and helped Catherine into the cart. Catherine wept until the township of New Norfolk was out of sight.

# 42

# HOBART TOWN

**1818**

'Do you like the house, Catherine?'

'Yes, Teddy, it is lovely, and more space than we had before, we even have a parlour like Mama and Papa have.' Catherine held baby Margaret close, so she could bury her face in the infant's swaddling. Teddy was happy, and she didn't want her tears upsetting him.

Tedder left the house at sunrise; the early winter air had a crispness that wasn't quite cold but left no doubt that warm autumn mornings were no longer to be expected. The streets were muddy from the rain the night before, but not impossible to walk on, although he was pleased he'd worn his old convict issue boots and not the new ones he'd bought from James Blay Jr. He stopped briefly to watch the rising sun play with the surface of the Derwent and cast shadows over the ship that was anchored at Victoria Dock. *The Lady Castlereagh* was one of many ships arriving in

Hobart Town carrying convicts, and as Tedder watched the ship in the morning sunlight, sailors were organising for the unloading of the cargo, which included human. He shuddered at the memory of leaving the *Indefatigable* with Blay, the terror that almost paralysed him and made it impossible to stand up straight.

'Well, look e here,' said a voice from behind. 'If it isn't the convict Tedder.'

Turning to face his nemesis, Tedder saw that Toothless had even fewer teeth, had lost almost all of his hair, and appeared to be wearing the same clothes he had on when he tied Tedder to a tree with the intent of drowning him in the Derwent five years earlier.

'Dressed up all nice, are ye Tedder? Goin' to a funeral? Didn't get to the one we had set up for ye a few years back, did ye? Disappointed in that, we are.' Toothless' gummy grin was copied by the others in his cohort. 'We might try and arrange one for ye while we are in this God forsaken hell hole this time.'

'Is that a threat? Are you threatening my person with violence?' Tedder moved toward Toothless with menace, keeping his back straight and glaring right into the other man's eyes.

'I can have you whipped for insolence. Lieutenant Governor Colonel William Sorell will not take kindly to a guard from a convict ship threatening the safety of a settler who supplies meat and flour to the Government Stores.' Tedder stepped back to relish Toothless' response.

'How can ye be a settler, ye haven't done ye seven years. I don't believe ye.'

'Well, man, it is of no concern of mine whether you believe me or not. I am a settler, not a convict, and you will show me respect. If you darken my path with your presence again while you are in Hobart Town this time or any other time in the future, I will have you charged with harassment. Now, get out of my way, I have work to do.'

Toothless and his cronies moved out of Tedder's way, with mouths agape, all displaying the remains of rotten teeth. Taking purposeful steps while being watched by the guards, Tedder breathed deeply as he made his way to the Government buildings. His shaking hands belied the confidence he oozed when he came face to face with the man who had almost killed him.

Toothless seethed as Tedder walked away, turning to the men in his group he promised revenge. 'That upstart convict will not make a fool of me. I will have the last say and see his funeral before my days are done.'

## 43

# NEW HOME

**1818**

Elizabeth Cullen and her daughter, Betsy, sat in the new kitchen at the table and chairs brought from their first house, while Cook busied herself with arrangements for dinner.

'Will Mr Cullen be back for dinner?'

'I am not sure, Cook,' answered Elizabeth 'put some food aside for him anyway.'

They'd been living in the new home James built for them for some months, it was three bays wide and two bays deep, symmetrical, like the mansions in England [Georgian]. Each room had a fireplace, and downstairs boasted a splendid parlour, a kitchen with a cooking fire designed so cooking pots hung easily a dining room where guests could be entertained away from the kitchen, and a separate room for bathing. Three bedrooms and a library upstairs completed the palatial home. Elizabeth spent days in Hobart Town looking through newspapers and catalogues from London to source items to furnish her house to the standard she and James wanted. In the parlour she had two giltwood armchairs, sitting either side of the fireplace, a mahogany settee with pink silk cushions, a mahogany games table and paintings and lamps bought from deceased estates in New Norfolk and Hobart Town. The dining room boasted a mahogany table with scrolled leaves over each leg, and eight matching chairs with pink silk cushioning. Elizabeth did sometimes wonder if the income from the crops and live-stock on the 104 acres her husband had in land grants was keeping pace with expenditure.

James had a contract with the Government to supply meat, but Elizbeth was not privy to the amount this brought in. James didn't hide these things from her, but she couldn't read what was in the ledgers. She did know what was growing on the farm: James had six acres planted with wheat, barley and beans, and four with potatoes. Ninety-three acres were pasture and on this were forty-one cattle and 430 sheep. She planned to speak with him over supper about the fortunes of the farm and the financial position.

'Good evening, Mr Triffitt,' Elizabeth greeted James' guest. 'Please join us in the parlour.'

'Thomas and I have some business to discuss, Elizabeth, could you please ask Cook to bring us some tea.'

Elizabeth didn't like being dismissed by her husband, and Thomas Triffitt, one of the first generation, born on Norfolk Island as her girls were, would recognise this too. However, she wasn't going to argue the point, they were respected members of the community, a small community that enjoyed dabbling in gossip. She would be gracious, so

Thomas would have no ammunition that could easily turn into scurrilous chatter when he returned to his father's home.

'Of course, James. I will attend to some mending in the kitchen while you discuss your business with Thomas.'

'I am sorry for dismissing you in that fashion, Elizabeth, but the subject of my meeting with Triffitt was too complicated and I didn't want any distractions.' James explained to his wife when they retired to the bedroom.

'So, I am a distraction, am I?' Elizabeth smiled coyly at her husband, but his solemn expression caused her to frown. 'What is it, James? You must tell me.'

'I have transferred our original sixty-five acres and our first house to Thomas Triffitt, to lease, in consideration of £400. We will continue to farm it, but it is his property, and I will pay him a share of the income from the land. He will take possession of it in ten years.'

'I knew things were not as they should be, and we spent all that money on this house and you encouraged me to buy the furniture and curtains and cushions. I would have been happy in the first house we had.'

'But I wanted you to have the things we talked about, the things we would never have been able to have in Dublin or London.' James tried to take Elizabeth in his arms, she turned away and snuffed the candle on her bedside table.

## 44

# HOUSEWARMING

Invited to the Cullen mansion for afternoon tea, Sarah Blay arrived wearing a blue dress of the new fashion she had ordered from an advertisement in the Hobart Town Gazette. The long conical skirt fell from just below her breast, the round neckline flattered her shoulders, which is where the dress puffed to meet the edge of the long sleeves. The hem was decorated with ruffles. She carried a patterned shawl and had her hair styled in the London fashion, with a part in the centre and tight curls over her temples. 'What do you think, James?' she asked her husband when he walked into the bedroom.

'I can't think. I don't know what to say.' He stood for a few minutes staring at his wife. 'I have never seen you look so beautiful. You are beautiful, but that dress, you look like a queen.'

'Am I overdressed for afternoon tea? Will they think I am being audacious wearing something so grand?'

'You are audacious, Sarah. Without that side of you, we would not be enjoying the success of living in Van Diemen's Land. To hell with what they think.' Blay took Sarah's hand in his, put the other behind his back, bowed to her, and kissed the hand of his brave, beautiful wife.

Pulling the shawl around her shoulders, checking her hair in the mirror once more, and carefully putting on her new slippers, Sarah tiptoed through the house to the carriage her son William had ordered for her. Her husband helped her board and paid the driver to take his wife on the short journey to the Cullen Farm.

As one of the servants Elizabeth Cullen had employed for the day helped Sarah from the carriage, she looked to see what the other guests were wearing. She was relieved to see they were all dressed up and looking remarkable. 'I am not overdressed.'

The ladies were led into the parlour of the Cullen mansion; the room easily accommodated the ten women Elizabeth had invited. Afternoon tea was laid out on the dining room table, and servants were walking through the group offering ciders, ale and iced tea. Sarah had never been to such an event in either of her lives: the one in England, or the one in Van Diemen's Land. She was giddy with excitement, it was a lovely opportunity for them to talk without the men. Sarah knew most of the women and Elizabeth Cullen, the perfect hostess, introduced her to those she didn't. She sat with Catherine Tedder who was pregnant with her second child, the first one, Margaret was with Betsy and Cook. Sophia Rayner, Catherine's older sister was pregnant with her third child, her two girls were also with their young aunt.

'How have you been keeping, Catherine, are you well?'

'Thank you, Sarah, I'm fine. Margaret keeps me busy and I have had to resettle us into another house since Teddy sold the one we were living in in Hobart. He wants the money to buy land to build a flour mill.'

Catherine wriggled in her seat and straightened her skirt.

Although Catherine's dress was not as grand as her own, Sarah did notice Catherine's hair was curled in the same fashion as hers, and the skirt had coloured feathers sewn across the hem.

'Do you not think it strange, Catherine, that most of us left England, and have no interest in returning, but we copy the fashions from there because we want to look like the ladies in London?'

Catherine Tedder smiled at Sarah, apparently not quite understanding the question.

Sarah continued, 'It was very generous of your mother to invite us today; we spend so much time working we don't often have a chance to dress up and socialise. You look lovely Catherine, your hair especially.'

Catherine giggled.

'How are you and Blay and the boys getting along on your allotment, Sarah?'

'James works very hard with the farming; he seems to revel in it and has no interest in returning to his trade. Our eldest, James Jr, is still in Hobart and working the allotment he was left by his master tradesman. I swear Mr William McCormack must have been witness to a side of young James that we did not see, to leave him his land grant in his will. William works alongside his father all day, and John does his part after he has finished his morning lessons. My husband received a Conditional Pardon two years ago. Were you aware?'

'Yes, Teddy told me. That is wonderful, and a relief for you, I am sure.'

'When he was charged and sentenced and put on that stinking, rotten prison hulk on the Thames waiting to be transported to what we imagined was the hell hole, arse end of the earth for the rest of his life, this reality, this future, wasn't even a dream.'

'Mama and Papa never told us what it was like on the hulks and then on the transport ships. Mama always said that how they got here wasn't important, the important thing was that they had us, each other, and a good living. But I worry about the living because I hear Papa has some debts to reconcile. Teddy has put Papa's livestock on his allotment to carry the cost of hay feeding and butchering.'

Sarah too had heard the rumours of the Cullen's financial distress 'I am sure your Papa will work things out, Catherine, he has managed very well up until now.'


Elizabeth Cullen gained the attention of her guests and ushered them into the dining room for afternoon tea. The New Norfolk wives of the Norfolk Island convict farmers had a splendid time gossiping, laughing and eating James Cullen's profit for the previous month.

# 45

# THE PARTNERSHIP

**1820**

'Catherine, I would like you to meet Mr Edward Yates. Edward and I are going to be partners in the flour mill.' James Tedder was bubbling with enthusiasm when he introduced his wife to his new business partner.

'Pleased to meet you, Mr Yates. I hope you and my husband run a successful business together. He has been planning this for many years. Excuse me, sir, my husband will prepare a drink for you, the baby requires my attention.'

'Very good to meet you, Mrs Tedder. Your husband and I will benefit each other, our families and the community if our business succeeds. Congratulations on the birth of your new daughter. Sarah, isn't it?'

'Yes, Mr Yates, thank you.'

Catherine left the parlour and made her way to the bedroom where her newborn daughter was screaming to be fed. Margaret, not yet two, was sitting on her parents' bed playing with different shaped and sized blocks of wood that James Blay Jr had made for her. He brought them when he delivered Teddy's new boots. He seemed a delightful young fellow, not showing the behaviours his parents complained about. Catherine opened the window to let the afternoon breeze from the Derwent into the room, the heat was stifling, and summer had only just begun. The baby tried to latch onto Catherine's breast, but the perspiration slipping down her chest made it difficult for little Sarah to suckle. She put the screaming baby back in the cradle and wiped herself with a wet cloth; the baby then suckled fitfully as Catherine tried to keep them both cool.

Tedder saw his guest off and walked into the bedroom just as the baby decided she'd had enough. 'Did you like Mr Yates, Catherine? Seems to me he knows what he is talking about with flour milling. He was a miller in Shropshire.'

'How long was his sentence and what was his crime, Teddy?'

'I don't know his crime, but he was sentenced to life, as was James Blay. If he murdered someone he would have been executed, so we assume it was theft or burglary. He received a conditional pardon in 1818.'

'As long as you think you can trust him, Teddy.'


James Tedder didn't ever remember being this excited any other day in his life. The day he married Catherine he felt joy and happiness, this was a different happiness. The birth of his daughters brought hope, happiness, and love, this was different, this was pure excitement.

He and Edward Yates had worked feverishly to finish the fit out of the building they had secured to use as a flour mill. The doors opened for business on Monday, 4th September 1820.

'This is the day, Edward, let us salute to a successful

business venture.' Tedder and Yates clinked glasses filled with rum and congratulated each other on how quickly their plans had been realised. Their partnership agreement indicated that Yates' primary responsibility was the book-keeping, and Tedder was charged with managing the receipt of wheat and its process into flour.

At the end of the first full day of trade, Tedder walked the short distance to his and Catherine's cottage in Murray Street. He had wheat husks in his hair, stuck to his breeches and up the sleeves of his jacket. Two-and-a-half-year-old Margaret squealed when her father walked into the kitchen and ran behind her mother's skirts.

'You look like a scarecrow, Teddy,' Catherine giggled as she coaxed Margaret from behind her. 'Was your first day productive?'

Tedder wrapped his arms around Catherine's waist, pulled her toward him and kissed her more passionately than he had done for some time.

'It was a most productive day, Catherine. Edward and I did not stop, we are working as hard as the grinding wheel.'

'That's wonderful, I am pleased for you. Now go outside and remove the husks from your clothes, then come in for supper.' She smiled at the back of his head as he made his way to the garden. 'I am very proud of you, Teddy.'

*Mr James Tedder Esq.*
*Murray Street,*
*Hobart Town, Van Diemen's Land, New South Wales.*
*September 1820.*

*Mr Henry Tedder Esq.*
*Newgate Street*
*London, England.*

*Dear Father and Mother*

*There is much news to relay to you since my last letter. Catherine and I have been blessed with the joyous birth of another daughter, Sarah, I named her after Mother. She is now nine months, and her sister Margaret is two years and a half. When they are old enough to travel, I will bring them, and Catherine to London to see you. We are prosperous here in Hobart Town, and although my conviction and subsequent sentence, of which the worst part was the prison hulk* <u>Retribution</u>*, were grim, I have no regrets about the turn my life took.*

*No doubt I would have married in London and perhaps had a family, but unless the opportunity arose for me to be a master tinsmith and have my own business, I would have laboured long hours working for another. I am a landowner in a place that has pristine water, clear skies that roll on and on, fresh air and hot summer days that transform into warm evenings when Catherine and I sit outside and marvel at the millions of stars above. And you would marvel at the strange animals and birds, and even the plants – they don't lose their leaves in winter – they stay green all year.*

*I have built a flour mill and have a business partner, Edward*

*Yates. He too was sent to Van Diemen's Land as a convict. We started milling flour two or so weeks ago and have been kept busy.*

*We have had our trials and tribulations, Catherine and I, and I struggled in the early days of my transportation, but all is well now, and we are happy.*

*Please write as soon as you can, I would love to hear news from the family.*

*Respectfully, your son*

*James.*

# 46

# BETSY'S WEDDING

Not sure how long she would stay with her parents, Catherine packed enough clothes for three-year-old Margaret and two-year-old Sarah to last a few weeks.

Tedder packed for a few days. The new mill was open, the fit out completed, and Edward Yates had taught Tedder the trade. They ground wheat into flour for bakers and settlers every day, except Sunday. Edward Yates had assured James he could manage a few days on his own.

They harnessed the two horses, packed the cart and set off around 5 am Saturday morning to try and avoid the heat of the day. Margaret sat between her parents, and Sarah sat on Catherine's lap. The journey from Hobart Town to New Norfolk usually took around three hours. Tedder knew they would have to stop many times for the children.

'It will be pleasant to see everyone for the happy occasion of Betsy's marriage to John Lilley Pearce, on Monday, don't you think so, Catherine?'

'Yes, I am looking forward to seeing Mama and Papa and to spend time with my sisters. John appears to be a good man.'

.   .   .

They'd made good time, Tedder was astonished at how well the children had travelled; they had seen their grandparents often, but it was when they visited Hobart Town. The girls had not travelled to New Norfolk before.

Betsy ran out of the house to greet her sister and nieces, they smothered each other in kisses and hugs. When the children started wriggling to remove themselves from Betsy's grasps, she noticed Tedder and gave him a polite curtsey. 'You are all just in time for dinner. Cook has created a feast, she says she is practising for the wedding party. Sophia is arriving tomorrow, and she's not even with child again.'

'Elizabeth,' Catherine chastised her sister, 'that is unkind.'

'Well, she's always having a baby. But she seems to be having a rest for a couple of years; she'll be able to travel comfortably. You're not having another baby, yet are you, Catherine?'

'No, I am not. Now help the little ones into the house, they are very hungry and thirsty, and Mama and Papa will want to see them.'

Turning to Tedder, who was smirking at Betsy's observations of pregnancy, she said, 'Was I that naive and excitable and silly when I married you? I was the same age as Betsy is now.'

'Yes, my dear, you were as impulsive and naive as your young sister is now, but that was part of the attraction because it accompanied innocence.'

'Don't be silly, Teddy. You and I both know I wasn't innocent.'

'That's not what I meant, but the memories of our loss of innocence are wonderful.'

She kissed him on the lips 'Will I get your manhood to show how happy he is to see me?'

Tedder pulled away, laughing. He held Catherine's hand and they walked into her parents' grand home.


**29 January 1821**

Betsy wore the same dress the other Cullen women wore on their respective wedding days. James Bryan Cullen cried more openly at this daughter's wedding, as much from the last child making her own way in the world, as from worrying about his financial position.

Reverend Robert Knopwood, the Colonial Chaplain who had been a friend of the Cullens since they arrived from Norfolk Island in 1808, noticed James' distress.

'Betsy looked lovely, James. As did your other daughters and your wife on their wedding days,' Reverend Knopwood said to his friend.

'Yes Robert, I am fortunate. I have been blessed.'

'But I sense unhappiness on this joyous occasion, James.'

'Do I speak to you as a friend or as a chaplain, Robert?'

'Am I not both? It will make no difference either way to what you have to say to me.'

'Let's go for a walk in the garden, Robert.'

James led the way outside while his guests ate and drank another quarter's profits. He offered the reverend a seat under the ghost gum and put back his head to take in the clear January night sky.

'It's amazing how the stars on this side of the world are so different. It's been so long since I left London that I forget what the night sky looked like. I am sure it was never as clear and full of stars as this.

'Elizabeth knows I owe money to Thomas Triffitt, but she doesn't know I am in debt to George F Read, nor does she know that Betsy's new husband has paid some of my debts and Catherine's husband, Tedder, has taken responsibility for some of my livestock and crops.' James Cullen took a deep breath and looked at his friend for comfort.

'I am sorry to hear of these troubles, James. You should go to Hobart Town and visit your solicitor, to see what steps can be taken to relieve you of this burden. Be prepared to learn that you may have to sell this beautiful house that you have for such a time, longed for,' Robert Knopwood counselled.

# 47

# THE STRUGGLE ENDS

**5 April 1821**

Elizabeth Cullen fussed over her youngest daughter who had come home to the farm to rest. The seventeen-year-old, pregnant with her first child, was sickly and spent most days in bed. Elizabeth prayed for a boy - James' and her only son had died in infancy - and the other two daughters, Sophia and Catherine had so far only had girls. In his advanced years, James would enjoy the company of a little boy. She looked over at her husband, sitting in his favourite chair by the fire reading a play. She didn't know what the play was, or why he took pleasure in reading at all but was glad she'd decided to get the servant to set the fire, the mid-autumn evenings were getting colder, earlier. He was nearing eighty years, and she was always concerned for his comfort, although he seemed stout enough. He worked the farm every day, read by the fire on cold nights, or outside under the stars on warm, balmy evenings.

James put the play he'd been trying to read on the games table Elizabeth had bought from a deceased estate in

Hobart Town. Using the arms on the giltwood chair she had ordered from London to push himself upright James announced he was going to lay down and rest until supper. Elizabeth watched as he climbed the stairs, almost laboriously, almost as if he was taking as long as possible to reach his destination. She thought his behaviour was odd but dismissed her concerns as an overreaction to his age, he was after all still working the farm.

On hearing the report of a pistol, mother and daughter rushed to the stairs. Betsy forgetting how sick she felt, picked up her skirts and took the steps two at a time.

Her beloved Papa lay on the bed gasping; the sight of his mutilated body, the hole where the bullet had entered his chest, the blood gushing from the wound and oozing down the edges of the bed to the floor, was more than a sheltered, protected child could suffer; she fainted, just as her mother rushed into the room to see her husband take his last breath.

*"On Saturday last an Inquest was held at New Norfolk, before A.W.H. Humphrey, Esq. Coroner, on the body of Mr J.B. Cullen, a Settler residing in that district, in consequence of a rumour that he had shot himself on the Thursday previously. After an impartial investigation, it appeared in evidence, that about 4 o'clock in the afternoon of the day stated, the deceased, with his wife and youngest daughter, were all very comfortable at home, the former sitting in the parlour reading a play; he, however, rose from his seat, and went alone into the bedroom, when shortly afterwards the family heard the report of a pistol; the daughter instantly hastened to the chamber, where she saw her unfortunate parent lying on the bed breathing his last. The room was full of smoke, and the blood was running off the bed profusely. Upon this awful sight, the young woman fainted and*

*fell down on the floor senseless; and, upon the family examining the unfortunate object of their anxiety, they found that the deceased had received the fatal wound close to his heart. It did not appear by the evidence of any of the witnesses, that the deceased was of a melancholy mind; but that he was perfectly steady at the time the unhappy affair took place. It was therefore considered, that the pistol, which was cocked and loaded, and had been placed some where about the bed, had accidentally gone off while the deceased was handling it, as it was found at the foot of the bed; and to which effect the Jury returned their verdict. The deceased, who came from Norfolk Island at the evacuation of that place, leaves a wife and three daughters, and was much respected throughout his neighbourhood; he had arrived at the age of nearly 80 years."*[1]

## Cullen Farm - 8th April 1821

The parlour wasn't big enough to welcome everyone who had come to offer their condolences after the funeral. The people, like extended family, who had been through the same obstacles to forge a life on Norfolk Island and Van Diemen's Land: James Triffitt and his family, Richard and Kitty Morgan, Abraham Hands, James Jordan, William Rayner Sr. Elizabeth slumped in her chair in front of the fireplace, staring at the empty seat opposite, where James had sat in the evenings to read. She'd been there since Sophia and Catherine helped her out of bed in the morning and organised her for the day. She hadn't eaten since James pulled the trigger and shot a hole in his chest. Cook spent most of her time struggling to get Elizabeth to drink tea.

Reverend Knopwood fussed over her; he had lost a good

friend and was trying to put his grief aside to conduct the service. 'I am pleased James' death was deemed an accident by the Coroner,' he said to Tedder who was standing to one side. 'I couldn't bear the thought of him not being buried in consecrated ground or of Elizabeth facing the judgemental gossip of the community. If only I'd listened more attentively and offered better advice when James shared his financial difficulties with me.'

Putting his hand on the Reverend's shoulder, Tedder said, 'How were any of us to know how desperate the situation had become.'

Sophia and Catherine made conversation with Elizabeth Cullen's guests, trying not to show any emotion that would send their mother spiralling even deeper into melancholia. They chatted, smiled, pretended to listen to stories about their father's exploits in Sydney Cove and on Norfolk Island and handed out refreshments.

'I didn't think they would ever leave, Teddy. Trying not to cry has exhausted me.' Catherine told her husband as they stood and watched the last of James Bryan Cullen's mourners depart.

Tedder put his arm around his wife, brought her in close, and kissed her forehead. 'Cook will help you and Sophia get your mother to bed, then we must all discuss what is to happen next.'


The three Cullen girls and their husbands and children crowded into the parlour their father had always craved, and yet enjoyed for such a short time. Catherine marvelled at how the clan had thrived and grown in this sometimes-harsh environment: Sophia and William Rayner Jr had three little girls, Mary, Eliza and Sophia Christiana, she and

Teddy had Margaret and Sarah, and Betsy was early into her first pregnancy, with her husband John Lilley Pearce. Their father had longed for a grandson, and Catherine had the feeling that his first would be Betsy's baby; the child their father would never see.

James Tedder brought the group to order. 'We are confronted with a situation that needs to be addressed. How are we to help and support Elizabeth during her time of mourning,' he scanned the faces before him. 'We three sons-in-law have businesses and farms to run, Sophia has three small children, Catherine two, and Betsy is most unwell carrying her first child. To ensure there isn't to be too much upheaval in Mrs Cullen's life, Sarah Blay has offered to come and stay at the farm to help Cook take care of Elizabeth for a few weeks. When she is strong enough, she can stay with Catherine and me in Hobart Town, if she is so disposed.'

'He didn't leave a will, Mrs Cullen,' explained James Cullen's solicitor, 'we'll have to apply for Letters of Administration to manage his affairs.'

'I will have to leave that to you, sir. I am not familiar with Letters of Administration,' Elizabeth Cullen said. 'I wonder if the repercussions of my husband's death will ever end.'

Tedder had attended the solicitor's office with his mother in law, forever grateful that his parents had seen fit to send him to school. James Cullen's death had left Elizabeth confused and befuddled, and not being able to read increased her reliance on others.

'I'll talk to the solicitor for you, if you wish, Elizabeth. We'll get things worked out.'

'Thank you, Teddy,' said Elizabeth, using the pet name Catherine had given him.

Tedder nodded to the solicitor, then reassured Elizabeth, 'Let's get you to our cottage for some refreshments, I'll come back this afternoon to make arrangements.'

Tedder helped Elizabeth out of her chair, she seemed to have aged physically, and mentally since her husband's death.

'What is to be done, Mr Cartwright?' Tedder later asked the solicitor.

'An advertisement in the newspaper indicating we are applying for Letters of Administration is all we can do at this stage, Mr Tedder. Any claims on the Estate will be received and therefore an indication of financial liabilities will be revealed. Apart from Mr George F Read Esq. to whom Mr Cullen owed £105.7.2, are you aware of anything else?'

'I know Betsy's husband, John Lilley Pearce paid some of Mr Cullen's debts. I have land adjoining and took on some of his sheep for management but will not be recording a debt against his Estate.'

'The land grants will be returned to the government for reassignment, because they can only be left to male heirs, as you know, Mr Tedder,' added the solicitor. 'The land Mr Cullen owned can be inherited by his wife and daughters, unless it is to be sold to furnish debts.'

Tedder left Mr Cartwright's office despairing of the bleak future in store for his mother-in-law.

.   .   .

'Mama isn't doing very well, Teddy. She is fearful of losing the house to pay for Papa's debts.' Catherine, while tending to their youngest, Sarah, was relaying her concerns to Tedder so quickly, he found it hard to keep track of what she was saying.

'She may well have to sell, Catherine. Mr Cartwright is not optimistic there will be any other way. She will reside with us or Betsy and John, or Sophia and William. I am saddened that your father reached the financial collapse attributed to him, but Mr Cartwright believes the expense of building the big house for your mother reduced his capacity to balance his income against his expenses.'

## 48

## THE BREAKUP

**April 1821**

'It isn't working as we had planned, Edward. You spend too much time away from the mill and leave me to do most of the work. The accounting is behind, we have monies not receipted and bills not paid. A tardy business is not going to be a good one, that I learned from my father and my master tinsmith. Our partnership needs to be reconsidered.'

James Tedder had been mulling over the situation at the mill for some days: if he severed ties with Edward Yates he would be doing all the work instead of most of it, but he would run a tight ship. He was disappointed their partnership had lasted only seven months, but ties would be better cut now than later. He was finding it difficult to worry about Edward Yates while working with James Cullen's solicitor to finalise his Estate.

Edward Yates took his hands out of his pockets and folded his arms across his chest 'I agree with you, Tedder. It is much more work than I expected, and my heart is not in it. We will visit the solicitor to dissolve the partnership.'

. . .

Catherine was less than gracious when Tedder told her of the partnership break down over supper 'Teddy, this is going to be more work for you, and the children and I will see you less. Perhaps you should speak to James Blay Jr about how he manages his business, he seems to have much spare time.'

'He is a rogue, Catherine, he cheats customers and suppliers, and will soon have no business at all. I am offended that you would want me to be like him.' Tedder rose from the table and went straight to bed, disappointed that Catherine wasn't more supportive.

Tedder thrived being the sole owner of the flour mill. The fears Catherine harboured about his time being consumed by the work, were not realised. He was assigned trusted convicts to work in the mill, and he managed the running of the business admirably. She was proud of him all over again; he had built up and managed a thriving business while taking care to ensure her mother's affairs were in order.

'I think we will be able to travel to England next year, Catherine. The girls will be old enough, and we will have the money saved for second class, not steerage, so the journey should not be too difficult.' Tedder told her of his plans after a particularly good day at the mill. 'Your mother should be recovered from her melancholia by then.'

Catherine breathed deeply and slowly, not wanting to alarm her husband. 'That will be lovely, Teddy,' she whispered, trying to disguise the fear that agitated her voice. She had no interest in England. She had no interest in carting her children to the other side of the world like Sarah Blay had done with her boys. She had no interest in leaving her mother.

*Henry Tedder Esq*
*Newgate Street*
*London, England*
*May 1821*

*Mr James Tedder Esq*
*Murray Street*
*Hobart Town*
*Van Diemen's Land, New South Wales*

*Dearest James*

*Many thanks for writing to us again, we enjoy hearing about your life in Van Diemen's Land. Mother thanks you for naming the second child after her and looks forward to the day when she can meet your wife Catherine, and your children. As you are aware, your sister Esther married John Millicent in July 1812 and they now have a daughter, Caroline, who was born on 6 March 1819.*

*Your brother William and his wife, Phoebe have a daughter, Martha born last year. Their son, James, named after you, is now five years old. I am still barbering, and Mother is well.*

*Mother and I find it odd when you say the seasons are the other way around. Coming in to summer here in England, knowing you are heading into winter in Van Diemen's Land is a strange thought.*

*We do hope Catherine and the children are well, and count the days when we might be able to see you again and meet your family.*

*With love, always*
*Mother and Father*

## 49

# MOVING ON

Elizabeth Cullen was grateful her husband's legacy would
live on in the son of Betsy and her husband John Lilley
Pearce – their little boy - born six months after the death of
his grandfather, was named James.

Her sons in law John Lilley Pearce, James Tedder and
William Rayner Jr had all contributed financially to the
continued running of the house but she knew the time
would soon come when it was necessary to sell.

'Let us go and sit outside in the warm winter sunshine,' Dr
Robert Officer encouraged Elizabeth. At the insistence of
her daughters, Elizabeth had accepted the offer of help from
Dr Officer; he would be a guest in the house while he
worked in New Norfolk, and in return for accommodation,
would ensure Elizabeth's health was monitored. She
followed him outside and sat in her rocking chair on the
front porch. Looking across the gardens, toward the
Derwent. She imagined James riding back from a day's work

on the farm, eagerly anticipating what Cook would have ready for supper. He'd loved coming home in the evenings to eat with her and talk to the children about their day's activities. The tears filled her eyes, and she wiped them away before they had a chance to materialise on her cheeks.

# 50

# FEAR AND LOATHING

**August 1822**

Toothless arrived in Hobart on 23 July 1822 on the *Prince of Orange* convict ship. His relish in the position of overseer of convicts grew with each voyage. Off-loading the human cargo into the responsibility of the Colony gave Toothless the opportunity to wander around Hobart Town and marvel at the growth and changes in the town since he first arrived ten years earlier, in 1812.

'Startin' to look a bit like a real place, instead of a blot on the English soul,' he commented to a friend. 'Wonder if Tedder is still here,' he said quietly to himself. 'I must find out.'

Walking down Liverpool Street away from the mill, toward home, with his head down against the biting wind blowing off the Derwent and his hands in the oversized pockets of his new winter coat, Tedder didn't notice the bald, heavyset man skulking in the alley between two commercial buildings on the other side of the street. Nor did he notice the man follow him to his home in Murray Street. The sight of his wife and children waiting for him with supper ready brought joy. 'I am blessed. This is a good and prosperous life.'

Toothless sat with his associates in a small establishment in Collins Street, drinking rum and planning his assault on James Tedder.

'We'll have to watch him over some weeks to see his routine and make sure we get him alone.'

Nods from his friends indicated agreement.

'His flour mill is in Liverpool Street, and his house in Murray Street, he walks between them alone. He has convicts working for him – imagine that – a convict running a business with other convicts doing the work. Don't seem right to me.'

Catherine was aware of a change in her husband's disposition. Coming home to supper after working in his beloved mill was always a joy for Teddy, but of late he had a fearful look and was wary entering the house, he looked around fervently before stepping inside.

'What is the matter, Teddy? You are so cautious of late it is as if you are being followed everywhere by a ghost.'

'I think I am, Catherine. I swear I am being followed by a guard from the *Indefatigable* who, the last time he saw me in Hobart Town, vowed to kill me. He tried to do it before I was assigned to your father to work in the Stores at New Norfolk.'

'Teddy, why have you not mentioned this before?'

Tedder moved over to his chair by the fire and allowed it to swallow him as he sunk into it.

'I recovered from almost drowning in 1813, and I demanded respect from him when I last saw him in Hobart Town a few years ago. He wasn't pleased. I didn't expect him to return.'

'Teddy, you must be extra careful, go to the constable and air your concerns.'

'I fear I am imagining things, Catherine. Why would a person keep sailing on convict ships to the same places?'

'Perhaps he enjoys the power he has over those under his authority,' Catherine mused quietly.

———

Tedder took more notice of his surroundings on his way to the mill each day; during breaks in customers, he stepped outside the mill to look up and down Liverpool Street to detect anything unusual. He kept a watchful eye on people as he walked home each evening, taking particular notice of the spaces between commercial buildings and houses where a person could slink and not be noticed.

'I was either imagining I was being watched or whoever it was has moved on to bother someone else,' Tedder said to Catherine after she had put the girls to bed.

'I have been careful to take more notice of my surroundings over the last few weeks and have not seen anything to cause concern.'

'Thank goodness, Teddy. It bothered me to see you so on edge. Now we can continue with our lives. You did remember the girls and I are going to stay with Mama at the house for two weeks from this Friday, didn't you Teddy?'

. . .

Tedder hadn't remembered, he had been so engrossed in his own fear and imaginings he had forgotten the little things in their lives. 'Yes, of course, I remembered. I will miss the three of you terribly, but your Mama does need the company and the girls always cheer her.'

---

**Friday 27 September 1822**

Opening the mill as usual Friday morning, Tedder left his most trusted, assigned convict in charge, so he could return home and help Catherine get the girls organised into the boat for the trip up the Derwent to New Norfolk.

'Teddy, we need to hurry, your dawdling along will make us late for the boat,' Catherine scolded as he walked up the path to the front door of their cottage.

He harnessed the pony to the little cart and loaded the bags into the back. Helping Catherine up to the bench at the front he hoisted up Margaret who sat next to her mother, and then Sarah who wanted to squeeze between Catherine and Margaret. Climbing up to the bench he looked at the girls in his life and smiled. 'I am so much in love with her and adore my beautiful daughters.'

Tedder stood on the banks of the Derwent until the little boat carrying his wife and children was out of sight. He walked slowly back to the mill, thinking how lonely the house would be without the squeals of happy children and the chatter of a busy woman.

---

'He's on his own now, his whore and brats left on a boat this mornin'. I don't know how long they'll be away, but lookin' at the bags, it will be more than one or two nights. We need to surprise him tomorrow when he opens the door, 'afore the convicts arrive to work.'

Toothless worked out the finer details of his plan with the other members of his gang. 'We need to surprise him and shut him up straight away, so he doesn't let out a yell and have someone hear and come pokin' round.'

**Saturday 28th September 1822**

Tedder wasn't as fond of spring in Van Diemen's Land as he had been of a London spring. It was often very windy here, and the days fluctuated between warm and sunny to cold and rainy. However, this Saturday morning was beautiful, there was a freshness to the air that brought the promise of a warm day. The sun's appearance over the horizon as it swept away the remnants of night, reminded him of actors appearing on a theatre stage when the curtains drew back. Although already missing his little family, it was hard to feel gloomy on a spring morning such as this.

As James Tedder put the key in the lock and opened his flour mill, to get ready for a busy Saturday of trade, two large hands in the middle of his back pushed him through the door, knocking him to the ground. One hand pulled back his head by the hair, while another hand went over his mouth. Hands belonging to two other people stood him up.

'Don't rough him up too much, lads, we want his clothes to be clean, don't want him lookin' as if he's been knocked about.'

Toothless grinned into Tedder's face. 'Told ye I'd see your funeral eventually, convict.'

The hand over James Tedder's mouth was replaced with a gag to ensure silence. He worried briefly about the cleanliness of the rag in his mouth, then realised it was the least of his problems.

Tedder struggled against the two men who dragged him over to the bags of newly milled flour. The bags were stacked ready for transfer to the Government Store.

'Don't get ye clothes dirty, convict,' Toothless ordered, 'we don't want anyone thinkin' some foul play has come of ye.'

Terrified and unable to escape from the clutches of the thugs who had him restrained, the realisation of what Toothless had planned for him hit James Tedder like a horse's hoof to the chest. He mentally rummaged around in his muddled brain to see pictures of his wife and children. He kicked and struggled against the brutes who restrained him.

Toothless pushed him, face down, into a bag of milled wheat, he held his head into the sack while the other two held down his thrashing body. James Tedder took his last breath in the flour mill he had built and made successful, in a town on the other side of the world, where he had been exiled ten years earlier.

*"Deaths – this morning at his mill in Liverpool Street, Mr James Tedder, many years a respectable and industrious inhabitant of Hobart Town, in which he had erected several houses, and a corn (sic) mill."* [1]

Elizabeth Cullen couldn't console Catherine, her grief was palpable, the whole house felt it, and grieved with her. The children, Margaret and Sarah, were looked after by Sophia, while funeral arrangements were made for Teddy.

For the second time in eighteen months, visitors crowded into the parlour of the Cullen home to pay their respects to a grieving widow. It was difficult to understand how a seemingly healthy young man could die so suddenly. They gossiped with each other about how fortunate it was that James Tedder had left a substantial Estate for his wife and children. They all agreed he would be a loss to the Colony; he was a respected businessman, attentive son in law to Elizabeth Cullen, and much loved by his wife and children.

Unlocking the door to their cottage and stepping inside, Catherine's senses picked up the presence of her husband. She could smell the pieces of wheat husk that used to attach themselves to his coat, the sweat from his body when he climbed into bed next to her, and she could taste his lips when he kissed her after she'd cooked his favourite meal for dinner. She could hear him laughing with the children when he tickled them until they could take no more She could feel his rough hands caressing her naked body and she could see him, standing before her, smiling, telling her how much he loved her. Catherine's knees gave way, she crouched on the floor, sobbing, with no attempt to stop the tears that flowed in a torrent.

---

James Blay Jr knocked quietly on the door of the cottage in Murray Street; he'd made new shoes for the girls, and a pair of summer weight sandals for Catherine.

'Good morning, Catherine,' James Jr took off his hat and bowed his head slightly when she opened the door. 'I have some shoes for the girls.'

Catherine invited her friend into the parlour. It had

been six weeks since Teddy's death, and she was having difficulty moving on. 'Thank you, James, that is very kind of you. Please, sit down.'

'I also have another reason for visiting, Catherine,' he said while taking the offered seat, 'I wonder if you would like me to help you write a letter to your husband's parents, informing them of his death?'

She took a deep breath before she responded, 'Yes, James. Thank you.'

## 51

### GROWING UP IN A CONVICT COLONY

Sarah Blay missed her eldest son but admitted to herself
that him being away, living in Hobart Town, eased a lot of
tension. He seemed to be doing well, he had land grants that
he managed, and on completion of his shoemaking apprenticeship, was selling shoes to the Government stores and the
people of Hobart Town.

William, now seventeen, had settled in well to farming
and took on most of the responsibility for running their
land holdings. It was interesting to see how her husband
had become an accomplished property investor; he bought
or built houses in Hobart Town and sold them at a profit.
Their life was comfortable, and apart from the sadness of
her friend, Elizabeth Cullen losing James under such tragic
circumstances, and their wonderful friend, James Tedder
dying, Sarah would be very happy. Sitting at the kitchen
table, with her youngest son, John, now fourteen, she asked
him if he missed London.

'No Mama, I don't even really remember London. I do
remember Grandmama but not living in London.'

Sarah was amazed at how her sons' accents had

changed. Gone was the distinctive London Cockney accent they spoke when they were little, although James Jr had more of his left than William and John. It was replaced with a cocktail of English, Irish and a Colony born twang that if spoken quickly was difficult to understand. She was glad she had kept up with their schooling and that they were able to read and write; she knew it gave them an advantage, especially when she saw how difficult it had been for Elizabeth Cullen when dealing with her husband's affairs.

'What are you thinking about, Sarah?' her husband asked returning from his trip to sell goods to the Government stores.

'I'm marvelling at the life we have built here for our sons and for us. I'm marvelling at how prosperous we have become. That would never have been possible in London.'

'I know,' he agreed as he bent over and kissed her cheek. 'Best thing I ever did was get knicked for trying to sell them boots.' He grinned.

# 52

# THE SECOND AND FIRST WEDDING

**February 1823**

The feeling of overwhelming joy was missing from Catherine's second wedding. It had only been five months since her beloved Teddy died mysteriously at the flour mill, but there were two little girls to think about, and her mother to help support. James Blay Jr had been helpful and friendly since she and Teddy had moved to Hobart Town, and he had very kindly written a letter to Teddy's parents on Catherine's behalf, to explain why their treasured son would not be returning to London to see them. He was very affectionate with Margaret and Sarah and showed a maturity far beyond his 20 years. Her little girls were only four and three when their father died; Catherine knew they would not remember him and would be likely to call James Blay Jr 'Papa'. She wouldn't stop them, but wanted to ensure the girls knew about their "real" Papa as they grew up. She had applied for Letters of Administration for Teddy's Estate, which was quite substantial, and accepted James Blay Jr's proposal of marriage knowing he had his eyes focussed on Teddy's land holdings and other wealth.

Catherine relied on James Jr to walk her through the myriad of paperwork around Teddy's affairs and quietly cursed her parents for neglecting her education. A sadness swept over her like the winter fog rolling off the Derwent. Teddy had never liked or trusted James Blay Jr, even though he had been very good friends with the lad's father. She forced a smile while her mother fussed.

Elizabeth Cullen helped her middle daughter into the dress she had chosen for her wedding to James Blay Jr. Catherine seemed older than her 23 years both in appearance and maturity. The pain Elizabeth had simmering in her heart since the death of her husband James a year earlier, erupted into agony when Teddy died. It enveloped her every time she looked at Catherine and little Margaret and Sarah. Marrying again was Catherine's path to financial security, she couldn't run a flour mill, and manage the 30 acres Teddy had in land at New Norfolk. Elizabeth knew James Blay Jr wanted to build his own wealth on the back of James Tedder's success, but she and her daughter had chosen to ignore his voracity, hoping the decision to marry would not be one Catherine would regret.

Catherine Tedder's soon to be mother-in-law Sarah Blay, joined Elizabeth Cullen in fussing over Catherine's hair and dress.

Sarah had picked some roses from the Government House garden and tied a piece of pink ribbon around the stems to cover the thorns. She handed the posy to Catherine and lent in close to kiss her cheek. 'I know the situation you find yourself in is difficult, Catherine, but wonder if it is difficult enough to make you consider marrying my eldest son.'

Although the relationship between James Jr's parents and he, had been fraught with difficulty since they arrived in 1814, Catherine thought she'd seen signs of improvement. 'He does seem to have genuine affection for me, Sarah, and he is very fond of the girls. Even when Teddy was alive, James Jr visited with gifts for the children.'

Sarah Blay smiled tenderly at Catherine, put the posy between her hands and clasped her own around the flowers as well. 'Yes, in his own way I think he is very fond of you. But he is an ambitious lad who doesn't really like hard work, and Teddy's Estate adds to his portfolio. If he doesn't make you as happy as he is promising, my husband and I will come to your aid.' Sarah kissed Catherine on the cheek, nodded affectionately toward Elizabeth, and left to join the other guests in St David's Church for the marriage of her eldest son and the middle daughter of James Bryan Cullen.


James Blay Jr had never been in love, and Catherine realised by the nature of the sex between them, that his only sexual experiences had been in the brothel. He was rough and inconsiderate and used her to relieve his needs, not to share intimacy. She hoped he would become gentler over time, perhaps when he realised he didn't have to hurry, that he wasn't in a queue and that Catherine would be there for him. She lay in bed next to her new husband, the bed she used to share with her beloved Teddy and crossed her legs to ease the pain of his rough, repetitive penetration. Her mind wandered to the wedding night she and Teddy had shared at the Cullen Farm, how embarrassed he was when she laughed at his nakedness because he still had his boots on. She remembered how concerned he was that he might be hurting her, all the while unable to control his manhood which sprung up every hour or so. But Teddy made love to her, she and Teddy didn't just have sex.

She wiped her eyes. James Blay Jr wasn't Teddy.

The story continues in Book Two of the Cullen / Bartlett Dynasty
*Love, Lies, and Legacies*

And
Book Three
*Time Tells All.*

Visit: *https://janeenannoconnell.com/*
for up to date information.
And my Facebook page
https://business.facebook.com/JaneenAnnOConnell/

Please be kind enough to review the book on Amazon.com, or Amazon.com.au, or Goodreads.

Thank you.

janeeno@outlook.com

# NOTES

## Chapter 1

1. Saunders Newsletter [England] 7 November 1810 (British Newspaper Archives)
2. Hampshire Chronicle (ENGLAND) 5 November 1810
3. Old Bailey on Line 'Summary of Sessions of the Peace, Middlesex, October 1810'.

## 2. The Shoemaker

1. Old Bailey Proceedings: Accounts of Criminal Trials 9th January 1811. www.oldbaileyonline.org
2. Shoemaker's Guild
3. Old Bailey Proceedings: Accounts of Criminal Trials 10th January 1811. Twenty shillings = one pound

## 3. The Shoemaker's Wife

1. Dysentery

## 12. New Norfolk

1. Historical Records of Australia Series 1, Volume 1 1788 - 1796., p. 274
   *Governor Phillip to Lord Grenville Sydney, New South Wales November 5th 1791*

## 19. The First Fleeter

1. Dysentery
2. "The First Fleet" by Rob Mundle page 198

# 22. Norfolk Island

1. *One quarter of an acre*
2. *The founders of Australia: a biographical dictionary of the First Fleet by Mollie Gillen*

# 23. Transported Again

1. *The founders of Australia: a biographical dictionary of the First Fleet by Mollie Gillen. Published Sydney. Library of Australian History, 1989*

# 25. Expansion

1. *In 1813, Major Geils appointed CULLEN a Superintendent of Government Stock of the Derwent. From :* Exiled Three Times Over *by Irene Schaffer and Thelma McKay*

# 26. Endless Delays

1. Sunday 21st August 1814

# 31. Dublin to New Norfolk

1. From: A Desperate Set of Villains: The Convicts of the Marquis Cornwallis. Ireland to Botany Bay 1796. By Barbara Hall.
2. *From: A Desperate Set of Villains: The Convicts of the Marquis Cornwallis. Ireland to Botany Bay 1796. By Barbara Hall.*

# 37. Orders

1. *State Records Authority of New South Wales. Colonial Secretary's Papers. Special Bundles 1794 to 1825.*

## 38. Bush Medicine

1. *http://www.bri.net.au/medicine.html (tea tree)*

## 47. The Struggle Ends

1. *Hobart Town Gazette and Van Diemen's Land Advertiser. Saturday 14th April 1821. (Trove.nla.gov.au)*

## 50. Fear and Loathing

1. *Hobart Town Gazette and Van Diemen's Land Advertiser, Saturday 28 September 1822. (trove.nla.gov.au)*

CPSIA information can be obtained
at www.ICGtesting.com
Printed in the USA
BVHW090819220221
600771BV00026B/1046/J

9 781034 454380